CATASTROPHE AT KILLDEER CAY

Nicolette Harpford

Copyright © 2025 by Nicolette Harpford

PRINT ISBN-13: 979-8-9876688-3-2

Cover Design: BookCoverZone

Editor: M. Perez

Edition: First

Printing: Second

Published by Avenue du Gui

CONTENTS

CHAPTER ONE

ABOARD THE SHIP

My father's callused finger pokes at the fleshy lemon on his plate, causing a fat seed to slide down the peel like a lonesome tear. My stomach curdles, and I set down my morning coffee.

"Stop playing with it," my mother nudges him with her bony elbow.

"I asked for a lemon with no seeds," he says before letting out a long sigh.

"Does it matter? You're just going to squeeze the juices into the water. Don't all lemons have seeds?" she asks.

Dad opens his mouth to argue, but he doesn't get even a small grunt out before Mom changes the subject.

"I talked to the shore desk, and they said we need to be at the gangway by eight o'clock *on the dot*!" she emphasizes. "That means we only have a quarter of an hour left to dillydally for breakfast." She takes a breath as she squints at a couple sitting at a table across the dining room. "Is that Linette?" She pinches my father's arm. "Doesn't your one uncle have a niece that travels a lot? Maybe she's on our cruise!"

Dad follows her pointer finger to a couple enjoying their breakfast in front of a picturesque window. Outside, ocean waves lazily dance and shift while the sun sends sparkles through the sky. It looks like everything in the world is blue.

Views like this remind me why I agreed to spend my precious vacation days on a cruise with my parents. I don't see them often, and I can't exactly afford a grand vacation on my miserly salary, so when they invited me and my boyfriend, Harry, on a Caribbean vacation to celebrate their 35th wedding anniversary, I didn't hesitate.

I had warned Harry ahead of time about my mother's incessant talking, and my father's strong opinion about fruit, but what I had failed to remember was how flaky my younger sister was. While my older sister had been tied up with business meetings, I had still been expecting my younger one to tag along, but at the last minute, she had called my parents and told them she would be in Dubai. Without her to help take the spotlight, I've had to endure multiple days at sea being the sole focus of my parents. It's been exhausting.

"It's not her," my mother says. "Linette's hair is much curlier. It's too bad your older sister, Kiera, couldn't come. She and Linette used to play when they were little, and I know she would love to see her."

While my mother can talk the day away, she isn't the best listener, so I don't bother to tell her that what she said doesn't make any sense. The woman sitting in the dining room isn't Linette, so Kiera couldn't catch up with her if she had come on the cruise with us all.

"Where's Harry?" Mom asks.

I'm surprised it's taken her so long to notice Harry hasn't arrived for breakfast. Normally, he's the first person she converses with at meals. Harry's been a good sport about it. He has yet to complain to me in private and still hasn't brought up the incident at dinner on our first night when my mother called him Henry for over an hour.

"He was feeling a bit sick," I say. "He said he would meet us at the gangway."

"He needs to get some of those ear stickers for seasickness, and some of the bracelets too," she says. "Before we left, I went to the store and got a whole box of them. I would lend you some, but I can't remember where they went. Maybe they're in your father's toiletry bag…" I let her voice turn into a lull in the background of the noisy dining room. She'll be talking for a while now.

When I had first invited Harry on this trip with my parents, I was a little nervous. We hadn't been dating that long, but my parents had insisted. I rarely have boyfriends, so it seems that they're determined to cement my relationship with this one as soon as possible. Harry hadn't been scared off though. He had been delighted, which only made me like him even more. He works a stressful job at a company that is hired out to collect evidence for cold cases. In fact, that's how we had met. He had been investigating a case at my Great Aunt Lois's historical home while I had been there to write about nuthatches for the birding magazine I work for.

"There are pills too," my mother's shrill voice breaks into my thoughts.

"Pills?"

"For seasickness. Didn't you say Harry was seasick?"

"Yes, last night—" I cut myself off. A crackle sounds from overhead on the ship's intercom.

The cruise director's bright voice takes over the room, "Good morning, ladies and gentlemen. This announcement is for groups A and B to begin making their way to the gangway. It's time to start loading the tenders that will take you away to Perfect Sands Islands!"

"That's us," Mom grabs Dad under the armpit and hoists him up. "Away we go!"

Chapter Two

A Change of Schedule

The cruise my parents had selected to celebrate their anniversary had an itinerary that included stops at several islands. The most unique of all the spots is this first one. The ship is planned to anchor overnight so that the passengers can enjoy not one, but two days on Perfect Sands Islands, a small collection of cays known for their secluded beaches and bright blue, shallow waters. In fact, the waters are so shallow around the islands that the cruise ships can't properly dock. They have to anchor out at sea and shuffle large groups of passengers to and from the main island using smaller boats called tenders. That's what my parents and I are waiting in line for now, to be taken ashore.

"What was the name of the island again?" my father asks while readjusting his fanny pack.

"Perfect Sands Islands!" Mom says loudly. "I'm starting to worry about you."

My dad lets out a long sigh. "I know that! I meant—"

"Then why'd you ask?" Mom shuffles forward in the line, knocking into a pair of elderly, twin ladies in the process. They give her dirty looks, but she doesn't notice.

"The tenders are taking us to the main island. It's called Lapis Rock because of the blue rocks that can wash up on the shore. There was a blurb about it in the daily newsletter they pushed under our doors last night," I say.

My father nods his head appreciatively.

"What happened last night?" Mom turns around, her backpack swinging near a man carrying a toddler. The child lets out a startled sob.

"I was just talking about Lapis Rock," I say as a group of young men in polos pushes by me in the line. I hadn't expected getting off the cruise to be so crowded.

"Where's Harry?" my mother asks.

"He said he would meet us here. He'll show up any second," I say.

"If he's late, we're not waiting. I went to guest services extra early yesterday to make sure we would be on the first tender to shore," she says. "The lines going!"

The line moves at a swift pace, and Harry is nowhere to be found. I hope he's okay. Last night had been rough for him. The ship had hit a squall, and he had spent a good hour in the bathroom, trying to settle his stomach.

"I'm going back to the room to check on Harry," I say.

"You'll miss the tender!" Mom squirms. She doesn't like it when things don't go to plan. "Then you'll lose your spot, and you'll have to wait for who knows when. Can't Harry just meet us there?"

Dad lets out another long sigh and gives my mother a look.

"Alright. I guess your father and I will meet up with you on the island. There's free Wi-Fi in a lot of the restaurants, so we'll send you a text around lunch."

The line surges forward, and my parents are carried away down the hall like floating flotsam.

It takes me a moment to remove myself from the tide of people by the gangway and make it to one of the ship's many staircases. I huff and puff up the endless flights of stairs until I have a stitch in my side. The room Harry and I are staying in is on one of the top floors, which probably didn't help Harry's seasickness last night. I take a left and follow along the narrow hallway. The doors and walls are paneled in a faux-wood that goes well with the swirling blue carpet. Everything on the ship evokes the idea of the ocean. Even the glassware in the dining room is a foggy green that resembles sea glass.

I get to an interior room tucked next to the guest laundry and flash my card against the door lock. There's an automated sound, and the door unlocks. I expect to see Harry as soon as I step inside, but only the furniture greets me. The room my parents booked for Harry and I ended up being a slender shaped cubby with just enough room for a pair of bunkbeds and a bathroom. I had been a bit nervous at first about the lack of space when we saw the room, but it turned out not to matter since there was so much to do on the cruise.

I poke my head into the bathroom to make sure Harry isn't heaving up his most recent meal again, but it's empty too. He must've gone down to the gangway while I was making my way up here. I would text him, but neither of us has bothered to splurge on the ship's Wi-Fi plan, so until we are on shore and sitting in a beach club or restaurant, I'll just have to hope to run into him.

"There you are!" a warm voice says in my ear.

I jump at the sound, but it's just Harry.

"I went down to the gangway, but I didn't see you anywhere," Harry says.

He looks much better than he did last night. His brown eyes have returned to their normal vibrancy, and the splashes of freckles that cover his skin are no longer covered with a sheen of sweat. He's dressed in white swim shorts and a matching shirt and hat. The smell of sunscreen tickles my nose as he gives my hand a squeeze.

"I think we missed our reserved time to board the tender," I say. "Honestly, the early tender was so crowded, it's for the best. We'll head back and see if they can fit us in on another one. We have lots of time to explore the island anyway, so there's no rush."

Harry smiles at me. "Sounds good. I was never a fan of rushing on vacation."

I laugh as he leads me back towards the stairs.

At the gangway, the crowd has dispersed. Harry tells me to wait by a map of the ship while he goes and talks to one of the nearby officers about what we should do since we missed our time to board. On the other side of the map, a woman paces quickly, her flip-flops clomping on the floor with every step she takes. Her hair is blown out into thick, dark waves, and she sports a tan that suggests she's recently been on vacation. I notice that the large handbag that hangs from her arm is designer, and the hoop earrings she wears have matching emblems.

"Ope!" A man with a slight paunch bends to the carpet in front of the pacing lady and picks up something. "Looks like you dropped this, miss." He holds up a shiny object that sparkles under the light, and the woman snatches it out of his hand. The small bald spot on the back of the man's head pinkens.

"Thanks," she slips whatever he found into her large purse. Her voice is cool and deeper than I imagined, suggesting that she's older than I originally thought.

Harry walks back over to me. "It looks like everything will work out. There's an extra tender leaving right now. There was a miscommunication in scheduling, and an extra one showed up. We should be able to get a spot since the mid-morning group isn't expected for another hour."

"That's great!" I say.

Harry and I go down the hallway where I had last seen my parents and through a checkpoint area staffed by security. The actual gangway leading off the ship to the smaller vessel is a sturdy gray bridge with thick metal handlebars. Harry helps me step onto it and follows me to the waiting boat where a couple people are already aboard.

The tender has two floors. The top floor is open to the elements while the bottom is closed off with windows. As soon as I step onto the boat, a man in a captain's hat greets me by grabbing my hand and helping me steady myself against the uneasy movement of the waves.

"Welcome aboard, mia bella." The captain reveals his smile. White teeth flash against tan skin and smooth lips while dark brown eyes crinkle with delight. The captain can't be much older than myself. A small blush creeps up my neck. I hope Harry doesn't notice.

"Signore," the captain nods his head to Harry as he helps him off the gangway.

He directs us to seats by the edge of the boat. "You are welcome to go downstairs as well. This will be a small group that I am taking to shore, but I must say sitting upstairs is the preferred way to travel on this tender. Who would want to miss out on the Caribbean wind caressing their cheeks?" He winks at me.

Harry doesn't notice. He's looking out at sea, his face turning a slight shade of green.

The pacing woman from earlier joins us on the boat, and the captain gives her the same greeting as us. I close my eyes as the vessel rocks back and forth. I've never been so thankful that my parents invited me on this vacation. I can't even fathom what article my boss would have me working on right now if I was at home. Spring is a busy time for *The BFF Birding Magazine* (*The Binocular Feather Feature Birding Magazine* is its full name, but how in the world a name like that ever got approved to be the title of a magazine is beyond my knowledge). I had been worried that my editor wasn't going to give me time off to go on this trip, but I had recently written a few big articles, so Mr. Hawking had given me the go ahead.

The captain claps his hands together and wakes me from my thoughts. I'm not upset that my mind has been pulled away from the office and back onto a boat in the middle of the Caribbean. "Welcome aboard the *Tempest Lady*," he says. He has a clipped accent. "I will be your captain today on this tender to the island. My name is Lorenzo Branca, and I am from Italy. You might be wondering how I ended up here in the Caribbean. I wonder the same thing."

There's a smattering of laughter from the few people on the boat. I notice the man most enchanted by the joke is the same one who had earlier helped the woman by the map. He must have missed the earlier departing tender as well.

One of the security officers from the cruise ship crosses the gangway and hands Captain Lorenzo some papers. They shake hands, and Captain Lorenzo gives him a smile and nod.

"Perfetto, we can now take off, and I can bring you to Lapis Rock. Enjoy your ride. Remember that just below us is some of the ocean's finest corals and aquatic life. If we are fortunate, maybe we will even see some special creatures!"

Captain Lorenzo disappears into a small, blocked off area so that he can pilot the boat. Slowly, we edge away from the cruise and out into the open ocean where in the distance, I can see the sandy beaches and the blue and pink loungers that dot the landscape.

Chapter Three

KILLDEER CAY

As the tender slices through the water, I realize that what I had thought was one long shorefront is actually two separate islands. The one with the beach umbrellas must be Lapis Rock while the other looks to be some sort of undeveloped landmass. Maybe it's a nature preserve. I wonder if there might be birding tours or nature walk excursions that explore the island. Harry and I will have to check that out when we get back to the ship later tonight. I'm so entranced by the growing scenery that I don't notice right away when the boat sputters to a stop. The lack of momentum allows the ocean to lap against the vessel and twist it from side to side.

The door leading to the small navigational quarters swings open, and Captain Lorenzo pops out. "Un momento," he says. He gives everyone a friendly smile as he heads down the stairs to the lower floor of the boat.

"Must be a mechanical issue," I say.

"It's probably something minor," Harry says. "The captain didn't look too concerned."

"We're still idling, so we'll be on the island in a blink. Maybe the propeller caught too much seaweed," the voice belongs to the older man who had helped the woman back on the cruise ship. He is seated next to Harry.

"I'm Bruce Misemueller," the man holds out his hand. "I have a boat back home." Up close, I see he has a large gap in his front teeth. "I'm retired. I take about two cruises a year. This is my first one to Lapis Rock. What about you two? Honeymooners?"

Another blush escapes me, and while I don't have a mirror, I'm sure I must be a nice fuchsia at this point. Harry laughs at the question. His pale lips spread into a smile, and some of the freckles near his mouth rearrange themselves. He's still handsome despite the hints of queasiness on his face like the small dots of sweat near his hairline or the unusually white color of his cheeks.

"No, we're here to celebrate Emma's parents. It's their anniversary. Emma and I are just dating." Harry squeezes my shoulder.

Bruce responds with a deep chuckle. His smile is gummy and small while his cheeks are large and ruddy. "You two sound like trouble! Enjoy it while you can. I still remember traveling when I was young."

There's a sudden thud on the steps as Captain Lorenzo appears. He's been running. His forehead is shiny, and he's pulling at the collar of his white uniform.

"We must reroute," he says.

"What's going on?" Harry asks.

"There has been something. It is not good. We will dock at the nearby island here." Captain Lorenzo waves his hand towards the undeveloped land.

"Excuse me," the woman who had paced in front of me earlier stands up. Her red flip-flops make plopping noises as she walks towards the captain. "What's going on? I need to get to Lapis Rock without delay. I was told this tender would get us there."

"We must detour. I cannot help it." Captain Lorenzo shrugs, but his face doesn't match his laissez-faire body language.

"This is unacceptable," the woman sits down in a huff. Her brown hair grows puffier in the humidity, making her look prickly.

Next to her, another woman crosses her arms. She looks uncomfortable. She chews her lower lip, some of the bright red lipstick painted on her mouth disappearing in the process. She's wearing a netted coverup that matches her makeup, and a red pendant necklace dangles over her chest. She clasps a hand around the stone and tugs at it. Across the boat, our eyes meet, and she quickly lets go of her necklace and threads her dark hands through her tightly coiled hair instead.

The tender lurches forward, and I fall back against Harry's strong chest. He folds his arms over me and gives me a light kiss on the neck. "If we're going to have engine trouble, I think the best place to have it is in the Caribbean," he whispers in my ear.

I snuggle against him and focus my eyes on the island coming closer. The tropical trees are starting to come into detail, and the world in front of me blooms into colors. The sand on the beach is as white as a newborn cloud while deep red flowers and tall, green grasses stretch into a nearby tree line.

But despite this, something feels wrong. A tightness aches in my stomach, and my heart sinks in my chest. I'm not sure why I'm so uncomfortable. I can't remember eating anything odd at breakfast, so I figure it must just be the way the water tilts the tender back and forth. I guess Harry isn't the only one prone to feeling ill out in the ocean.

The tender lines up with the dock, and Captain Lorenzo dashes back down the stairs. He tosses a rope from the boat to the dock and begins ensuring the vessel won't float away with the tide as he loops and ties.

"He better not think we're going to get off on this island," the woman in red flip-flops scoffs.

It's only a moment before Captain Lorenzo is back on the top deck with the rest of us who have remained seated. The collar of his white shirt is upturned and flattened against his neck. The happy face that greeted us when we boarded the vessel has been replaced by one that is flustered.

"We have a problem, so we will need to stop here. I will need to explain more, but it is best if we leave the boat."

"We're getting off here?" a man who looks to be in his late twenties asks. His hair is a coppery blond, and his nose dips foreword on his face as if it might touch his lips.

"Safer than the boat," Captain Lorenzo says.

"What does that mean?" Harry asks.

Captain Lorenzo holds a hand over his face in a dramatic pause. As he lowers it, his eyes glow glossy. "It would be best if we leave the boat before we discuss things."

"I'm not getting off this ship until I know what's going on. It doesn't look like anyone has set foot on this island for a few decades, so unless there's a real emergency, I'm staying right here," the lady with the red flip-flops fumes.

"There has been an emergency," Captain Lorenzo says. "I believe there has been a murder."

The guests on the boat all stare at Captain Lorenzo in a quiet daze. A murder happened on the boat in the short time it took the tender to leave the side of the cruise ship to reach this island?

Bruce is the first one to speak, but he doesn't say any words, instead he lets out a chuckle.

"This is not a joke," Captain Lorenzo says, his eyes full of the same darkness that must live on the bottom of the ocean. "We experienced mechanical problems, so I went downstairs to check the engine, and I found more than an engine in trouble."

"Is there a body down there?" the young man with the long nose asks.

Captain Lorenzo puts his hand back on his face again. "No. There is no body."

"How do you know there was a murder then?" Harry asks. He's standing up now, and he's starting to sound like the private detective he is outside of his free time.

Captain Lorenzo turns towards Harry. "Because when this boat left, it had seven passengers, and now there are only six."

This time, instead of a stunned silence, a cacophony of voices breaks out on the deck. The woman with the pendent necklace looks close to tears while the other woman's face is red with rage. Bruce, the retired man who had sat near Harry and I, looks confused while the younger man with the long nose looks blankly at Captain Lorenzo.

"We must not disturb anything. The lower part of this boat is now a crime scene. We will take the stairs and exit the craft immediately." Captain Lorenzo places his hands on his hips and shakes his head. "The laws of Perfect Sands Islands are very strict when it comes to crimes such as this. *Do not touch anything,*" his strong accent emphasizes the syllables.

Captain Lorenzo leads the group of us down the stairs. I want to gaze out into the water and away from the scene, but curiosity overcomes me, and I steal a glance at the lower deck. There's not much to see. I expect thick blotches of blood smeared on the floor as if someone was dragged across and dumped into the ocean, but the deck looks the same as the upper one with the exception of a small trail of blood on the seats near the edge of the tender. The sight makes me nervous. It seems all too easy to disappear at sea with little trace. A small Caribbean breeze brushes against my cheek, but it feels icy and cold. I've been involved in sticky situations before, but I've never seen or felt such an eerie emptiness come over me at the simple sight of something. Harry must sense it too because he gently rubs a hand down my back, letting me know he's still right behind me.

When we're on the dock, I pull Harry to the side as Captain Lorenzo helps the others off.

"Do you think Captain Lorenzo is right? Do you really think someone was murdered?" I ask.

Harry looks off into the distance where the bright blue ocean meets a sky of a similar hue. "I don't see why he would announce a murder if there wasn't one, and there was blood on the lower deck."

My conversation with Harry is cut short. Captain Lorenzo has assisted everyone off the boat and is leading us away from the dock to a pathway. While the island looked wild and uninhabited at first glance, I see now that it has been partially developed. Trees and grasses have been cleared where a narrow path cuts through the landscape. On a nearby tree, a black smooth-billed ani watches us with curiosity. It looks like a raven who has taken a tumble in a dryer and come out shrunken. Captain Lorenzo stops by the bird, and it disappears into the thick tangle of twigs and bushes.

"I hope you all don't mind. I wanted to give us space away from the vessel. It is not good if we stay too close to the scene. The police would not like that," he says.

"I don't think anyone wants to hang around the boat!" Bruce chimes in loudly. "Spooky stuff!"

"Where are we?" asks the younger man.

"We are on a small cay not far from Lapis Rock," answers Captain Lorenzo. "The law dictates that when an event like this happens in the waters around these islands, the vessel is to go to the nearest land." Captain Lorenzo looks around, noting the barren path. "I know there is not much here, but I have to follow the law."

"So do we just wait here until the police show up?" Harry asks. "How long will that take?"

Captain Lorenzo shakes his head. "I radioed the authorities when we were out on the water, right after I discovered...everything, but I will call again now that we are on land." He lets out a deep sigh and rubs his forehead. "I will be honest, sometimes these things do not move as quickly as they should."

"You've got to be kidding me!" The woman with the red flip-flops snaps.

"I am sorry, Signora," Captain Lorenzo says.

"That's Mrs. Opal Halladay to you! I can't believe I am stuck here on this sand dune!" She stretches out her arms and dramatically turns in a circle. "There's nothing here!" A nearby warbler lets out a raspy chirp. "Except stupid birds!"

"We must respect the law, and we are not as unfortunate as you think. This island was once a beach club. It has many amenities. It only closed recently. Come," he beckons with his hand to follow him down the path, "I will show you."

The small group of us trails behind him. Everyone seems to be reacting to the catastrophe in their own way. Bruce looks dazzled, almost entertained by the idea of something so exciting happening to him while the woman wearing the pendant necklace looks ill. There's only seven people in our party, but on this quiet island, it feels like we could make up the population of the world.

Some low palm leaves hang in the way of the path, and Captain Lorenzo holds them back for us. As we step past the leaves, the path disappears and a beach greets us. The sand is white and light like the soft sugar on a doughnut. There's a small spattering of lounge chairs out on the beach, but they look like they could be in better shape. One of them has a rip through it while the others have been tossed along the beach by wind. Off to the side, there's a bar and a small group of tables set up under a large, thatched roof. Other than that, there's not much.

"There are some cabanas on the far side of the beach, and behind the eating area is a small kitchen. There are bathrooms too if you keep following the footpath," Captain Lorenzo says. "Usually it is kept nicer, but right now, there is not much business."

"I'll be in one of the cabanas," Opal Halladay storms off. Her flip-flops sink into the white sand as she stomps away.

"Mrs. Halladay!" Captain Lorenzo shouts at her retreating figure.

But Opal isn't interested in whatever the captain has to say. She keeps wobbling down the beach. She even disturbs a group of seagulls, causing them to flap into the air and swoop around her large sun hat.

Captain Lorenzo turns back to us, dejected. "Well then, welcome to Killdeer Cay."

CHAPTER FOUR

THE SEVENTH PASSENGER

The passengers left in our group and the captain sit around one of the wooden tables in the shaded eating area. Bruce had wanted to gather up the lounge chairs and sit on the beach, but one look at his sunburnt bald spot led to Captain Lorenzo suggesting the cool shade as a better place for us to convene.

"I am very sorry for all this trouble," Captain Lorenzo has just returned from his phone call with the police, his cell still in his hand. "This is very bad. I have not had this happen before."

"No worries, Cap'," Bruce thwacks him on the back. "It's not like you killed anyone."

Harry shifts in the seat next to me and catches my eye. I'm not sure what he could be thinking.

"The cops will be here soon, and everything will work out," Bruce says. "At the end of the day, it'll all be a funny story."

Bruce's comment makes the woman sitting next to me burst into tears. Her dark, curly hair shakes as she sobs.

"Dear me, I didn't mean it like that," Bruce gives her a thwack on the back.

"It's very upsetting, but Bruce is right," I say gently.

Harry raises his eyebrows at me.

"Bruce is right about the police being here soon, not the part about it being funny," I clarify.

"It's not that," she takes a deep breath and her weeping slows. "It's all horrible, and it's all so wrong, but also..." She wipes the tears away with her hands. "Excuse me, I need a moment." She stands and walks towards the path, heading in the direction of the bathrooms.

It seems that everyone will be spread across the island if people keep leaving abruptly. I can't imagine that's what Captain Lorenzo had in mind when he harbored the boat here.

"Captain, did the police say when they would be here?" Harry restarts the conversation.

"That is the trouble. When I called, they told me there had been an incident on Lapis Rock, and it would be a while before they could send someone here."

"Do we know anything about the person who disappeared? Is there some sort of passenger list you keep in case of emergencies?" Harry asks.

"Of course," Captain Lorenzo says. He pulls out a folded paper from the pocket on the chest of his uniform. He lays it out on the table and smooths it over.

"Everyone is on here. The cruise security gave it to me before we departed. We have Emma Finch and Harry Starling from the same cabin, so that must be you two." Captain Lorenzo points towards us.

"Mr. Bruce Misemueller,"

"That's me," Bruce waves a hand in the air.

"Dane Cassigan," Captain Lorenzo looks up as the young man with the long nose and coppery blond hair gives him a salute. "And then the two ladies that left, Mrs. Opal Halladay and Ms. Samara Loweton."

Captain Lorenzo shifts in his seat. "That leaves one name left." Captain Lorenzo clears his throat, "The name of the man missing is Lloyd Alapha."

As Captain Lorenzo says the name, the wind ripples the palms high in the trees. The large, green leaves make a light noise across the island like a gentle rustling chime. I sink lower into my seat. This is far from the tropical vacation I had imagined. I've never been to a more beautiful place, but I doubt I'll enjoy a moment of it.

"I cannot apologize anymore for what has happened, but we all must wait." Captain Lorenzo looks off into the turquoise shallows.

"Did the police give you any idea of when they might arrive?" Harry asks.

Captain Lorenzo shakes his head. "No, the police on the islands are stretched thin. It can take them several hours to arrive for something of this nature."

Harry nods his head. "Hours is better than days."

Bruce leans forward, and as he does so, his stomach lets out a loud grumble. "Ope! Pardon me. My body is on cruise time!" He chuckles. Whatever happened to Lloyd Alapha doesn't seem to be bothering him much.

"I believe the kitchen is stocked if you are hungry," Captain Lorenzo says. "The beach club only closed a week ago. I cannot guarantee there will be anything fresh, but they should have something."

"If you all don't mind then," Bruce scootches out from the table. Despite sitting under the shade, the bald spot on his head is redder than when we all first landed on Killdeer Cay. He weaves in between the sets of table and chairs until he disappears behind the wooden bar. Strings of fairy lights are strewn around the bar's edges, but none of them are turned on.

I wonder why the beach club closed in the first place. The island is one of the most tranquil places I've ever seen or even imagined.

Harry must notice my mind turning because he grabs my hand under the table and gives it a tight squeeze. His thumb traces invisible lines along my fingers, and I refocus my thoughts.

He stands up. "If you don't mind, Emma and I are going to take a walk on the beach. It might clear our heads."

Captain Lorenzo replies, "I will be here in case you need me. Be careful though. We cannot have anything else happen."

CHAPTER FIVE

THE KILLDEER NEST

The water tickles my toes as it inches back and forth across the sandy beach. Underneath my feet, the sand is soft and firm. I gaze out over the horizon and see where the light blue water turns into a navy before it touches the sky. There isn't a cloud in sight, but it feels dark to me.

"Do you think Lloyd's body is out there?" I look over at Harry.

He runs a hand through his hair, ruffling it. In the bright sun, the streaks of auburn stand out against the darker brown strands. A light pink brushstroke is forming on the length of his nose as if an artist has streaked him with paint.

"I hate to think of it," he says. "It's rather bizarre, isn't it?"

"Murder usually is," I say.

Harry stares at the sand as we walk down the beach. "I don't understand how someone could've been murdered on that tender. There were only a few of us on it, and I think I would've noticed someone sneaking downstairs."

"I've had the same thoughts," I say, "but I wasn't looking at the others while we were on the water. I was looking at the scenery. I suppose I'm not the best witness."

Harry frowns. "I'm in the same boat. I didn't feel well, so I wasn't paying much attention to the movements of the others, but that doesn't mean someone else didn't see something."

"Should we ask the others if they saw anything?"

Harry turns to me, and to my surprise, his eyes are twinkling, and his smile is spread wide across his face.

"What?" I ask.

"Emma, I know we've found ourselves in the middle of mysteries before, but we don't need to go investigating what happened to Lloyd. Remember, the captain said the police would be here in a few hours." He laces his fingers through mine. "I think for once we might be caught up in a murder that we don't need to investigate."

"I guess old habits die hard." I give Harry a small peck on the cheek, and we keep walking down the sandy shore.

I smile up at Harry, but something doesn't feel right. Like the waves hitting the nearby rocks, my anxiety smashes against my stomach. Harry is right. Whatever happened on the lower deck will be handled by the police, and it's not anything I should be worried about, but for some reason, something is gnawing at my gut. Something is telling me I shouldn't forget about what happened. Something is telling me Harry and I may not be completely safe here.

A scream breaks through the air, and Harry and I startle apart.

"It sounded like a woman," I say. "It must be one of the women who went off alone."

Harry looks towards the thick bushes where the scream originated. I pull him towards the trees. My thoughts move as fast as my legs. There were only eight people on the tender, and there are seven people on this island now. That means that one of them might be a murderer, and no one is safe.

The dry grass scratches at my calves, and a hot burning itches my skin where small cuts must be appearing, but Harry and I don't stop. Another high-pitched scream travels through the air as we tumble out of the weeds and back onto the island path.

Not too far away, Opal stands shaking. She's clutching her purse so tightly that the pinks of her nails are white. She glances up and sees Harry and me.

"Help!" she yells, her voice shrill. She rushes towards us. Her face is covered in sweat, and she's missing one of her flip-flops.

"Are you okay?" I ask her.

"Did someone hurt you?" Harry looks behind Opal, checking to see if anyone is there, but no one is.

Opal trembles, and the dark waves of her hair shake. "That thing attacked me!"

She points to the undergrowth and unkempt grasses by the path. I expect to see reptilian eyes or a mammalian head poking out at me, but I don't see anything.

I take a slow step towards the bushes.

"Emma, be careful," Harry says while Opal gasps.

I bend down towards the area where Opal had pointed, and suddenly something white and brown flops on the path, screeching and squealing and somersaulting.

"Get away from it!" Opal yells. "It's about to attack!"

A bout of giggles takes over me. It's a plump bird with a white stomach, brown wings, and striped collar. It shuffles witlessly on the path with its wings flapping about before it disappears back under the underbrush.

"You're not thinking straight! That thing could've hurt you!" Opal fans her face with her hand.

I fold my arms over my stomach. I'm laughing so much that my abdomen hurts.

"She doesn't understand the danger she was in. Look at how she's laughing." Opal pulls at Harry's shirt desperately.

"It was just a bird," I manage to squeak out between giggles.

"And most likely a deadly one at that," Opal shakes her head. "I cannot believe how close I've come to death today. Twice in a row, and they say things come in threes."

The laughing finally subsides, and I'm able to take a few deep breaths. "It's a killdeer," I say.

"No, it was too small to be a killer deer," Opal awkwardly pats me on the shoulder. She is near enough to me that her floral perfume overwhelms my nose. "This island has caused her to lose her mind," she shakes her head. "It's a horrible place. I don't know what that captain was thinking, dropping us all here."

"No, it's not a deer, it's a killdeer. It's a type of bird," I say. "When they're nesting and have eggs, they pretend they're injured and make loud sounds. We must be near its nest. If we walk over there again, it'll do the same thing. The island must be filled with them, hence the name, Killdeer Cay."

"This place is absolutely treacherous." Opal reaches into her purse and grabs a pair of sunglasses that she slips over her eyes.

Harry and I return back to the kitchen area of the beach club, but it's empty. Bruce and Captain Lorenzo must've gone off somewhere. I have no idea how large this island might be, but I have no doubt that there are lots of nooks and crannies considering the intricate paths that carve their way through the dry shrubbery.

Harry plops onto a nearby lounge chair and pulls his phone out. I grab my own phone from my pocket. I know I won't have service on the island since I don't have an international plan, but there could be an off chance that the beach club hasn't disconnected their Wi-Fi yet. I type in my password, and sure enough, I'm able to login to the nearby network.

The first thing I notice is a slew of missed texts from my mother.

MOM: AT THE PORT!
MOM: MEET AT SUNSHIN SANDS BACH CLUB.
MOM: SORRY FOR SPELLING.
MOM: BARTENDER VEY FUNNY!
MOM: WHER DID YOUR FATHER GO?
MOM: FOUND HIM BY BATROOM!

I debate sending a text to my parents to tell them what happened, but I decide against it. I don't want them to stress on their vacation. Plus, it sounds like they are having fun wherever they are on Lapis Rock.

"What's new?" Harry asks me. He's peaking over my shoulder.

"Mom sounds like she's having fun. I'll text her in a bit. I don't want her get worried about us."

Harry lays his head back against his chair and closes his eyes. A light pink spreads across his pale shoulders, and he has more freckles on his nose than he did this morning.

I lay my head back too and try to relax like Harry, but I can't stop thinking about what might've happened on the lower deck of the tender. How was it possible for someone, Lloyd Alapha according to Captain Lorenzo's passenger list, to be murdered without anyone noticing? It wasn't like the boat was huge. Sure, Harry and I were both distracted, and the captain would've been navigating the waters, but someone must've noticed a person sneaking around.

"Are you still thinking about what happened?" Harry asks. He's looking directly at me with a twinkle in his amber eyes and a small grin on his face.

"It's difficult not to think about it," I say.

"Let's explore the island then. Sitting here isn't helping either of us."

I raise an eyebrow. "Does that mean you were thinking about it too?"

Harry's grin widens. He stands up and grabs my hands, pulling me to my feet.

"Let's go on the paths," he leads me away from the blue water and back to the inland. "Maybe we'll see something interesting. Like some birds," he winks at me. I know Harry isn't into birdwatching the way I am, but he tries.

Despite our earlier encounters with several bird species, the island is eerily quiet. Not even the sound of cicadas breaks the silent hum of the still air. Harry and I pass by gnarled trees with twisted limbs and tall, yellow grasses that have been dried out from the harsh sun, but there are no animals in sight.

Finally, the path we are on ends abruptly at a weather-worn bench. We both take a seat, sweat pooling at my temples and on the hollow of Harry's neck. We can't see the ocean, but we must be close to the water. The quiet shush of the waves running and retreating off the sand can be heard.

"I'm not too surprised this place shut down," I say. "There's not much around here."

"Maybe if we went to the other side of the island there might be more," Harry says. "Several people left the main eating area, and they didn't go back, so they must've found somewhere to wait."

"Should we try the path again?" I ask.

Harry gives me a simple nod, and we both stand up, but as we do, someone walks into sight. Farther down the path, a woman appears. It must be Samara Loweton. Her curly hair is disheveled and pressed against her dark skin from the heat. She's biting the nails on her one hand while the other clings to her pendant necklace. When she spots Harry and I, she stops and turns around, but then she seems to change her mind and turn back to us.

"Samara," I give her a friendly wave.

Her eyes grow large, and she freezes on sight. I look behind me, wondering if some animal is approaching, but nothing is there. It must be Harry and I that are making her uncomfortable.

As we get near her, she takes a step back.

"There's not much to do around here, is there?" I say, trying to be friendly.

She eyes me up and down. Small red veins climb around her dark irises. She looks as if she's been crying a good bit since we last saw her.

"Is everything okay?" I ask.

"How did you know my name?" She pulls at her pendant necklace.

"Captain Lorenzo shared the passenger list after you left. There were only three women, and I know you're not Opal Halladay, and I know you're not me, so I assumed you were Samara."

Samara's shoulders relax, and she lets go of her pendant. "Right, right," she says. She tucks a loose curl behind her ear. "I'm getting paranoid out here. What were your names?"

"I'm Emma, and this is Harry."

"I'm so embarrassed." Samara lets out an uncomfortable laugh. "You two are obviously a normal couple, and I'm freaking out at everything. It's this island."

"Harry and I were just thinking about walking to the other side to see if there's anything over there. Do you want to come with us?"

Samara doesn't hesitate. "Yes, yes. If I spend any more time alone, my thoughts will eat me."

"We were feeling the same way," Harry says. "Emma and I tried to relax by the beach, but we couldn't stop thinking about what happened."

Samara frowns, her lips pulling at the sides of her face. "Whenever I think about it, my heart goes fast." She brings her hand back up to her pendant and clenches it.

"It can be disturbing, but the police will be here soon like the captain said," Harry reassures her.

"Right, right," she tucks another curl behind her ear.

The three of us take to the path, but there's no ignoring the awkwardness that breathes around us. Samara keeps glancing around her, her eyes dodging left and right, and her head turning every so often as if someone is following us. We reach another rickety bench on the path, and Samara runs over to it before bursting into a violent bout of tears.

"I'm so sorry," she hiccups.

I sit down next to her on the bench and sling a comforting arm around her shoulders. "It's okay. These things are awful."

"Why are you sorry?" Harry asks. Unlike me, he isn't sitting next to Samara but has remained standing on the path.

"I just feel so terrible," she cries.

"Why? Did you do something?" Harry raises a brow.

I glare at him. His inner detective is coming out, and it's certainly not the right time. Samara is crying and alone on an abandoned island. The last thing she needs is an interrogation. Can't Harry see how upset she is?

"She didn't do anything wrong," I snap. "She's upset because of the murder. Anyone would feel terrible after that. If they didn't, that would be a problem."

Harry clamps his mouth shut. He might be angry at me, but we can talk about that later. Right now, Samara needs to be consoled.

Samara takes a shaky breath. "I can't keep walking around the island. I have to tell someone."

Harry opens his mouth to say something but closes it again when he sees me catch his eye.

"You can tell us," I say.

Samara gulps and takes another shaky breath. "I think I was the one who was supposed to be murdered."

Chapter Six

An Inheritance Awaits

I'm suddenly aware of the humid and suffocating air on Killdeer Cay making it difficult to breathe. Why would Samara think she was the one meant to be murdered? Had she done something? Seen something? Did she know the other passengers personally?

"I know it sounds strange, but if I explain everything to you, it will make sense," Samara says.

"We're here to listen," I say.

Harry takes a seat next to me on the bench. His earlier apprehension towards Samara has evaporated.

"I'm not here because I'm on vacation," Samara starts. "The reason I scheduled this trip was to come to Perfect Sands Islands so that I could meet with extended family. My grandfather is, I mean was, from the main island. I recently inherited a large estate after his death, and I wanted to see the property without some of my other family members knowing. I thought taking a cruise would be a good cover. No one could prove that I had been intending to come here to see the land. I even went ahead and scheduled full-day excursions in case anyone in the family asked about my cruise plans."

Samara pauses to wipe a tear off her cheek.

"I've made my fair share of mistakes in life, and several people in my family cut me off, but my grandfather was never one of them. When he passed not too long ago, my great aunt, my grandfather's sister, was upset that he kept me in his will. She's made it clear to me that she and her husband will do anything to prevent me from getting the estate. It doesn't matter that my grandfather was a wealthy man and left her several of his vacation homes. In her eyes, I deserve nothing."

"What makes you think your great aunt would resort to such violence?" Harry asks.

Samara shudders, and a few more tears fall from her large eyes. She blinks them away. "My great aunt isn't like most. She is twenty years younger than my grandfather, and she's spent her life making him feel horrible for the privileges their parents bestowed on him and not her." Samara pulls at her pendant necklace. "There are other reasons too, things that haven't added up when I think about them. People close to her who have gone through things that they shouldn't have. Friends of hers that have died too young."

Samara lets go of her necklace. "I've said too much. I know no one will believe me, but it's my gut. I was supposed to be the person killed on that boat, and for some reason, they got the wrong person."

I'm not sure how to respond to Samara. I don't know anything about her great aunt, so what she's saying could be valid, but it's also possible her nerves have run away with her thoughts.

"Did you see anything suspicious when we were on the tender?" Harry asks.

Samara closes her eyes for a second, but then she shakes her head. "No, no. I was so concerned with how I would get to my grandfather's estate that

I wasn't paying much attention to what was going on." Samara's shoulders shake and more tears fall from her eyes. "Imagine if I had taken a seat on the lower deck? I wouldn't be on this island now. I would be dead!"

"But what matters is that you didn't, and you aren't hurt," I say softly.

"But I could be at any moment," Samara says.

"You think you still might be in danger?" Harry asks. "From someone here on Killdeer Cay?"

Samara looks at us and lowers her voice. "When we docked, we were missing one, only one, person, and that person had been murdered. Someone on this island is a killer."

My heart thumps against my chest. Obviously, I know what Samara says is true, and it shouldn't come as a surprise, but it does. Someone on this island could be a danger to not only Samara, but everyone, and there's no way for us to run or hide. We're all stuck on Killdeer Cay whether we like it or not.

"We can stick together then," Harry says. "If there is danger on this island like you say, one person won't be able to take on three."

"Harry's right. There's safety in numbers."

"Let's keep exploring," Harry says. "If we want to feel safe, we need to know the territory. It'll also distract us from our thoughts."

We all stand and continue on the walkway towards the opposite side of the island. Eventually, we come to a small cove with a rocky beach and some abandoned fishing equipment. The ocean is active here. It slams against the black rocks that jut up out of the water, sending crystallized saltwater spray into the air.

"The water is rougher on this side of the island. We must be facing a different direction," Harry says.

"Look!" I point to something on the horizon. "You can see Lapis Rock from here."

"If only we were close enough to swim," Samara says." We would be able to escape."

"There you three are!"

I turn and see Bruce. As unbelievable as it may be, he is even more sunburnt now than he was when Harry and I last saw him. I hope he packed some aloe or else he will be feeling crispy rather than chipper.

"We wanted to explore the island," I say. "Were people looking for us?"

"Just dear old me!" Bruce says. "I got a bit bored with the Cap' and that other guy. I thought I would do some exploring myself. This little beach here is neat. Maybe we could go for a fish!" He nods to the fishing rods and tackle box leaning against the palm trees.

Samara crosses her arms at the sight of a newcomer. I'm not sure why she decided she could trust Harry and me, but she may not warm up to Bruce the way she did to us.

"I went and had a look at the other side of the island. It has more beach cabanas and a reef sectioned off for snorkeling. I bet this place wasn't too shabby when it was up and running. I wonder why it closed." Bruce puts his hands in his pockets and looks out towards the ocean. The Hawaiian shirt he is wearing blends in with the turquoise waters.

"It's a bit funny we ended up here. I had planned to go on an excursion to a different beach club today. It's like I got upgraded to my own private oasis." He chuckles. "Zany stuff!" Bruce leans back on his heals. "I never thought I'd be part of a murder. Vacations can sure take a turn!"

Unlike Samara, he doesn't act bothered at all by what happened on the tender. I'm not sure if that points to guilt or innocence.

Harry mimics his stance and puts his hands in his pockets. "Makes you wonder what happened," he says to Bruce. "Did you see anything odd yourself?"

I fight the urge to raise my eyebrows. Harry had been the one to remind me that we weren't going to investigate what happened. Why is he now asking Bruce questions? Could he really think we are as unsafe as Samara thinks we are?

"Welp, I wish I'd seen something. I was busy looking out at the horizon." He pats his belly. "I ate some shrimp for breakfast that were a bit off. I was trying to calm the seas so to say. I feel much better now that we're on land."

Harry removes his hands from his pockets. "I think I might check out the cabanas like you suggested."

"Okie dokie! They're out that way," Bruce gestures to a part of the island path that is shaded by palm trees and runs on the edge of the island. "See you three around! Don't be strangers!"

He gives us a friendly wave before going over and inspecting the fishing gear. I glance back one final time as we walk onto the path. He's bending down and examining the contents of the tackle box, lost in his own world.

CHAPTER SEVEN

TO THE NORTH

On the other end of the island, Samara, Harry, and I find the cabanas that Bruce had mentioned. They're not in the same good shape as the ones on the main beach. They have wooden slats for walls and straw roofs that could use some TLC. There are three in total, each painted in a soft pastel. The closest cabana is painted the pink of a conch shell.

"Should we go explore?" I turn to Harry and Samara.

"Might as well," Harry says. "It's not like we have anything else to do."

Closer up, I see that the pink cabana needs a lot of maintenance. The steps leading up to the airy room are rotting, and the plywood floors are covered in a thick layer of sand. I skip over the bottom step, trying to avoid the rot, but I slip on the second one, flying backwards onto the sand.

"Are you okay?" Harry rushes over and helps me up.

I sweep my legs off. "I would've thought sand was softer, but I'm alright."

Harry brushes some sand of my back and tucks a loose strand of hair behind my ear. "It looks like you might've injured yourself," he looks down. "You're bleeding."

There's a small scrape on the top of my foot. Bright blood dots my skin like a line of ladybugs. Next to my foot, a large piece of rotten wood lies in the sand. When I fell, I must've dislodged the slat on the second step. The step now sits crooked, and something red is sticking out from underneath it.

"There's something under the stairs," I point to the bit of red poking out.

Harry grabs the edge of the second step and tugs at it until the wood comes loose. He picks up a small, red journal. The book is weatherworn, and the leather on its cover has gone soft with age.

"Looks like a forgotten diary," Harry flips through the book. "It's just filled with a few pages of random numbers." He opens it up to a section and shows it to me and Samara.

"Probably just some tourist playing a prank," I say. "Maybe it leads to lost treasure." I give him an exaggerated wink.

"In that case, I better keep it," Harry returns my wink.

I roll my eyes playfully at Harry.

"Realistically, someone came up with some sort of silly code and left it here to see if anyone could crack it. I can work on it while we wait around the island," Harry says.

"Do you think it could end up being important?" I ask.

Harry smiles. "No, but there's not much else to do around here, is there?"

"I can't argue with that," I say.

Harry tucks the journal safely away in his backpack before we go ahead into the cabana, but there isn't much to find. The lounge chairs are in good shape, and it's an ideal spot to get out of the sun while still enjoying the ocean views, but none of us are in the mood to relax today. The other two cabanas, one a mint green and another an Easter blue, look identical.

Out of the corner of my eye, I see Samara fidget. Maybe if we keep mapping out the island, she will stay distracted until the police arrive. I don't know if Harry and I will be able to calm her down if she breaks down a second time.

"Do you think there might be anything else on the island?" I ask.

"I'm always down to explore," Harry says.

We set back out on the path, but we don't make it far. Just around the corner, Bruce pops out from behind some sort of flowering plant with large, pink petals. He really should consider sitting in the shade instead of wandering the island. His nose is lobster red and so are his ears. He'll be in a lot of pain tonight if he doesn't find some aloe.

"Fancy us running into each other again! Did you find the cabanas I mentioned?" Bruce asks.

"We did," Harry says. "Did you get any fishing in?"

Bruce laughs deeply from his belly. "I thought about it, but then I realized, there's a greater chance of me becoming a fish's meal than one becoming mine!"

Harry smiles politely as Bruce chuckles at his own joke.

"Oh! Before I forget again!" Bruce reaches into his back pocket and pulls out a folded piece of paper. He holds it out for Harry to take. "When I was having a look around the kitchen, I found some maps of the island. I grabbed a few and thought I'd give them out to prevent people from getting lost."

Harry opens the map so that both I and Samara can see it. From far away, the island is the shape of a kidney bean. The beach that Captain Lorenzo brought everyone to is on the side of the island that bulges out into the ocean while the cabanas we just explored are at the bottom near a reef, making it a perfect place for scuba diving. The little cove with the fishing gear is the island's bay.

"We've only seen about half of the island," I point to the spot on the map that we stand in now.

"It couldn't hurt to make our way to the other side," Harry says. "Knowing the territory is always helpful."

"Let's get started on the main path here," Bruce's large index finger jabs at one of the trails on the map.

Harry clears his throat but doesn't speak. I know he hadn't been planning on inviting Bruce on our expedition, but it would be rude not to let him tag along.

"I've had enough exploring for now," Samara says. "I'm going to find a place to rest for a bit."

She eyes Bruce, failing to disguise the guarded distrust she must be feeling towards him. I'm surprised that she wouldn't rather stick with us than stay by herself, but maybe she senses something about Bruce that Harry and I don't. Or maybe she's decided she doesn't trust Harry and I and is hoping to wait out the arrival of help in a space that is more private.

"Are you sure you don't want to stick with us?" I ask.

Samara's large eyes don't look into mine. They are trained on the ground. "I know someone on this island has it out for me. I can't take any risks," she whispers so that only I can hear.

She drops back from the group as we start to make our way towards the other side of the island. The message is clear. For one reason or another, she doesn't want to go with us. Whether it's paranoia or a secret she knows, we'll find out eventually.

The path narrows. It looks as if this section may not have been designed for tourists to explore. It is ill-maintained and filled with holes and cracks. I take care to watch where I step. I can't imagine twisting my ankle while we're alone on the island.

We pass a wall of flowers blossoming from a collection of tall bushes. The petals are buttery yellow and sink into the center of the blooms, giving the flowers cup-like structures. They remind me a bit of daffodils. I wonder if

Lapis Rock will be similar to Killdeer Cay, or if the natural beauty around me is rare in the islands. It won't be long before the police arrive, and we can view the main island for ourselves.

As we turn a corner, Bruce calls out in pain. He falls to the ground and grabs his ankle.

"Ope!" He cries. "I've rolled it. Must've been one of the dips in the path."

Harry crouches down to take a closer look at Bruce's ankle. While it appears fine for now, if he's truly injured it, it won't be long before it swells.

"Let me help you up," Harry offers him his hand.

Bruce attempts to step on his bad ankle, but he crumples back to the ground.

"It's a bad one," he says with a grimace.

"I'll go get Captain Lorenzo. He probably has a first aid kit somewhere," I say.

"I'll come with you," Harry stands back up.

"I'll go alone. We shouldn't leave Bruce by himself," I reply.

I take off down the path at a run, retracing the steps we took here. At least, that's what I hope I'm doing. Everything is looking the same. The grass is all overgrown and a paled, dried yellow color. The shrubs and trees are unfamiliar, and there aren't any animals around, not even the killdeer that scared Opal earlier.

A sharp stitch hits my side, and I pause to take a breath. The island is big, but it's not big enough for me to panic. Eventually, I'll have to pop out at one of the many beaches and be able to reorient myself. Something behind me rustles, and I flip around. The low bushes shake, but the air is still. Maybe a killdeer is on the edge of the path, nesting with its eggs.

I ignore the distraction and push on. I pass large hibiscus plants with pink faces that stretch towards the sky along with a small family of warblers. The land around me explodes with hues bright enough to inspire the dullest of artists to experiment with their color palette.

Eventually, I stumble out onto a beachy area just a little way down from the main beach. This must be where the other cabanas are that Harry and I didn't get around to exploring. The same ones that Opal Halladay stormed off to earlier. Unlike the ones on the private beach that were painted in pastels, these are done up in bright oranges and blues with complementary white stripes. I wonder if Opal might be in one of them.

As if she can hear my thoughts, Opal pops her head out of the orange cabana right in front of me.

"Oh, it's you." She frowns. At her side, she still clutches her oversized purse. A large sun hat casts a shadow across her face, and her white dress wrinkles in the breeze. "I heard some sounds out here. I thought someone was sneaking around, but you don't seem the type." She lowers her sunglasses so that she can have a better look at me. "No offense. You just seem a bit...simple."

"Thanks," I mumble, unsure if that was an insult or a very odd compliment.

Opal shrugs her shoulders before disappearing back into the cabana. It's peculiar, but I don't have time to analyze her behavior. I have to get help for Bruce.

Farther down on the main beach, Captain Lorenzo is sprawled on one of the lounge chairs. Dane Cassigan is sitting next to him, fiddling on his phone. When they see me, they both sit forward.

"Is everything okay, mia bella?" Captain Lorenzo stands.

"Bruce tripped on one of the paths. He hurt his ankle."

Captain Lorenzo puts his hands on his hips. "This is not good. I will grab the first aid kit from the kitchen. Will you be able to show me the way?"

My head stops mid nod. "I got a bit lost coming back here."

"That's okay," Captain Lorenzo says. "Tell me where you were headed when it happened, and I will be able to find them."

"We were trying to check out the northern end of the island."

Something dark flickers across Captain Lorenzo's face, but then it disappears like a small cloud covering the sun, fleeting.

"You stay here, and I will go by myself. Keep Mr. Cassigan company. I will not be long." He sprints off. I watch him disappear into the kitchen for a moment before coming back out with a small, red box with a cross on it. Then, he's gone onto the trail, heading north.

I take a seat next to Dane on a lounge chair. The mesh material is warm against my skin. I hope it doesn't take Captain Lorenzo long to find Harry and Bruce. I imagine he knows this island a lot better than I do.

Next to me, Dane texts furiously on his phone. Deep lines etch his forehead, and he cracks his neck several times. Abruptly, Dane sits up and tosses his phone on the end of his chair.

"Everything okay?" I eye the discarded phone at his feet.

"As good as it will ever be." He lets out a sigh.

I don't want to press into his private business, so I lay my head back against the lounge chair. I close my eyes against the bright sun. Behind my lids, I can still see the luminous flowers and birds that call the island home. The sun warms my cheeks, and I wonder how long my sunscreen will hold up until I need to reapply it. And if I need to reapply it soon, Harry definitely will too. He is much paler than me. Hopefully when—

"It's frustrating," Dane interrupts my thoughts. "I'm not trying to have a pity party for myself, but at this point, I have nothing to lose."

I glance over at him. The lines of his face have grown deeper, and he's shaking his head while staring off into the distance.

His phone buzzes, and he snatches it up.

"I'm going to power off my phone. Nothing I do will make her happy," he gestures to his phone that now lies in his lap. "We've been married less than five days, and she's no happier than she was before."

"I take it you're on your honeymoon?"

"One heck of a honeymoon." He clenches his fists. "She's furious. She doesn't believe that I'm stuck here on this island. She thinks I'm off hiding from her or something."

"I'm sure your wife is just worried."

"Nope. Not Jill. She can't trust me. I mess up one time, and everything is my fault."

I dig my toes into the sand and avoid looking at Dane. I'm not exactly an expert on romantic relationships. I rack my brain for ways to deflect the conversation, but birds and flowers are the only topics I can think up.

"I came back to the room late last night because I was catching the rest of the game in the sports bar, and she accuses me of being with another woman. She knows I was at the bar. I *told her* I was going to the bar." Dane lays back in his chair and huffs. He crosses his arms and flairs his nostrils like a bull readying to charge.

"Lucky me, I get to be on the boat where someone got murdered." Dane throws his hands in the air. "I missed my original boat because Jill and I had a big blowup fight at breakfast, and I couldn't find where she went. I searched all over that ship, and it turns out she had gone ahead and gotten on the tender. Now I have a slew of messages accusing me of lying." His eyes bulge a bit. "Like I actually want to be here instead of with her."

I nod my head awkwardly.

"And that jerk at dinner last night didn't help." He looks at me as if I had been sitting right next to him during supper, sharing appetizers and toasting champagne.

"He just waltzed right up and made a big mess, and then he did it at breakfast again!" Dane looks out onto the water, his light eyes a striking blue in the bright sunlight. "I guess I don't have to worry about him anymore though," he murmurs under his breath.

Thankfully, there's a buzzing in my pocket. "So sorry, but I've got to take this," I hold my phone up to show Dane the incoming call.

I scamper out of the lounge chair and to the eating area. There's no way I'm going to spend any extra time with Dane if I can help it. Whatever is going on between him and his wife is something that can't be fixed while he's stranded on Killdeer Cay.

Once I'm out of earshot, I answer my phone.

"Emma Finch?" a rough voice I would recognize anywhere greets me. It's my boss and editor, Mr. Hawking.

"Mr. Hawking? Is everything alright at the magazine?"

"It will be as soon as you turn in your article," he says.

"My article? I'm on vacation, remember? I went to the Caribbean with my parents."

"Did you put in for time off? Because I need that article, Finch."

I sputter. How could Mr. Hawking forget that he had approved my vacation leave? I had talked about it with him multiple times. Before I can answer, Mr. Hawking cuts in.

"Boston cream!" He shouts down the line. "All over my new shirt too. Mrs. Hawking will have a field day when I get home."

I hear a series of scrapes and shuffling in the background. Mr. Hawking tends to be prone to food-related accidents. He really should just eat spill-proof things like protein bars and apples. Although, he would probably spill those somehow too.

"Mr. Hawking?"

There's no reply, and the call ends. Great. Now I'm stuck on an island with a possible murderer, and my boss wants me to write an article for him. I'm not sure which one is worse. I plunk down in one of the seats in the eating area when my phone buzzes in my lap. I expect it to be Mr. Hawking calling back, but it's my parents. It had slipped my mind that they had been patiently waiting on Lapis Rock for Harry and I to meet them this whole time. Guilt stretches its fingers through my chest. I hope that they aren't too worried.

"Emma?" My mother's voice comes through the phone.

"I'm okay," I say quickly, trying to dispel any worry she might have about why I haven't turned up on the main island yet.

"You will not believe what happened! Your father and I were on the beach, you know, the part where that little bar in the shape of a dolphin is?"

I glance down at the time on my phone. A couple hours have gone by since my parents left the cruise ship on their own, non-murderous tender. Have they not wondered where Harry and I have been?

"The bar has these little lights that are pink and blue. The bulbs are in the shapes of octopuses? Or is it octopi? I'll have to ask your father what the word is," my mother continues her monologue. Clearly, neither her nor Dad have been too concerned about my whereabouts.

"Your father and I were sitting right at the bar top, having the most delightful drink. Mine was called something cute, an orange sunshine burst, something colorful like that, and I look to my left, and the most dashing man is sitting next to me. He looks like one of those movie stars. Dark hair, almond shaped eyes, perfect skin."

"Mom," I try to cut in, but she doesn't hear me, or if she does, she ignores me.

"I'm looking, gawking really, at this gorgeous man, and I'm thinking to myself, what movie have I seen him in? When it hits me!"

"Mom," I cut in again, but she keeps talking.

"It was your friend!"

"My friend?" I ask.

This time she either hears me or is willing to acknowledge what I said because it fits with the course of her conversation. "Your friend Charlie. The one who is a chef!"

"Charlie is a food writer, not a chef. But that's beside the point, Charlie is on Lapis Rock?"

"I couldn't believe it either, but then I asked. I leaned forward and I said *Are you Charlie Kim?"* My mother laughs loudly. "He about jumped out of his seat, so I explained to him who I was. He was delighted! He can't wait to see you and Harry!"

Charlie is a good friend of mine. I met him at the same time I met Harry when I was visiting my Great Aunt Lois's home. We had all been stranded together by a windstorm. Charlie is a world traveler, so it shouldn't seem too shocking that he tends to show up in the most random of places.

"What's he doing on Lapis Rock?" I ask.

"He's here for a food festival or something. I don't remember exactly, but anyway, I have to run! They're about to start the dance-a-thon. The prize is a free crab dinner!"

The phone clicks off.

I let out a groan. I guess my parents are one less thing that I have to worry about. They're not wondering at all where Harry and I have gotten off to.

There's a rustling over by the path, and Captain Lorenzo walks my way. He's carrying the red first aid kit and has a serious look on his face. I stand up to greet him.

"How'd it go?" I ask.

"I couldn't find either of them," Captain Lorenzo says.

"What do you mean?" I know that the trails have twists and turns, but I thought for certain that Captain Lorenzo would be able to navigate them without issue.

"I searched all over the area that you said they were in, but no one was there."

"They had to be somewhere around there. Bruce could barely walk when I last saw them."

"Maybe they took a break on one of the beaches." Captain Lorenzo shrugs his shoulders. "No one can leave the island. We are all stuck here together."

Captain Lorenzo means his words to comfort me, but they do the opposite. There is no way for anyone to leave the island. If Harry and Bruce weren't where they were supposed to be, something could have happened to them. Whoever hurt Lloyd on the tender could've gone for them. Or even Bruce could've faked his injury to get Harry alone. Samara had seemed incredibly suspicious of him earlier. Did she know something about him?

Chapter Eight

THE HOUSE OF SAFETY

D own on the beach, Captain Lorenzo and Dane throw pieces of lost driftwood back into the sea. I know Harry had told me not to think too much about what had happened on the tender, but with Harry now missing, it could be his life in danger. Maybe I shouldn't feel so comfortable trusting these people around me. After all, every single one of them is a stranger, and a stranger killed Lloyd Alapha.

The skin on the back of my neck prickles. Whether the cause is the strong sun or my racing thoughts, I'm not sure. It's been close to an hour since I last saw Harry, and right now, sitting on the beach in Killdeer Cay is anything but relaxing. I know it's not the smartest move, but I'm going to go look for Harry.

I head north on the path. The farther I go, the more the island comes alive. I come across two more killdeer nests with overenthusiastic parents who squeak and flap their wings when they see me approaching. If Mr. Hawking insists that I write an article for the magazine, I might end up doing it on the killdeer. They might not be the typical bird people find in their backyards, but they're definitely full of personality. Along with the birds, there are pink and red flowers in bloom that decorate the lowest branches of the trees. The grass is healthier too. It's dark green and greedily reaches towards the sky.

After a short time, the path beneath my feet grows sandy, and the tall grasses thin. In their place, dark rocks and small boulders scatter the ground, and the ocean can be seen once again. I understand why this part of the island was never developed. The water is full of jagged limestones and sharp coral.

Up ahead, on the edge of the rocks, a small structure stands erect. It's made of whitewashed stones and appears rather old. As I near it, I see that there is a plaque on one of its walls. It reads:

Here Stands The House of Safety

Built in 1877

Killdeer Cay was once a popular stopping point for ships during bad weather. Lapis Rock's shallow shores were difficult to navigate. If ships came to harbor and couldn't reach the main island, they would stop at Killdeer Cay. Small stone houses once dotted the island, but now only one stands. In 1894, a strong hurricane hit Perfect Sands Islands, and the House of Safety was the only structure left standing. The house was named by those who took refuge on the island as it was known to be used by sailors seeking shelter during storms.

There's no door on the one room house, just an open archway. Inside, a healthy cross breeze makes the tiny hairs on my arms stand up. Not much furniture is in the space. There's a rickety desk and a bare bench. The floorboards beneath my feet aren't very thick either. They give slightly as I walk towards the window overlooking the sea. The wood under the window is in the worst shape, puckering at the sides. One of the slats is so loose that it needs to be nailed down. Otherwise, anyone could come along and pluck it from the floor. In fact, it reminds me a bit of the rotting step out by the cabanas.

I bend down and tug at the plank. It comes away with ease. Beneath it is a small hiding space. I'm not sure what I thought I'd find, maybe another journal, or some ancient letters, but what lies beneath the floor is the last thing I thought that I would see.

A dagger, red with blood, sparkles in the light coming in from the open door. My stomach turns, and I slam the wooden plank back down. It's not the type of thing I expected to unearth in a place named *The House of Safety,* and it's not the type of thing I wanted to find on Killdeer Cay, but it confirms what I've known all along. One of us on this island is a killer, and no one is safe until the police get here.

With chills running down my back, I go back outside. I know the gusts of wind coming off the water haven't become colder, but I'm shivering either way. I need to find Harry. I don't know what I'll do if something happens to him.

I step out onto one of the boulders that juts into the sea near *The House of Safety* and look down the shoreline. Seagulls loop and dip in the air and bubbles surface in the swirls of the ocean. Farther down the beach, I see two people hobbling on the shoreline. I squint, and can make out that one of them has brownish hair while the other looks to be balding. Could it be Harry and Bruce?

I don't hesitate. I climb off the boulder and sprint down the shore towards them while a million thoughts cruise through my head. Why are Harry and Bruce so far from where I last left them on the path? Why did they leave the path and end up on the beach in the first place?

When I'm close enough, I call out, "Harry!"

Harry stops and turns around. A huge smile breaks across his face when he recognizes me. I smile back, but as I get closer, my smile falls.

Harry's face has a large scratch on it, and his cheek is bleeding.

"Are you okay?" I ask and grab him in a tight hug. "Did someone attack you?"

Bruce breaks out into a chuckle. "He took a little spill! He fell just like I did." Bruce thwacks Harry on the back. "Unlike me, he took the blow with his face! Looked like one of those funny movies." Bruce laughs heartily.

"I'm happy you're okay." I squeeze Harry even harder.

"Why would you think someone had attacked us?" Harry asks, a look of concern threading across his face.

I open my mouth but then quickly close it. The last thing I want to do is tell Harry about the dagger I found right in front of Bruce. Bruce seems friendly on the surface, but like the ocean around us, it's impossible to know how deep his secrets may stretch.

"Captain Lorenzo went looking for you, but he said he couldn't find you."

"That would be my fault," Bruce says with a smile, the gap in his teeth showing. "Silly me thought we could make our way back, but we got turned around. Some sort of aggressive bird jumped out at us on the path, and we couldn't figure out which way was up or down after that!"

I exchange a look with Harry. It sounds like they came across a killdeer nest. The poor birds probably aren't accustomed to so much foot traffic near their homes.

"I'm happy I found you," I say more so to Harry than Bruce. "I was starting to think the worst."

Harry gently runs his hand down my arm before lightly caressing my hand. Going forward, I won't leave his side. Killdeer Cay isn't the place to be left alone.

The three of us orient ourselves and trek back to the main beach. Captain Lorenzo and Dane are still there. They've moved away from the lounge chairs and have taken up residence under the thatched roof of the dining area. Between the two of them, there sits a bowl of chips and guacamole.

"Where'd you two come across that prize?" Bruce steps right up to the table and grabs a chip before slathering a large helping of guacamole on it.

My stomach grumbles at the sight. It feels like years have passed since I was at breakfast with my parents.

"I am happy to see everyone is back," Captain Lorenzo stands up. "Please, have a snack. Mr. Cassigan and I did what we could with what we found in the kitchen."

"It must've been your lucky day! Finding fresh avocados in there." Bruce chomps down on a chip.

"I am happy to see that you are feeling better, Mr. Misemueller," Captain Lorenzo glances down at Bruce's ankle.

Despite the heavy fall he took earlier, there isn't much swelling. He's also moving around on it well. His fall must've not been as bad as it looked.

"Misemuellers have always healed quicky," Bruce says. "The one who has the biggest injury is this one here," he jabs his thumb at Harry.

Captain Lorenzo's eyebrows shoot up when he sees Harry's scraped up face.

"It's nothing," Harry says.

"Nonsense. I can help you." Captain Lorenzo opens the first aid kit. He sorts through it, looking for band aids and ointment. Once Harry is cleaned up, the scrapes and cuts don't look so bad.

"Has there been any news on the police?" Harry asks Captain Lorenzo.

Captain Lorenzo doesn't have time to answer. The phone clipped to his belt rings. He makes an apologetic face and excuses himself from the table.

This is the perfect time to get Harry alone so that I can tell him about the dagger that I found while exploring the north end of the island. With Bruce and Dane distracted by the guacamole, I pull Harry towards the beach.

When we're out of earshot from the others, Harry turns towards me.

"What's wrong?" he asks.

"I found the weapon that might've been used to kill Lloyd Alapha."

"What? How?"

"There's a historic building on the island. I was looking for you and Bruce when I came across a dagger under some floorboards."

"Tell me you didn't touch it," Harry's eyes are intense, pleading with my own. He runs a hand through his hair, ruffling it.

"I wouldn't dare," I say.

He relaxes a bit and drops his shoulders.

"It confirms that someone on this island killed Lloyd." I take a step closer to Harry. "It also confirms that we need to keep our eyes wide. We can't sit back and expect everything to be solved once the police arrive. By then, it might be too late."

CHAPTER NINE

A CALL FROM A FRIEND

B ruce finds a pack of cards in the kitchen, so we play a few rounds of Cheat out in the eating area. Captain Lorenzo wins every time because neither Bruce nor Dane are very good liars. Bruce chuckles whenever he puts down a false card, and Dane has a tell where he shifts in his seat. I lose because I have bad hand after bad hand.

We're on our fourth round of the game when Captain Lorenzo's phone rings. The sound is similar to that of a windchime.

"Un momento," he holds up a finger to us.

I watch as he heads down to the beach. He's managed to keep his cool throughout this whole thing. Could it be possible that he had something to do with what happened to Lloyd? No, that's not possible. He was driving the tender the whole time.

"Ope! I think I might've gotten a bit too much sun!" Bruce interrupts my thoughts. He pats the top of his head, just now discovering his sunburn.

"I might have extra sunscreen in my bag," Harry says. "It won't reverse what already happened, but it should prevent the burn getting worse."

Harry and I had packed a small backpack for our day on Lapis Rock. We included things for the beach like sunscreen, water, extra towels, a novel for Harry, and a crossword book for me. Harry had been wearing the backpack ever since we arrived on the island.

As Harry sifts through his pack, Captain Lorenzo comes back up from the beach. He's still on the phone, but he's holding it away from his ear, and it is now on speaker phone. Captain Lorenzo sets the phone on the table as he finishes up his call.

"No one must touch the murder scene," whoever is on the other side of the phone speaks. They have a strong accent. "We will arrive when we can, but we have to take care of the situation here first."

"Thank you, officer," Captain Lorenzo says. "Will you call again with updates?"

"Yes," the phone crackles. "We will call. Goodbye." The call ends with a click.

"Was that the police?" I ask.

Captain Lorenzo nods. "It was. They are still on the main island."

I sink lower in my chair. How much longer would it be before the police arrived on Killdeer Cay? Every second that passes is a second that gives the murderer more time to come up with an alibi. Or worse, it is a moment they can use to murder again.

"Shoot," Harry says as the red journal he found earlier tumbles out of the backpack. "Sorry Bruce, but I can't seem to find the sunscreen."

"That's okay," Bruce says. "I'll just stay in the shade."

"If I find it, I'll let you know," Harry says.

I hope he finds it soon. Bruce isn't the only one with a sunburn. Harry is looking much pinker than usual.

Harry sets his backpack on the sandy ground and stretches his arms over his head, his biceps flexing. Bruce shuffles the cards in preparation for another round of Cheat, but both Dane and my phones go off, sending the table vibrating. Dane snatches his off the table and hurries away. I have no doubt it's his new wife calling. I hope they're able to work out their problems before their whole honeymoon is ruined.

I take up my own phone and find a private spot near a couple of trees and tall grass.

"Hello?"

"Emma!" A familiar voice sings through the telephone. It's my friend Charlie. I would recognize his voice anywhere.

"Charlie! My parents said they ran into you in Lapis Rock?"

"Ding, ding!" Charlie says. "I was stopping by a place known for their famous sunshine bursts. They are these drinks that come in tropical colors, and they're made with a special sugar that is harvested on Perfect Sands Islands. As I'm in the restaurant, getting ready to take my first sip of my pineapple sunshine burst, I notice this woman keeps eyeing me. I know I'm handsome, but I'm not handsome enough to be ogled at the way this woman is making eyes at me. That's when she burst forward and asked me if I'm Charlie Kim! I had no idea your mother was so fun, Emma! You've kept her quite the secret."

"I can't believe how small the world is," I say. "Did you come all the way to the Caribbean to try a drink?"

Charlie laughs. "If only! No, I'm here for a pepper festival!"

"Pepper festival?"

"I'm here to get pepped up for peppers! Some of the rarest peppers known to the cooking world will be on display. I've had my tickets for this event for years. You never know when these things might sell out."

"I'm happy you managed to snag one of those tickets," I say. I try my best to keep the doubt out of my voice that the pepper festival may not be as popular as Charlie thinks.

"Enough about me," Charlie says. "Why haven't I seen you on the island? Dare I say, are you and Harry off on a romantic excursion?"

I can almost hear Charlie's eyebrows wiggling through the phoneline. If only Charlie knew how badly I would've liked Harry and I to actually be on some sort of romantic adventure instead of stuck on Killdeer Cay.

"The tender we were on ran into some trouble when we were being transported from the cruise to Lapis Rock." I keep my answer vague. I don't want Charlie worrying about Harry and I, or worse, telling my parents that Harry and I are stranded.

"What a shame," Charlie says. "At least no one got murdered. You do tend to attract that horrible business."

"Right," I mumble. Going down memory lane with Charlie when it comes to murder mysteries is one of the last things I want to do right now.

"Emma?" Charlie's voice sounds suspicious. "What are you not telling me? Did someone get murdered!"

I stifle a groan. How can I possibly explain to Charlie what has happened without sounding like I've lost my mind?

"Emma Finch spill. What is going on?"

I bite down hard on my lower lip. There's no point in hiding the truth from Charlie. He's pretty good at sniffing out fibs. "Someone was killed on the lower deck of the tender while we were enroute to the main island. The boat had to stop at the closest cay according to Perfect Sands Islands' law. We've been stuck here since then. We can't leave until the police show up."

"Why haven't the police shown up? This seems like a pressing matter!"

"They're tied up with something happening on Lapis Rock. Captain Lorenzo has been keeping in touch with them periodically."

Charlie is quiet. It's not like him to let silences lap into conversations.

"Emma, what are you not telling me?"

Even though Charlie isn't anywhere around, a blush still heats my cheeks.

"Emma?"

"I'll tell you, but you have to promise not to tell my parents. I can't let their anniversary be ruined because they're worried about Harry and me."

"I would never betray the closest confidence of my dear friend," Charlie sounds offended.

"There were seven passengers and one captain on the tender, and somehow, someone murdered one of the passengers without anyone noticing."

"How is that possible?"

"I don't know. Basically everyone, except the person who was murdered, was on the top floor of the deck, or so they say."

"Someone is lying," Charlie says. "It can't be the captain because he would've been controlling the ship, and it's obviously not you or Harry, so it must be one of the four remaining passengers. You need to get close to each of them and learn as much as you can."

"I would, but—"

Charlie cuts me off. "No buts! You and Harry are stuck on that cay. You can't trust anyone. Someone there is a murderer, and who knows why they did what they did! They could be deranged. Don't trust anyone, and play detective. Emma, this could be your life at risk."

The air on the island feels too humid and suffocating. Could Charlie be right? Is it only a matter of time before Harry and I are next?

CHAPTER TEN

NOTES IN THE KITCHEN

I put my phone back in my pocket when I hear someone speaking nearby. I peer through the leafy bushes so that I can see into a small grove. It's Dane. He's on the phone and pacing back and forth across a sandy section of land.

I crouch on the path so that Dane doesn't see me on the off chance that he looks my direction. I can't be caught eavesdropping. Normally, I wouldn't dare listen in on his phone call, but I can't get the seed out of my mind that Charlie planted. What if Harry and I might be in trouble? I can't be ignorant to what's happening around me. It could mean my life.

"Melissa, how many times do I have to tell you? We won't ever have to deal with that again! Can you drop it?"

Melissa? I thought Dane's wife was named Jill?

I lean forward a bit on the balls of my feet. A pesky bug zips around my head, making my ears ring and my skin tingle. It's one of the first ones I've noticed on the island. I hope it's just curious and not attracted to my sunscreen or scented shampoo because I can't risk running away and revealing to Dane that I've been crouching in the grass this whole time.

"Not a word of this to anyone. Understand?" Dane says, his voice deep and serious. "He's taken care of."

The phone call must end there because I hear the sound of feet shuffling, and everything stills. I stand up slowly and stretch my legs out. If there's one thing I learned from Dane's phone conversation, it's that he can't be trusted. For all I know, the *he* that he referenced during his call is Lloyd Alapha.

I head back to the main beach, passing a smooth-billed ani with a lizard in its mouth. Normally I wouldn't find a lizard appetizing, but I am a bit jealous that the bird found lunch, and I haven't had anything to eat in some time. Maybe there will be a new bowl of guacamole out when I get back to the main beach, but when I arrive, Opal and Bruce are screaming at each other near the lounge chairs. Opal wags her finger at Bruce and tears her sunglasses off her face, waving them around aggressively. Bruce doesn't appear any less heated. His face is the same red color as his sunburnt bald spot, and he shakes his head back and forth.

"It was there one moment, and it was gone the next!" Opal bellows.

"But why would you think I took it?" Bruce's voice hitches an octave.

"Because the last time I saw it was right before you came barging into my cabana like some sort of circus elephant," Opal spits.

"I came to the cabana to give you a map of the island. I didn't go to your cabana to steal your things!"

Opal eyes him up and down. "I bet someone like you would just love to get your hands on a phone like that."

"I have my own phone," Bruce waves his cellphone around in the air. "Why would I steal yours! I don't even know anyone on your call list. You think I want to sit around and call all your friends?"

Opal looks down her nose at Bruce. "You are exactly the type of person who would love to socialize with my set of friends."

Bruce shakes his head. "You're out of your mind, lady."

He turns around and walks down the beach. He's heading in the opposite direction of the cabanas. Opal crosses her arms and lets out a loud humph as she heads in the other direction.

"What happened?" Harry is standing behind me.

"Where'd you go?" I ask.

"I ran to the bathrooms when you left to take your phone call. When I came back, Opal and Bruce were storming across the beach."

"I know about as much as you do," I say.

I glance around the area and notice that Captain Lorenzo and Dane are not around either. I wonder where everyone has gotten off to. My phone call with Charlie couldn't have lasted that long.

Harry's stomach growls loudly. "Do you want to explore the kitchen? I could use some lunch."

"I couldn't be happier that you suggested that. I'm starving," I say.

I follow Harry off into the small building behind the bar. It's clean but sparse. An array of bowls and cooking instruments are neatly arranged against the far wall, and a large utilitarian sink takes up a corner of the room. Harry goes to the nearest counter and opens a drawer, looking for any sort of snack. I open a different door that leads to a pantry with some dry goods. There are canned vegetables and fruit along with the staples like flour and oil.

"Did you find anything? There's food in here, but I doubt it's the kind you want," I call out to Harry.

"Emma, come here!" he calls back.

I exit the small pantry and go back into the main kitchen. Harry is holding a piece of scrap paper up to the light, his previous hunger pangs forgotten.

"What's that?"

"Look," Harry gestures for me to come closer.

Under the light, the paper looks thin and fragile, almost like a butterfly wing. Upon further inspection, the paper contains a long list of numbers. Whoever wrote them out has fairly loopy handwriting.

"Is it a phone number?" I ask.

"It's too long," Harry says. "Wait," he looks at me expectantly. "Let's compare this to that journal we found earlier. Maybe they're connected."

We go to the dining area. Harry's backpack is here, exactly where he left it not long ago. While someone on the island along with us might be a murderer, at least we know our belongings are safe.

Harry bends down and sifts through his things. He places a light blue beach towel patterned with dolphins on the chair closest to him along with a metal water bottle that clangs like thunder when he sets it down, and a large book of crossword puzzles. He must've put the journal in the bottom of the bag because it won't be long before everything we've packed is piled on the chair.

"Here it is," he says with his arm plunged deep into the bag.

"Tada!" He pulls a book out and frowns. It's a novel I threw into the bag late last night. I forgot I had packed it in the backpack.

"*Midnight Murder at Mallard Beach*?" Harry raises his eyebrows. "I didn't know you liked cozy mysteries."

My cheeks fill with heat, and I swipe the book from his hand. "I didn't know you were so snobby when it came to book genres."

Harry smiles up at me, his grin boyish and playful. "I think it's cute. My birdwatching, murder-solving girlfriend reads birdwatching, murder mysteries."

I give him a light bop on the head with the book. "Did you find the journal or not?"

Harry takes a moment to dig around in the backpack again, but all he manages to produce is another towel. This one is purple and decorated with octopi wearing tiaras.

He stands up and runs his fingers through his hair, ruffling it. "It's gone."

"The journal is gone? How is that possible?"

"Someone must've taken it from my bag." Harry looks around as if that someone is standing on the beach, but other than the two of us, no one is in sight.

"It could've been anyone," I say. "Captain Lorenzo, Bruce, and Dane have all been around here most of the day. Opal has too."

"Why would someone want it though? It wasn't worth anything."

I frown. "We don't know that for sure. If it has something to do with that paper you found in the kitchen, maybe it's worth a lot more than we realize."

Harry takes a seat on one of the rickety chairs and stares out towards the ocean. The longer Harry and I stay on the island, the more Charlie's words echo around my head. What if Harry and I are at risk of getting hurt? Someone was brave enough to go through Harry's backpack. What if they think Harry and I are getting in the way of whatever they're plotting, and they decide to get rid of us too like they did Lloyd?

"It has to be Samara," Harry says.

"Samara?" My mouth drops open. "You think she took the journal?"

"She was with us when we found it. She would be the only one who knew about it."

I shake my head. It can't be Samara. She's been so quiet and flighty. Anyone who had just killed another person wouldn't act that way.

"I can't believe she would do that. What if someone else was looking for something in your bag and just happened upon the journal?"

"That's a huge if," Harry says.

"But it's still possible," I say.

Harry leans back in his chair and continues to look out to sea. I wonder if his thoughts are a whirlpool like mine.

CHAPTER ELEVEN

NAMES IN THE SAND

I must've drifted off because I wake with my head resting against the tabletop. My body is warm to the touch from the heat, but I can't complain. Had I fallen asleep in the lounge chair, I'd be as red as a raspberry.

Harry is no longer sitting next to me, but he hasn't left me alone. He's down by the shore, tossing pieces of driftwood into the waves. His body is tense and rigid. I know when we found the journal under the steps by the older cabanas, he had acted like it was nothing, but I know better now. He thinks it's connected to Lloyd Alapha's death on the tender, and he's mad that it's gone.

The police will be here any moment to sort out the murder, and Harry had said we should stay out of it, but not thinking about Lloyd Alapha is akin to pretending like a giant polar bear isn't standing next to you. Not only that, but Charlie had pointed out Harry and I could be in trouble. The discovery of the bloody dagger adds to that argument. What if when the police get here, they think I am the murderer? My fingerprints are all over *The House of Safety,* and if the murderer is smart, they would've made sure not to leave a trace of themselves. Despite the Caribbean heat, a chill settles in my chest.

I pull myself off of the chair in the eating area. My skin is sticky and moist and peels away uncomfortably, but I can't focus on the stinging that spreads across the back of my thighs. I march right over to Harry who has just found a sun-bleached piece of wood under a small hill of sand and is preparing to launch it into the tide.

Harry drops the wood when he sees me. "What's wrong?"

"We have to figure out what's going on." Harry opens his mouth, but I keep talking. "Yes, Captain Lorenzo called the police, and yes, eventually they will get here, but they're not here right now. Harry, we could be in trouble. Someone has stolen that journal we thought was just a joke from your bag, we've found odd coded notes in the kitchen, and my fingerprints are going to be all over the house where that dagger is hidden."

Harry opens his mouth again, but I hold up my finger.

"We don't have to go full-on detective. We could just talk through some things. The first being how is it even possible that someone was murdered on that boat?" I finish with a huff.

Harry picks up the piece of driftwood he had dropped earlier and turns it over in his hand as if it is valuable scrimshaw. "I disagree." He flings the driftwood into the ocean where a wave swallows it hungrily.

"You just want to be sitting ducks then?" I plunk myself onto the sandy beach. Can't Harry see how important it is that we don't stick our heads in the sand?

Harry plops down beside me. "No, I think we shouldn't be ducks. We need to be owls."

"What?" Is Harry trying to make some sort of bird joke? If so, it's not going well. I'm not in the mood for a comedy routine.

"Bad comparison?" He asks me with a grin.

"Harry, can we be serious?"

"We need to be owls. Everyone loves owls. They have those big eyes, and they hoot, and I think every kid secretly always wanted one as a pet, but at the end of the day, they're hunters. They hide in trees and wait until it is dark and quiet and then they snatch their prey." Harry looks at me, the amber in his eyes catching twinkles from the sunrays. "I think we should go full-on detective."

I burst into laughter. "I don't think I've ever been more in love with you."

Harry's grin disappears and his eyebrows raise. Oh no, now I've done it.

I can't believe I just told Harry *I love him*. We haven't even been in a relationship that long. He's going to think I'm one of those wacky girls who obsesses over guys after only a few months.

"I didn't mean that!" I cover my mouth in horror.

Harry's eyebrows fall, and he looks hurt. Maybe I should've just stayed with my original line. Would I make it worse if I back tracked again?

"Harry—" I start, but Harry holds up a hand.

He smiles, but it doesn't exactly reach his eyes. "It's okay, Emma." He gives me a soft peck on the forehead and slings his arm around me, cuddling me close. "Let's focus on what's happening on the island for now."

As difficult as it may be, I try to redirect my thoughts to the murder. I'm sure I'll have plenty of quiet time later to ruminate on the humiliation of telling Harry I love him and not being told it back. I need to focus.

How could Lloyd possibly have been killed? The sentence echoes in my mind like it's trapped in a dark cave.

"Let's go person by person," Harry says.

He squats down and writes three names in the sand.

Harry

Emma

Lorenzo

"We know I didn't kill anyone, and we know you didn't kill anyone. Lorenzo couldn't have either. He was driving the vessel."

Harry wipes away the names. I think it's my imagination, but he swipes my name a bit harder than the other two. Could he still be thinking about how I said I love him? I can't read his face though. It's stony with concentration.

Harry replaces the forgotten names with four news ones.

Samara

Bruce

Opal

Dane

"Let's start with Samara," he says. "When it comes to what happened on the tender, she's been the most upset about the murder."

I nod my head. "Her immediate reaction was to suspect herself as the intended victim due to an inheritance dispute. If she's telling the truth, which I think she is, that points to her being innocent."

"A murderer wouldn't be worried about being the victim of the next murder," Harry says as he swipes sand over Samara's name.

"Bruce, while managing to tickle the nerves of Opal, isn't exactly the murdering type," I say.

"While that could be an act, you're right. We have nothing to go off of when it comes to Bruce."

"Same with Opal," I add. "She might rub people the wrong way, but she hasn't done anything to make me wonder if she's a murderer."

Harry erases both names.

"Dane is the only name left," I say. I fill Harry in on the rocky relationship the honeymooner has with his wife. I don't forget to include the phone call I overheard in which he claimed to have taken care of someone while talking to a mysterious woman named Melissa.

"Dane is a point of interest. It's possible the fights he is having with his wife and this Melissa person are related to Lloyd somehow." Harry is quiet for a moment. "Sometimes relationships start easy before the tides turn."

My stomach flips. Was that last sentence loosely directed at me? At us? I put my hand to my forehead. It's hot with anxiety.

"We need to see where he was during the murder." Harry leans back on his elbows. He looks out to sea and avoids my eyes. "We also need to talk to the others and see what, if anything, they noticed. We've both worked on cases like this before. The smallest thing might turn out to be the biggest clue." Harry's gaze travels behind us towards the dining area. "Should we get started then?"

I follow his stare and see that Opal Halladay is strutting around the chairs and tables, looking for something. She's holding her purse and sun hat in one hand while the other plays with a strand of frizzy hair. Her hair is far from what it looked like earlier on the ship when it appeared freshly styled.

Normally, I would avoid talking to Opal, but right now, she's an attractive distraction. If I keep talking to Harry in private, my mind will keep reminding me of my big mouth that proclaims it's love for people at inopportune times. "Do you need help?" I call over to Opal.

Opal startles and clasps her hat and purse to her chest before realizing it's just me and Harry approaching.

"If you must know, I'm starving," she says once I'm standing next to her. "When I was grabbing breakfast this morning, I went on the lighter side. Had I an inkling that I'd be spending my day trapped on this tiny island, I would've opted for more than half a croissant."

My own stomach growls in response. I clutch my hands over it in embarrassment.

"We found some food earlier in the kitchen, but it was mostly dry goods," Harry says. He's joined us under the thatched roof that shades the tables and chairs.

"Great," Opal flops into a chair. "What are we going to do?"

"Let me check out the kitchen once more," Harry says. "Maybe I can figure something out. Emma, why don't you stay here and keep Opal company?"

Harry and I must be thinking the same thing. He wants me to talk to Opal alone and see what I can learn from her. I won't have a lot of time though. Harry can only pretend to hunt around the kitchen for so long.

After Harry leaves, I take a seat next to Opal. The table we sit at is square and wooden and situated towards the bar. Above us, a thick fan slowly spins with the wind.

"This is all pretty wild, isn't it?" Maybe if I prompt Opal, she'll open up easily.

"Yeah, wild as a horse," she mutters while inspecting her nail polish. I guess she's not much of a talker.

"I don't even understand how someone could've committed murder on that tender. Harry and I didn't see anything, and it's a small boat."

"A true shame," she blows on her fingernails, clearly indifferent to the conversation.

"Did you see anything weird while we were on the boat?" Internally, I cringe. Could it be any more obvious that I'm trying to get information out of her?

If Opal notices how uncomfortable I am, she's a good actress. She slides her sunglasses up onto her head, and her eyes appear glazed and bored.

"The boat? No, nothing weird. I was sitting next to that man." She smacks her lips together. "That rude one who stole my phone."

"Bruce? That can't be right," I say. "He was next to Harry and I." The memory of him introducing himself to us flashes through my mind.

Opal shrugs her shoulders. "I'm sure I was sitting next to him. I remember his knee kept bumping into my leg. Rather uncomfortable, but whatever." She pulls her sunglasses back down, but not quick enough for her to prevent me from seeing her roll her eyes.

I'm not sure where to steer the conversation. It's like telling Harry I love him all over again. My tongue feels like its stuck to sticky paper and immobile. Why does this keep happening to me? Why do I keep getting tongue-tied?

"I managed to whip something up," Harry arrives just in time. He puts a bowl on the table without looking at me.

"What is it?" Opal gives the contents of the bowl a sniff.

From where I sit, it smells sweet, like syrup. Inside the bowl is some sort of soup with yellow and red chunks floating around in it.

A pink blush colors Harry's cheeks. "I found a bunch of canned fruit and combined them together. It's a fruit surprise!"

"Yum," Opal deadpans.

Despite her disappointment, she grabs one of the utensils Harry brought outside and plunges a fork into a piece of fruit. She must be starving because she goes in for seconds and thirds. Opal is about to stick her fork into the communal bowl again when it clatters to the ground and she lets out a scream.

"Bees!"

Fat, yellow balls of fluff fly through the air, buzzing around Harry's fruit bowl. Opal jumps up and flaps around like the killdeer we ran into earlier.

"They won't bother you if you don't swat at them," Harry says to little effect.

"I'm allergic!" She squawks.

"I've got it!" I turn around to see Dane as he rushes towards us from the pathway. He's coming from the southern part of the island, so he must've been at the old cabanas or the hidden cove. I'm not sure if he can see the bees divebombing us from faraway, but he might be able to figure out what's going on based on Opal's erratic swiping.

Once Dane reaches the dining area, he lunges towards the table and grabs the bowl of fruit. The bees swarm around him like a dark cloud. Dane holds the bowl away from his body and scuttles back onto the pathway and disappears.

"That was interesting," Harry mumbles.

Opal rips her sunglasses off and glares at him. "He saved our lives. Unlike you, who just sat there bumbling."

"I wasn't bumbling. I was giving you advice," Harry protests.

"Poor advice, I might add," Opal fluffs her hair as if she's making sure no wayward bees have been caught in it, but her fluffing makes the frizz worse. "What were you thinking? Putting a big dish of liquid sugar out to attract all those bugs?"

Harry splutters, and his lips stretch thinly across his freckled face, but he doesn't say a word. He's smart enough to know that Opal is the type of person who knows exactly what button to push to get a rise out of someone.

"I don't think Harry made that dish with the intention of attracting bees over here," I say.

"Nice to hear someone on this island other than me is also *thinking* for once," Opal continues to poke at her hair.

Dane reappears at the edge of the pathway. He's covered in a light layer of sweat, and he's breathing heavy. The bowl is in his hand.

"We were just talking about how nice it is to have at least one real man on the island," Opal drawls.

Dane looks a bit confused, and Harry bites his tongue. I take a deep breath. Ignoring Opal is the best way to go. She's just looking for attention.

"I poured that fruit dessert out and rinsed the bowl. There's a watering spicket up on the path that was meant for washing sand off feet. The bees should leave us alone." Dane sets the bowl on the table. "This happened once when I was on a date with my wife. I made a fruit salad and brought it to her while she was tanning by the pool. We ended up crying because we were laughing so hard" A shadow of a smile passes across Dane's face before it disappears.

Dane takes a look around the empty tables. "Where did that captain go? I'd say it's time to contact the police again. I walked all over the island, and there's barely anything here. In a few hours, the sun will be closer to the horizon than the top of the sky. It'll be our luck if we all got caught here at night."

"Finally! Someone else with some sense," Opal bursts out. "Everyone has been blundering around here like we're at a five-star hotel. We're in the middle of nowhere, people!" Opal gestures wildly with her hands. "Where's Captain Lorenzo? He's the one who got us into this mess."

"Technically whoever murdered someone got us into this mess. Captain Lorenzo is just following the law," Harry says.

Opal crosses her arms and turns her back on Harry. "Where is everyone? This island is the size of my closet. How do people keep disappearing?"

Harry holds up a finger. "Opal, you were the first one of us to run off to be by yourself in the cabanas."

"Rhetorical question! Every heard of it?" Opal snaps at Harry.

"I have," Harry gives her a boyish grin, but she doesn't appreciate the irony.

"Where did that one girl go?" Dane asks. "Come to think of it, I haven't seen her since she ran away in tears."

"That was Samara," I say. I stop myself from telling Dane that she's off on her own. His phone conversation earlier about taking care of someone may mean he's not trustworthy. If Samara's theory about her being the intended target is right, I don't want to let Dane know she is alone in case he has something to do with Lloyd's disappearance.

"I don't like to point fingers, but she was acting strange," Dane says. "On the ride over here, she was restless. I'm not saying for certain that she killed someone, but there was something not right with her."

"If she had killed someone on the tender, wouldn't you have noticed her get up and go downstairs?" I point out.

Dane's theory doesn't make much sense. In fact, him suggesting other people so confidently makes him seem even more suspicious. I would be interested in chatting with Samara to see if the two of them really were sitting next to each other on the tender.

"Guess I'm not much of a detective," Dane says. "Not much good at anything these days."

"Hopefully someone around here is," Opal speaks up. "This murder needs to get solved soon or else I might murder someone myself."

I study Opal's sharp eyes and pursed lips. Who is to say she hasn't already?

Chapter Twelve

A Faint Clue

The path to the bathrooms is in disrepair. Weeds bite away at the trail so aggressively that in some spots it is difficult to see where the path ends and the vegetation begins. Harry had wanted to walk me to the bathroom, but I insisted he stay in the dining area with Dane and Opal. While I understand the danger that may be lurking on the island, I don't want my boyfriend escorting me to the restroom. Not only that, but I'm hoping that I'll find Samara somewhere along the way and be able to ask if she saw anything during the trip on the tender. Dane's behavior has been anything but innocent, and he claimed to have sat beside Samara during the trip. If he's to be believed, Samara needs to verify that.

There is, of course, another huge reason I wanted to head off to the bathroom by myself. Recently, I find that when I'm near Harry, I start sweating profusely. I don't know what I'll do if he brings up what I said to him on the beach about being in love. I'm not even sure why I said it. Sure, I really like Harry, but I've never even wondered if I'm in love with him. Why would my big mouth go and say something like that?

I turn a corner on the path, and a small, rundown building comes into sight. Vines lace their way around cracked, yellow walls that are dirtied with mud. For some reason, I had imagined the bathrooms to be in good shape, but they're almost as derelict as the cabanas on the southern shore. I open the door to the restroom, and it squeaks loudly. The hinges are a rusted orange, most likely from all the salty air that hangs around Killdeer Cay like a malignant ghost. Inside, my footsteps echo. The tile floors are dusted with sand, and the walls are in need of a layer of paint. Visible cracks run from the ceiling to the floor.

"Samara?" I call out.

There's no answer. I approach one of the stalls, but it's empty as is the one next to it. If she's not in the bathroom, I wonder where else she could be hiding. I turn around and almost jump out of my skin. Samara is right behind me. How did she get so close without making a sound?

I let out a deep breath. "You startled me," I say.

Samara toys with her necklace. "I was standing by the sinks." She nods towards an area further down from the stalls. "Are you okay?" she asks. "You look a bit unwell."

"I do?"

I glance in the mirror. Samara is right. My face has lost its rosy hue and is pale and clammy. Dark circles shadow my eyes, and my lips are dry. Now that I think of it, I don't feel like myself. Maybe staying out in the sun for so long is taking its toll.

I turn away from the mirror. Looking at my reflection isn't making me feel much better.

"Samara, can I ask you a question?"

Samara tilts her head, probably contemplating why I'm suddenly being so forward. Usually, I'm a bit more discreet when I investigate. Maybe I am coming down with the flu or something.

"I guess," Samara says. Her voice sounds neutral, but she clutches at her pendant.

"Who were you sitting next to on the tender when we were out at sea?"

Samara reflects for a moment. "I wasn't paying much attention. I was nervous about my great aunt finding out about me coming to visit the estate, so I wasn't watching what was happening around me."

"You can't remember at all?"

Samara twists her pendant and suddenly stops. "I think it was that blond man. I had been looking out at the beaches, and I remember the person next to me had hair that was almost the exact same color as the sandy shores."

Samara must've been sitting next to Dane. As far as I can see, I don't see a reason for her to lie, which means Dane must've been telling the truth about sitting next to her. But that doesn't make Dane innocent. Samara had been so distracted by her thoughts that she could've not noticed Dane getting up and moving around.

"Are you sure that you're feeling okay?" Samara takes a step closer.

I instinctively take a step back. I'm not sure why, but my heart is racing.

"I think you should sit down." She gently grabs my shoulder.

My breath hitches, and I hiccup. The room spins a bit, and black edges into my vision. I let Samara guide me to a nursing bench near the door. I lean my head back and watch as the lights on the ceiling sparkle.

"Did you maybe eat something that disagreed with you?" Samara asks.

I can't remember eating anything unusual. Actually, I can't remember eating anything since breakfast.

"I think we need to get you back to the beach. We shouldn't stay in the restroom alone. If you pass out, we could be in trouble."

I hear Samara's words, but they sound like bubbles floating far away, just out of my reach. I close my eyes, and cold air envelops me like a blanket.

The breeze tickles my face and above me, green palm leaves sway slowly in the wind. There's not a cloud in the sky. Everything is blue for miles, but it's also incredibly bright. Too bright. I squeeze my eyes shut. My head is thrumming, and my stomach is in knots.

"You feeling better?" Harry has his hand on my forehead, checking my temperature. He tucks one of my blonde curls behind my ear.

"What happened?" I sit up, but wooziness comes over me. I lay back in the lounge chair. The last I recall, I had been in the bathroom with Samara. How did I get back to the beach?

"You fainted. Thankfully, you were with Samara when it happened. She said you were only out for a second, but you were wobbly when she brought you to the beach. We gave you some fluids, and you fell asleep. I've been with you since."

Harry's words paint a dreamy picture in my head. My memory is thick as fog, but I do remember stumbling back to the beach while Samara propped me up on her shoulder. An image of Harry's concerned face swims in my mind.

"I'm so embarrassed," I mumble.

"Don't be embarrassed." Harry gives me a light kiss on my forehead, but it feels a bit awkward. "We were both distracted by so much going on. We'll make sure you don't get dehydrated again." He passes me the metal water bottle we had packed in our bag. "Stay out of the sun too."

I reach a finger up and trace the healing cut on Harry's face from when he fell on the path helping Bruce. He pulls away from me as if it hurts. "Neither of us is doing too well on Killdeer Cay," I say.

I attempt to sit up again, but this time, a sharp pain crawls through my wrist like a thousand tiny claws. "Ouch!"

Harry frowns. "I forgot to tell you. Samara said that when you fell, she tried to catch you. She managed to prevent you hitting your head, but your wrist took the brunt of the fall. Try not to put too much weight on it until we can get it checked out."

"I have to say, this might be the worst vacation I've ever had."

Harry gives my shoulder a squeeze. Another groan of pain escapes me.

"Shoot," Harry says. "Sorry about that. She said you also fell a bit on your left shoulder. I should've known you might be a bit tender there."

"It's alright," I say.

"There's something else I should tell you," Harry says. "I found another one of those strange notes."

"Where was it?" I ask, keeping my voice low.

"It was on some scrap paper near one of the trash bins by the kitchen. I saw it blowing in the wind, about to fly away, so I picked it up to toss. That's when I saw what it was."

He takes the paper out of his pocket and discreetly presses it into my hand. I glance down. This one is different from the journal and the paper we found in the kitchen. Unlike those, this one has long numbers scrawled on them along with letters. Lots of lines and sections are crossed out as well.

"Harry," I look into his amber eyes, "I might know what this is. I might know what all these numbers mean."

Chapter Thirteen

SECRET CALLS

"It's a cipher," I say. "You know, like a secret code. I remember my sisters made one up one summer so that they could write letters to each other without me knowing what they were saying. Each number corresponds to a letter in the alphabet."

"You're right." Harry takes a closer look at the paper, holding it up so that the sun makes the paper semi-translucent. "This scrap must be from someone trying to crack a code."

"Which makes perfect sense! Think about it. That journal we found was written in code, but it probably didn't come with the key to solving it. Someone is trying to figure out the code, and these scrap papers are their attempts at cracking it. Whatever is written in that journal must be important if someone took the time to write so cryptically." I look over at Harry who is tracing some of the numbers with his index finger. "Do you think it's somehow connected to Lloyd's murder?"

Harry peers up at me, but he doesn't have time to answer.

"Emma, mia bella, how are you?" Captain Lorenzo is walking our way. His long legs stretch across the sand. Harry shoves the papers into his pocket.

"I talked to Samara, and she said you took a fall in the ladies' room." He makes a motion with his head, indicating someone up in the dining area.

Samara is sitting at one of the tables, nursing a water bottle. She must've decided to stay here after she helped me back from the bathrooms. I can't help but feel indebted to her. I know how badly she wants to be away from people on Killdeer Cay, but she's stuck around for me.

"I'm alright now," I say. "I took a nap under the trees and in the shade, and Harry has been keeping me hydrated, so I'm on the mend."

Captain Lorenzo gives me a large smile. His tan has darkened since landing on the island, and he looks even more like a TV star than he did at the beginning of the day. "This is good to hear. We have now had four accidents, and we've only been on the island a few short hours. Any more, and I might lose my job."

"Four?" Harry asks. "Are you counting Lloyd?"

"If I count the murder, that makes five." Captain Lorenzo's smile disappears at the mention of the crime on the tender.

"Who else got hurt?" I ask.

"Harry and Mr. Misemueller fell on the paths, you fainted, and now Mr. Misemueller is ill. He is not having a good day."

"He's sick?" Harry asks.

"Si, after his fight with Mrs. Halladay, I went to check on him. He was over in the fishing cove. I am not sure what happened, but he was..." Captain Lorenzo trails off. "Expelling his breakfast."

Oh no. If Bruce is throwing up, it might not be long before others are too.

"He is resting now. I left him once his stomach calmed."

"It's too bad that he's not feeling well," Harry says. "Captain, have there been any more updates on the police arriving?"

"I called again, but they are very busy on Lapis Rock. They wouldn't give me details. It is frustrating. Today was not a good day for a murder." Captain Lorenzo shakes his head.

"I don't think any day is," Harry says.

"Si, no day is," Captain Lorenzo agrees. "I am going to check the kitchen. It is well past noon, and people will be looking for food soon."

"Emma and I checked in there earlier, but all we found was canned food."

"I see," Captain Lorenzo says. "We will have to make do with what we find. Excuse me," he heads back up the beach.

I glance up and see that the sun is past its peak in the sky. Time is going by fast, and so far, we aren't any closer to solving what happened to Lloyd, and it seems that the police aren't any closer to Killdeer Cay either. Equally worrisome is that when the police do arrive, they're going to find my fingerprints all over the house where the dagger was discarded. Harry and I need to figure things out fast or hope that the police believe me when I tell the truth about how I found the weapon.

My phone buzzes in my pocket. I pull it out and see that Mr. Hawking is calling. I had completely forgotten about the article he had asked me to write. While my job is important to me, and I'm finally starting to make some strides at the magazine, I don't have time to whip up an article on backyard birdwatching for Mr. Hawking. I slip my phone back into my pocket.

"Who was that?" Harry asks.

"No one," I say.

Harry raises his eyebrows.

"It was Mr. Hawking. He forgot I went on vacation."

The last thing I want on my mind right now is the magazine. I don't have a laptop, and I don't have a notebook to write an article. I suppose I could type out something on my phone, but either way, I would end up working on my vacation. Mr. Hawking will just have to wait. Someone else can take care of "The Backyard Bird Blurb" while I'm stuck on Killdeer Cay.

"Have some more water," Harry holds the metal bottle out to me. "You're looking a bit ill again."

I shake my head. "It's not that. I was thinking about work and Mr. Hawking. I can't believe he forgot I was on vacation."

Harry sets the bottle in the sand. "Sometimes bosses are busy. One time, my boss went on a two-week vacation to France and forgot to tell everyone. It was in the middle of a big missing person's cold case. We all thought he'd been kidnapped."

"You and I aren't exactly in the same line of work," I point out. Harry works on gathering evidence for mysterious cases that have gone cold. I imagine there's so much going on in his office that sometimes things slip the mind. A birding magazine isn't exactly the rat race of the writing world.

"You would think that after all these years, and after some of my more recent articles, he would at least value me a bit more on the magazine."

"I think he does. He just isn't the most organized mind, so he forgets sometimes," Harry says.

A large wave crashes into the shore and retreats back into the ocean, depositing shells and a few sand dollars in its wake. I want Harry's words to be true, but I know they aren't. I can't even remember how many years I've been stuck writing "The Backyard Bird Blurb." If Mr. Hawking really was impressed by my writing, wouldn't I have a better job by now?

"Emma, you're good at your job. Stop worrying."

Harry's probably right, but it doesn't feel that way.

The smell of smoke tickles my nose. I turn around to see that Captain Lorenzo has fired up a grill situated on the edge of the dining area. He is laying pale yellow, oblong strips on the grill. As he puts each one down, a sizzle erupts.

"Wonder what those are," Harry says.

I wonder too. "They look like bananas."

Off to the side, Dane comes out of the kitchen with some cans of food.

"Let's join them," I get to my feet.

As soon as I do though, I gasp. Harry catches me by the elbow.

"You should sit back down," he says.

"It's not that. I forgot to go to the bathroom earlier. I didn't realize I still had to go while I was sitting down." I glance in the direction of the restroom. "I'll be right back."

"Let me come with you," Harry continues to hold my elbow.

"I'd really prefer to go by myself." As much as I like Harry, I think bathroom retreats are something I want to keep private. Not only that, but for some reason that I can't exactly put my finger on, I think I want a moment alone. I know he's concerned after my fall, but he feels off. It's almost like something happened between us that I can't put my finger on. I hope we didn't get in a fight right before I fainted and now I've forgotten. I shoo the thought away. I'm probably overthinking again.

I wave goodbye to Harry, and I make my way through the sand and up onto the path.

Not much water comes out of the tap as I wash my hands, but that should be expected. I doubt freshwater on the island is common, and the beach club being shuttered for some time probably isn't helping the situation.

I wipe my hands on my shorts since there are no paper towels in sight. I move my eyes to the mirror to check my hair one last time when I jump.

Opal Halladay is behind me. Her sunglasses are on her head, and she wears a look of boredom. "I followed you in here to make sure we were alone," she says.

I'm not sure if she means this as a threat or a simple fact. It's impossible to tell with her monotone voice and lack of eye contact.

"I need to borrow your phone," she says.

"My phone? You could've asked me for it on the beach. I would've let you use it there."

I unlock my cellphone and hold it out to her. She takes it from my hand and types in a number, her long finger nails clicking against the screen. She holds the phone up to her ear for a moment before mumbling something and passing it back to me.

"They didn't answer." She flicks her sunglasses back over her eyes. "Well, thanks even though you weren't much help."

"Why did you have to follow me into the restroom to use my phone?"

Opal ignores my question and swishes her hair as she heads towards the door.

"Opal, why did we have to be alone for you to use my phone?"

Opal lets out a dramatic sigh and turns to look at me.

"Because," she says, her voice low and dangerous, "someone stole my phone, so someone doesn't want me making phone calls. That means to make a call, I have to do it in secret."

She looks at me and for a moment, something sinister glimmers beneath her sweet, red lipstick smile.

Chapter Fourteen

CAPSIZED IN THE COVE

"When she left, she had this smile on her face," I tell Harry. "I can't describe it with words, but in my gut, I knew something was wrong." I recall what happened with Opal in the restroom.

Harry leans against a thin tree. We're both obscured by a patchwork of bushes a little way down the path and away from the eating area. After my chance meeting with Opal, I had walked back to the beach to find everyone except Opal gathered around a table and eating a meal of plantains with beans and rice that Captain Lorenzo had made. I had a small serving myself. I couldn't risk passing out again, but when Harry and I were done, I knew we needed to speak in private.

Something doesn't feel right between us. He stands farther away from me than he normally would, and his eyes look at the sand by my feet, the leaves that rustle in the wind, the flowers that bloom in the soft, yellow light, everywhere but me. I have a horrible itch in my mind that something happened between us before I fainted, but I can't recall what it was. I would've remembered if we'd had a fight, right?

"Do you think Opal might have something to do with the murder?" Harry brings me back to the current conversation.

"I'm not sure, but we can't rule her out. Her behavior has been anything but normal."

"It looks like her and Dane are on the top of my suspect list then. Dane because of the phone calls you told me about and Opal because she can't seem to get along with anyone on the island," Harry says.

"It's still not much evidence," I point out.

"I know," Harry agrees.

I'm about to say something more when Harry brings a finger to his lips.

"Did you hear that?" he whispers.

I hadn't heard anything, but I hold my breath, waiting to see if what he hears comes to my ears. After a second, the sound manifests.

Someone is yelling.

"What direction is that coming from?" I ask.

"It sounds like it's near the cove," Harry says.

I grab his hand and pull him down the path, but Harry slows me before we make it into a sprint.

"What's wrong?" I ask.

"We can't run. You just fainted, remember? You also hurt your shoulder and wrist. Let's take it easy."

"I feel fine, Harry, really." I give his arm another tug, but he doesn't budge.

"Fine, I'll go without you."

I know it's not the nicest thing to say, but it's the only thing I can think of at the moment. I'm unlikely to faint again, and whoever is screaming sounds like they need help. Harry follows close behind as I rush. The trees thin, and the hidden beach comes into view. There's no one around, but a sparkle in the water catches my eye. I squint and see that something green is floating in the water. But what is it? An animal of some sorts?

"Over there!" I point out the green mass floating in the water and move closer to the shoreline.

"I think that's Bruce!" Harry wades into the shallows.

"Bruce? That's not possible. That thing is green."

Harry shakes his head. "No, it's a kayak. Bruce has capsized."

I follow Harry into the shallows to get a closer look. Something orange bobs up and down next to the overturned, green vessel. It is Bruce! I can make out his sunburnt head and arms waving in the air.

"How can we help him? I don't think it's safe to swim out. There could be rip tides."

"I have an idea."

Harry runs back up the beach and disappears into a small grove. He emerges a second later with a paddle. Behind him, he drags a kayak. This one is a lime green just like the one floating in the ocean.

"Should I go get more help?"

"I've got it," he says as he pulls the small boat into the waves.

Once it's deep enough, Harry hops in. Water splashes his shirt, and the fabric clings to his skin. He paddles quickly out to sea. I know he's moving fast, but it feels like he'll never reach Bruce who is all but a dot now.

"Hurry, Harry," I yell.

Harry's kayak bobs over a wave and dips into the clear waters. The last thing I want is for Harry to end up stranded out in the ocean along with Bruce. Another wave comes and tilts Harry's kayak, but he keeps it steady. He's almost to Bruce now.

Finally, Harry steers the kayak alongside of Bruce who is just a floating orange dot. The Kayak isn't a two-seater, so I'm not sure how Harry is going to get Bruce to shore, but they seem to navigate the issue fine. It's not long before Bruce is clinging onto a rope connected to Harry's kayak as Harry tows him back to land.

Once they near shore, I run through the water to meet them.

"Is everyone okay?" I look from Harry, who is covered in sweat and panting, to Bruce, who is close to the color of a watermelon and looks worn down. He's still holding onto the short rope behind Harry's kayak.

"I think we will be now," Harry hops out of the boat.

"I had a bit of an accident." Bruce gets to his feet. He's unsteady, and he sways with the waves. "I thought I would get myself to Lapis Rock, but the kayak I was in had plans of its own. Pesky little thing." Bruce looks back to where the tip of his abandoned kayak is about to disappear under the water.

"Why were you trying to paddle to Lapis Rock?" I ask. While Lapis Rock and Killdeer Cay aren't far from one another, they're definitely more than a short kayak paddle away.

"We can't wait around here forever, can we?"

"No, we can't," Harry says after he's dragged the kayak back onto the sandy beach. "But that doesn't mean we go out into the ocean on small watercrafts and risk getting hurt. What were you thinking?" Harry crosses his arms. He sounds more like Bruce's father than someone who could be Bruce's grandson. He's not happy at all.

Bruce sputters. "I was thinking I wanted to get out of here!"

"We all want to get out of here, but we have to wait like the captain said. Imagine if you had made it to Lapis Rock. It would've looked odd for you to have run away from the island during a murder investigation, wouldn't it?"

Bruce makes a dismissive gesture with his hand. "I would've been fine had the kayak not tipped. You young people worry about everything. You're just as bad as that Opal lady accusing me of stealing her phone."

Bruce shakes some water out of his hair. "The people on this island are all nuts!"

Bruce stomps off to the path, leaving Harry and I behind.

"Well, that wasn't exactly how I expected things to go," I say.

Harry huffs. "He thinks what he did was okay. He could've gotten really hurt. I could've gotten hurt. We don't know anything about the waters around this island. He's reckless."

I grab Harry's hand and give it a tight squeeze. "You did the right thing by helping him. He's probably in shock right now. Once he has a moment to calm down, he'll realize you were right about what you said."

Harry tightens his jaw, but he gives my hand a tight squeeze back. Let's hope the next few hours on Killdeer Cay aren't as eventful as the most recent ones.

Chapter Fifteen

NIGHT FALLS

Harry paces back and forth on the beach. A small path of flattened sand appears where he treads. After Bruce stormed off, Harry and I stayed near the cove. I ended up having to sit down in the shade of a coconut tree. With my head leaning against the smooth trunk, the pounding behind my eyes lessens, but not by much. I should have listened to Harry about taking it easy after fainting. I have a horrible headache.

"There's something wrong," Harry mumbles as he paces.

"Of course there's something wrong. There's been a murder, and we're all trapped here. This is almost as wrong as it can get."

"How could someone have killed on that boat? You and I were next to each other. Dane and Samara were next to each other. The captain was driving. Bruce was next to us. All that leaves is Opal, but do we really think she committed murder? Opal can barely keep her thoughts to herself let alone hide a murder." Harry runs a hand through his hair, ruffling it in stress.

"Wait," I grab hold of his arm to stop him from pacing. He's about to make me lose my last nerve by going back and forth the way he is, and it's not helping my headache either. "Opal told me she was next to Bruce on the tender. How could Bruce have been next to the both of us?"

Harry thinks for a second. "Opal could be lying."

"Or, she could be telling the truth."

Harry looks at me in confusion.

"Think about it! If Bruce was next to Opal at one point, and he was next to us at another point, that means he moved while on the boat! He acts silly, but that would be the perfect act for a murderer. Who would ever suspect the jolly, retired man trying to enjoy his vacation as a killer?"

"That would make sense," Harry says. "It would explain why he took Opal's cellphone if that's true."

"We should talk to him," I say.

"I'm not sure telling him we think he's a suspect is the best idea."

I shake my head. "No, we need to talk to him to see if we can establish a motive. As it is now, all we know is that it's possible that Bruce could've snuck down to the lower level of the boat, but realistically, that's not much to go on." I take a deep breath. "Without a motive or a reason to kill, the idea of Bruce murdering someone seems about as possible as a cowbird being raised by cowbirds."

"What?"

My face flushes. "It was a stupid bird metaphor. Cowbirds lay eggs in nests of other bird species and make those birds raise their young."

Harry nods his head. I can tell he's playing along and trying not to hurt my feelings. My headache must be messing with me because I swear Harry is looking at me in a way he hasn't before. Almost as if he feels sorry for me. I let out a huff, my cheeks growing warmer by the second. If Harry doesn't think I'm a nerd already, he must by now. And worse, the gnawing feeling that I've done something stupid in front of Harry won't leave me alone. What could I possibly have done that I now can't remember?

"The point is, I don't think it's possible for Bruce to be the murderer just because he walked around on the boat. Unless we can learn more about him, I think he's innocent, but he's also the best guess we have," I say.

"A parrot couldn't have said that better." Harry gives me a grin, but something about it feels a bit pitiful. "You're not the only one who can make bird jokes."

I smile softly back at him. Leave it to Harry to try and make me laugh when things feel like they can't get much darker. Harry helps me up, but I keep my raging headache and anxiety to myself. I just need to hydrate. I can't have Harry worrying more than he already is, and I can't let myself get carried away with silly thoughts.

We return to the path. Bruce is most likely in the dining area. While he wasn't too happy with Harry the last time we met with him, if he truly has the ebullient personality he portrays, then getting him to converse with us shouldn't be an issue.

To our surprise, when we reach the dining area, everyone is at the table nearest to the bar. Opal is sitting next to Samara who is twiddling with her pendant. Captain Lorenzo and Dane are across from them. Dane has his phone out again and is texting madly. I guess he's still in trouble with whoever is on the other end of the line. Whether that person is his wife, Jill, or the mysterious Melissa remains to be uncovered. Bruce is at the end of the table. His head has drifted to the nook of his shoulder where he is fast asleep. He's probably exhausted from his watery jaunt that ended in him being stranded.

Captain Lorenzo sees us and gives us a wave. "Buonasera, come join us."

Harry gives him a cordial nod, and we both take a seat at the end of the table.

"How come everyone is here?" I ask. "Did we miss something?"

Opal chortles. "You seem to miss a lot. Maybe you should pay attention occasionally."

I ignore her. Her personality is too hot and cold for me to analyze. If she ends up having something to do with Lloyd's murder, time will reveal it. Opal is just a distraction. Harry and I need to focus on Bruce for now. He's the only person who could've snuck to the bottom floor of the tender.

Bruce chokes on a snore and wakes himself up. He coughs heavily, bending towards the sand as he hacks. He reminds me a bit of my sister's cat when he needs to pass a furball.

"Ope! I dozed off for a moment! Did I miss anything?" Bruce beams around the table. His eyes are red and watery from his fit.

"After being asleep for ten whole minutes, we're still all trapped on this island. Shocking!" Opal laughs at her own sarcasm. Next to her, Samara shifts uncomfortably.

"It is getting late," Samara looks to the sun. It hovers close to the horizon. "Will the police be here soon?"

"I will call again, but there are no guarantees," Captain Lorenzo says.

Opal stands up in frustration. "If they don't get here soon, what will happen?"

Captain Lorenzo looks at the ground. "We will have to keep waiting."

Opal's mouth drops open. "Do you mean to say we have to sleep on the island? This abandoned island?"

Captain Lorenzo doesn't look at any of us. He keeps his eyes on the ground. "Unfortunately."

The quiet beach breaks into a symphony of sound with everyone talking at once. The island hasn't been this loud since Captain Lorenzo first told us there had been a murder.

"Are we supposed to sleep in the wild?" Opal gasps.

"Is it even safe?" Samara grasps her necklace.

"My wife is going to kill me," Dane groans.

"I can't sleep without a firm mattress," Bruce chimes in.

Harry and I exchange a look. Being stuck on Killdeer Cay has been stressful, but being stuck here at night? That might be treacherous.

CHAPTER SIXTEEN

TOWELS AND CUSHIONS

"The lounge chairs in the cabanas all have cushions. I believe there are towels around here as well," Captain Lorenzo gets up and peers behind the bar.

"Towels and seat cushions! Why didn't you say so earlier? It'll be just like a five-star hotel," Opal huffs and puffs.

"Not to be a thorn in anyone's side, but my back could give out if I don't have the right mattress," Bruce speaks up.

Dane shoves his shirtsleeves up and unbuttons the top of his shirt. "Why did this have to happen to me?" He pulls at his shirt, trying to exchange the trapped heat with the rapidly cooling beach air.

"I found the towels." Captain Lorenzo pops his head up from behind the bar and deposits a stack of thick, royal blue towels on the bar top. He unfolds one and holds it up so everyone can see. "They are large."

Opal shakes her head, causing her frizzy hair to bobble. "Large towels! Well, had I known the towels were large then I wouldn't have complained." She stomps one of her flip-flop clad feet.

"Maybe we should call the police again," Harry steps into the middle of the group. "I could talk to them."

"Right, because if you talk to them, they'll run on over here," Opal bites. "We all forgot you were the head cop in Perfect Sands Islands."

Harry's cheeks stripe red. "I was trying to help."

"The only thing that could even be remotely helpful would be if we could get off this island," Opal says.

"Stop!" Captain Lorenzo holds up his hands to all of us, but his eyes look at Opal. "We must make the best of this. Things run slower in Perfect Sands, and we will respect that." Everyone quiets at his outburst. "We will assign cabanas for the night."

"I'm taking the one down the beach. I already spent most of the day there," Opal says. "The rest of you can sleep in the coconut trees for all I care."

"I suppose I'll grab the cabana near Opal then," Bruce says.

"Naturally. You want to have the opportunity to steal more of my things," Opal tilts her head.

Bruce crosses his arms. "I was being polite by letting you go first, but who is to say I can't stay in the nicer cabana you've been hoarding to yourself all day? Maybe I'll just go ahead and sleep in there!"

"Stop!" Captain Lorenzo is looking at Bruce this time. "I will pick the cabanas."

Opal and Bruce glare at each other. I look down at my toes and study the small granules of sand stuck to my pink nails. Seeing adults bicker like children isn't exactly the most comfortable thing to witness. It also isn't helping my headache.

"There are six cabanas in total, three on this beach and three at the other beach. Why don't the ladies, Mrs. Halladay and Ms. Loweton, stay here. This beach has the best lighting and is most comfortable. I will stay here as well in case they need anything. Then the men and Ms. Finch," he looks at me, "can walk to the other cabanas. Does this work?"

There's a stretched silence as some sort of bird coos in the bushy vegetation off the path.

"As long as I get to stay in my cabana, I won't complain," Opal says.

I bite my tongue. It's hard to imagine Opal not complaining.

"I don't mind that arrangement, but I plan on sticking around here until nightfall," Bruce says. "There's no point in trotting all the way to the other end of the island when the police could show up any minute."

"He has a point," Dane says. "The sun is still technically out."

Out across the water, a small inch of the orange sun hovers over the horizon. It resembles a curious tabby cat peeking out a window.

"It's just as well," Harry says. "I had some questions I wanted to ask the group."

Opal smirks. "Here we go again."

"What does that mean?" Harry asks.

"You think you're in some sort of cozy mystery. I've noticed you running around the island playing detective. It's cute, but in my opinion, rather irritating." Opal's smirk grows larger.

Harry brushes her off. "Someone was murdered on the tender, and if I have to be blunt, the murderer was most likely one of us who is standing here right now. I'm not taking any chances. I'm going to do what I can to protect myself and Emma, and if anyone finds that irritating, so be it."

"He's got a point," Dane speaks up. "We really all should be on the lookout." He eyes each member of the group.

"You've got to be kidding me!" Opal scoffs. "You're okay with him interrogating us?"

"I have nothing to hide," Bruce says humbly.

"Nor do I," Dane says.

"Personally, I find it atypical that you are so unwilling to be questioned," Bruce holds a chubby finger in the air. "Some might say you're acting suspicious."

Opal narrows her eyes at him, but she doesn't say anything.

Harry clears his throat. "I'll be blunt. Did anyone see anything at all irregular when we were on the tender? I know Emma and I were next to each other the whole time, and Captain Lorenzo was driving."

"I didn't see anything," Dane says. "I was next to Samara. She was restless, but at no point during the journey did she get up and go downstairs."

Samara nods her head. "That's true. I was next to Dane. He didn't get up either."

"I was next to him," Opal looks at Bruce with a look of disgust.

"But he was next to us," I speak up.

"That's because I was next to both of you," Bruce says. "Originally, I sat next to Mrs. Halladay, but she kept hemming and hawing, so I switched seats."

"He's telling the truth," Dane says. "He brushed my shoulder when he got up."

"That's an oddly specific memory to have," Opal says to Dane.

Dane shrugs. "Honest. I remember because it caused me to send a text to my wife with a typo in it. She's been giving me heck since."

"Who is to say that *you* didn't sneak downstairs after I moved seats?" Bruce sternly assesses Opal.

"Me? You all think I go around killing people on my free time?"

Dane shakes his head. "If it was Opal, we all would have heard her flipflops on the deck." Opal glares at him. "Sorry, I have to be honest."

"If everyone is accounted for, then how was someone murdered?" Harry looks around the curious faces in the circle.

The pressing humidity in the air is covered in thick silence. No one can answer Harry's question. How can they? It seems as if a murder on the lower deck is impossible, but it happened.

A cicada buzzes in a nearby tree, and a thought strikes me. "Maybe multiple people murdered Lloyd on the lower deck, and they're all covering for each other."

"*Great*," Opal elongates the word. "It's not good enough for one person to confirm you aren't the murderer. Now the whole boat has to verify it. In that case, we're all murderers."

"None of us knew each other before the sailing. It doesn't make sense for any of us to go commit a murder together," Dane says. "We all just have bad luck."

I don't have the energy to argue my point. It seems like the dull ache in my head is spreading by the minute.

"What Emma said isn't impossible," Harry says.

"Maybe you two did it," Opal says. "You seem to know the answer to everything. The murderer would know the answer to everything."

"If we did it, why would we keep talking about it? Wouldn't we want everyone to forget it happened?" Harry says.

Opal gives the air a little sniff in annoyance.

"Let's look at motives. Does anyone here have a reason to kill Lloyd?" Harry asks.

"No one knew Lloyd," Dane says. "Why would anyone want to kill him?"

"That's easy enough to say, but some people have been acting odd since we've arrived on Killdeer Cay," Harry glances around the group that's now filled with offended faces.

"Not me," Bruce pipes up. "I'm just a retiree on vacation."

"Please, you stole my phone. That's suspicious," Opal says.

"You also tried to kayak all the way to Lapis Rock, and Harry had to rescue you," I add. Even though my headache is searing, I can't let that little fact slip away. What Bruce did with the kayak was bizarre.

"You tried to kayak to the other island?" Captain Lorenzo's eyebrows shoot up. "Why would you do that? That's incredible dangerous! You could've died!"

"How else are we going to get off this island?" Bruce clenches his fists.

"I have told everyone again and again. The police are coming," Captain Lorenzo says. "I can call them again to reassure you?"

"I'm the least suspicious person here. Opal is the one we should be looking at. She has just the personality to kill." Bruce points a finger at Opal.

Opal smirks. "Deflecting. Something a murderer would do. I like my life the way it is. I wouldn't do something to mess it up like murdering a stranger on a boat in the middle of the ocean."

"What is it you do?" Bruce leans towards her. "You have lots of flashy clothes, but you haven't once mentioned a job. Maybe you're a trained killer!"

Opal laughs. "Is anyone else hearing this man? I like designer labels, so I must kill people? Bruce, you are deranged."

"Then tell us what you do! I'm a retiree. See it's easy to share."

"I don't need to defend myself to you," Opal spits out at Bruce.

"We're getting off track," Harry speaks up. "Not liking a person isn't evidence that they're a killer."

"What other evidence is there?" Opal presses. "Bruce has been acting senseless. Maybe he didn't like Lloyd, and he went insane and murdered him."

"Stop!" Captain Lorenzo holds his hands up. It's starting to feel like he's a referee rather than a sea captain. "We will not discuss this if we cannot be civil. If people have concerns about one another, so be it, but the concerns must be presented fairly."

Bruce crosses his arms and turns away from Opal while she gives him the once over and looks away too with an unimpressed expression on her face.

"I have a concern," Samara speaks up. Her voice is small, and her nerves radiate around the circle. "I've been keeping this a secret, but I think I was the one meant to be murdered."

There's a small mumbling amongst the group. Samara's news doesn't surprise Harry or me. What does surprise me is her choice to share it with everyone. She's spent almost the whole day hiding, why reveal her secret now?

"I'm visiting Lapis Rock because I inherited a large estate from my grandfather, but his sister doesn't want me to have it. I don't trust her, and I wouldn't be surprised if she sent someone to try and get rid of me. Dumping me into the ocean is just the type of thing she would do."

"I doubt that," Bruce says.

All heads turn in his direction. Samara is trembling. It can't have been easy for Samara to express herself, so why Bruce feels the need to publicly denounce her is beyond me.

"No one asked you," Opal flicks her hair at Bruce.

"Not the story about your family," Bruce clarifies. "I doubt that someone would have mistaken Lloyd for you. Lloyd was a fella, and you're a lady. You'd have to be dense as a pound cake to make that mistake."

"Now that that's solved, why does your family hate you so much?" Opal purrs.

Samara blinks her eyes a few times and stutters. Leave it to Opal to direct the conversation somewhere unnecessary.

"She doesn't have to share if she's not comfortable," I speak up.

"She does," Opal says. "If we are trying to solve a murder, we all have to share. I shared, Bruce shared, Samara's turn." She smiles impishly.

Samara threads her necklace through her forefinger and thumb before taking a big breath. "My great aunt dislikes me because when I was young, very young, a school girl, I was caught shoplifting. I had been hanging out with a group of girls that I shouldn't have been with. They were a bad influence, and they had shown me how to pickpocket and steal. When I was caught, I was ashamed. I couldn't believe what I had done. My parents pulled me from the private school I had been attending.

"My grandfather was paying for school at the time, and my great aunt thinks I wasted his money not only because of school, but the lawyers who helped me with my charges as well. That's why she thinks I shouldn't have been left anything in the will."

Samara's story explains the mistakes she had told Harry and I about early in the day, but still, the treatment from her great aunt seems harsh. Samara must be in her mid-twenties, which means the shoplifting happen over a decade ago, and she had been a mere child at the time. Who would ever hold a petty error that someone did as a child against them as an adult?

"That's a rather boring story." Opal fakes a yawn. "Who is next in the hot seat? Captain Lorenzo?"

Captain Lorenzo looks surprised that he's been selected to participate. "I shuttle people to and from the island daily. I have no reason to kill someone and risk my job."

Dane bursts into laughter. His laugh is rough and a bit raspy. "He was driving the boat. We would've noticed if the boat stopped so that he could take a break to murder someone," Dane says.

"I see you've added some personality to your repertoire," Opal turns to Dane, having lost interest in Captain Lorenzo. "Maybe you did it?"

"I didn't," Dane's flat, monotone voice has returned. "I'm not even going to entertain your idea."

I play with a piece of gravel near my right foot. Now would be the time to say something about all of Dane's phone calls that I've overheard. Even when Harry and I went over everyone in private, he seemed the most suspicious. I take a deep breath.

"There were a couple things I wanted to ask you," I say to Dane.

"I'm as open as they come. Go for it." He moves his neck around, lightly cracking it.

"I wasn't trying to spy, but I overheard you having an intense conversation with someone named Melissa, but earlier you had told me your wife was named Jill. You even said something about a man being taken care of? And when I talked to you earlier, you mentioned a man who had ruined your dinner?"

"And now you're thinking Lloyd was the guy who disrupted my dinner, and I went ahead and *took care of him* by shoving him off a boat." Dane doesn't seem flustered in the slightest, almost as if he expected the accusation to be coming. "I admit, if I didn't know myself, I would be suspicious of me, but I had nothing to do with Lloyd's death. Melissa is my sister. She called me about our father, who is currently in the hospital. He has a gambling problem, and he's broke. Some of his bookies beat him up. I paid his medical bills and paid the bookies. I *literally* took care of him, and I didn't want Melissa to say anything to Jill while we are on our honeymoon."

"Family secrets run deep with this bunch," Opal whispers theatrically. "Who was the jerk at dinner though? Maybe it was Lloyd?"

Dane shakes his head. "The jerk at dinner was Bruce."

"Me! I've never met you!"

"Last night you cut my wife and I when we were waiting in line at the dining room. She was already mad at me for some trivial thing. She wanted me to tell you off, and I wouldn't. You made everything ten times worse than it already was!"

"I think that solves it," Opal says. "Dane is the murderer. He holds grudges against line cutters. Who knows what Lloyd did to him. Maybe he cut in line while he was boarding the tender."

"That's ludicrous! If you haven't noticed, Bruce is still alive. If I was going to kill him, I had all day to do it. I don't kill people for cutting in line."

"That leaves Harry and Emma," Opal's eyes cut across to us. "Tell us why you did it."

"We didn't do anything," I say. "Like I said earlier, if we were murderers, we wouldn't keep bringing up the murder. You've said it yourself, you think Harry and I are playing detectives. Why would the murderer go and investigate their own murder? That would make a very boring game of detective."

"I think we should take a break," Captain Lorenzo says. "I will call the police again to see if they can arrive sooner. Okay?"

Everyone is in agreement. We all slowly drift off in our own directions, careful not to stray too far from the dining area or main beach. Harry and I take up a set of lounge chairs away from the others. I couldn't be more relieved when Harry pulls a water bottle from the backpack and offers me a sip. I do more than sip. I gulp it down.

Settling my head back against the lounge chair relieves the pressure in my skull, dulling the loud drum that beats through my mind. Above us, a few tiny stars sparkle in the darkening sky. I hope Captain Lorenzo manages to convince the police to come soon because if things keep going the way they are, who knows what will happen next.

Chapter Seventeen

BONFIRE CHATS

S lowly, the blue sky morphs into a calming purple. The waves gently scrape against the shore, and the few birds that were chirping are replaced with croaking tree frogs. The scene isn't fitting for a murder. Paradise seldom is.

Now that my achy head is closer to normal, my thoughts rumble. They won't leave me alone. Who was Lloyd? Why would someone kill him? And lastly, how did someone kill him? Our open discussion left me with more questions than answers. Was it possible that two, or maybe three, people went and attacked Lloyd at the same time? If they did, how did no one notice?

Harry's breath turns rhythmic as he drifts off in the lounge chair next to me. His chest slowly ebbs and flows against the breeze coming off of the water. I wonder if his sleep is dreamless or filled with riddles and clues that need to be solved.

My phone buzzes in my pocket. Charlie has texted me a picture. He and my parents are in front of a giant rock on the beach making silly faces. It didn't take them long to become friends. I stare up at the stars blinking back at me. The world, despite how large it is, sometimes seems small. It's wild to think that Charlie happened to be visiting Perfect Sands Islands at the exact time as me, and it's even wilder to think about how he and my parents went to the same bar at the same time and sat right by each other. People could be anywhere at any moment, or in the opposite way, missing from exactly where you expect them to be.

I close my eyes against the dark sky, but only for a moment. My heart splashes into my stomach, and I sit up. My movement is sudden enough to rouse Harry from his sleep.

"What's wrong?" He asks groggily.

"Harry, I've got an idea!"

He blinks sand away from his eyes and sits up.

"I was lost in thought, thinking about how Charlie and my parents met on Lapis Rock. What are the chances, right? One of my friends from back home running into my parents in such a random place?"

"You think your parents or Charlie have something to do with Lloyd?"

"What? No. That's absurd. My dad couldn't kill a mouse if it pinched him, and my mother, while capable, could never be that organized."

"Then what do they have to do with Lloyd?"

"You and I were supposed to be on Lapis Rock, right? Samara, Dane, everyone else, they were also supposed to be on Lapis Rock. If I had never contacted my parents, I would think that by now they would be a bit worried about me. That means Lloyd was supposed to be on Lapis Rock, but, obviously, he's not. Someone must be wondering where he is, and that someone might know who would want to hurt him."

Harry grimaces. "While that's true, we have no proof if Lloyd was traveling with anyone. Look at Charlie. He came all the way to Perfect Sands Islands alone, and maybe Lloyd did too."

"We could at least ask Charlie to ask around. Maybe he might run into someone."

Harry shakes his head. "I think anything going on in Lapis Rock needs to be handled by the police. Killdeer Cay is different. We're stuck here, and you may have had contact with the murder weapon. You and I are backed into a corner, so we have to investigate. That doesn't necessarily hold true for Lapis Rock."

I bring my knees to my chest and wrap my arms around my shins. I guess my great idea wasn't as great as I thought, but I don't drown in my thoughts. There's a sound of clattering wood from farther down the beach. Captain Lorenzo has plopped a stack of chopped wood next to a rusty firepit.

Harry and I get up and walk to Captain Lorenzo. It's not long before the rest of the group joins us. Captain Lorenzo drags the nearby chairs together to make a circle, and we all settle in. Soon, a campfire licks the night sky with orange and yellow flames. While I'm not exactly cold, the air temperature has dropped, so the heat from the burgeoning fire feels nice.

Harry pushes his chair so it's touching mine, and he wraps an arm around me as he settles into his seat. The sweet smell of ash and embers fill my lungs. I lean my head against his shoulder and close my eyes, but his body feels stiff and uncomfortable, like something is bothering him. Despite this, I'm so exhausted from the day that my eyes grow heavy, but sleep isn't to come. Opal has other plans for the group.

"With the way things are going, maybe the island will catch fire," she says. "Is there a reason we are playing campfire time?"

"I thought we could all use something to distract us. You are supposed to be on vacation, so the fire is the least I can do," Captain Lorenzo says.

It's difficult for me to see his face since he's sitting directly across from me, but I can easily see Bruce. He has already dug his feet into the sand, and he's stretched back against his chair. All the tension he held earlier has melted away. I can't say the same for Samara. She's on the other side of

Harry, and she's squeezing her hands together so tight that they look more statuesque than human. I had expected her to be more relaxed after so many people pointed out that it would have been unlikely for a murderer to mistake her for a man.

"What did the police say when you called them again?" Harry asks.

I sit up straighter so that I can see Captain Lorenzo's face, but a large flame obscures him from view.

"They said they will be here in the very early hours of the morning. This is the first time they have given me an expected time. I am taking this as good news."

"The morning!" Opal howls. She looks more like a wolf biting at the moon than a woman. "That's absurd!"

"It is the best they could do," Captain Lorenzo says.

"This little excursion to the island is the biggest waste of time. This Lloyd probably jumped into the ocean. Ruining our vacations!" Opal blabs. She swings her arms wildly around. "We've already established it was impossible for any of us to be on the lower deck. Obviously, he jumped off the boat himself. The police will come to the same conclusion! We've wasted the whole day!"

Bruce nods his head. "I usually don't agree with anything that comes out of her mouth," he eyes Opal, "but I think she's right. We know none of us could've been down in the lower part of the tender when all this happened, so it clearly isn't a murder."

"We might have an idea here," Dane leans forward in his chair, putting his elbows on his knees. "We all saw the crime scene. There was blood, but what if it was some sort of traumatic nose bleed?"

"Maybe, maybe someone snuck onto the boat," Samara's voice cracks. "They snuck onto the boat and attacked Lloyd while he was on the lower deck."

"Was it a merman?" Opal laughs. "How would someone sneak onto a moving boat in the ocean?"

"A stowaway?" Samara squeaks.

"Stop!" Captain Lorenzo is standing again. "All of these are things to be left to the police. We must focus on ourselves until then."

"Cap', you were the one that jumped to murder when it first happened," Bruce says.

Captain Lorenzo exhales. "I jumped to murder because of the blood. I know now it might've been a nose bleed like Mr. Cassigan suggested, and maybe Mr. Alapha fell overboard, but I still think this should all be left to the police. Not us. Either way, a man is missing."

Harry has been quiet this whole time. It's not like him to be silent. I wonder if it's for the same reason I am. While the theory that Lloyd could've jumped is possible, it doesn't explain the knife I found in *The House of Safety*. A stowaway is something Harry and I hadn't discussed though. To see if it would be possible for someone to hideaway on the boat, Harry and I would need to investigate the crime scene, and that would be a no-go.

My phone buzzes in my pocket, and I glance down. I have a missed call from Mr. Hawking. I don't think he's ever called me this late at night. The article he had asked for earlier had completely slipped my mind. Hopefully, he'll remember I'm on vacation this time around and assign "The Backyard Bird Blurb" to someone else, preferably someone not stuck on an island in the middle of the ocean.

"Are you okay?" Harry whispers. His lips brush gently against the lobe of my ear.

I hold my phone up so that he sees who's calling. Trying to be as inconspicuous as possible, I ease myself out of my seat and walk quietly across the sand until I'm alone in the dining area.

"Hello?" I answer.

"Finch!" Mr. Hawking's voice comes so loudly from the speaker that I yank my phone away from my ear.

"Hello, Mr. Hawking. Is everything okay?"

"It's not okay! I'm looking at my desk, and there's no article from you. How is the next issue supposed to hit the stands without "The Backyard Bird Blurb?""

"I'm on vacation, remember? I asked for time off a while ago, and you approved it."

"I can't play games any longer. I need that article. Marketing got results back from a customer survey this week, and it turns out your little blurb is one of the biggest draws to the magazine."

"Mr. Hawking, I'm sorry, but I told you. I'm in the Caribbean. I don't have access to my work computer." I bite my tongue before adding that I've also been absent from the office for several days now. How has he not noticed? Am I really that forgettable? Apparently, "The Backyard Bird Blurb" isn't.

"I never thought it would come to this," Mr. Hawking drops his voice, and the other end of the line grows silent.

A fiery hand of nerves claws at my chest. I've worked so hard the past few years trying to establish myself at the magazine. Will it all be for nothing? Is this the moment Mr. Hawking lets me go?

The silence grows before me into a canyon.

"Mr. Hawking?"

There's no answer. I slide my phone away from my cheek and see that Mr. Hawking has hung up on me. I should've just typed out something about robins or cardinals on my phone and sent it to him. No one reads the Backyard Bird Blurb anyway. Mr. Hawking probably read the marketing report incorrectly.

I swallow the panic that rises from my stomach, but it gets stuck in my throat like a big balloon. Have I just lost my job? I know it was far from glamourous, but working at the birding magazine was steady work, something not easy to come by as a writer.

What will my parents think when I tell them? Or worse, where will I live? I can't exactly move back home. My parents have no fixed address. They're on a permanent vacation around the world, and there's no room, or money, for a third wheel to traipse along.

And Harry. What would Harry think? I bite down on my tongue. Should I even tell him? This trip hasn't exactly been going well. First, my parents have been overbearing. Second, the cruise put us in a room with bunkbeds. Third, we got stranded on an island because someone was most likely murdered, and lately, he's been acting strange, and I think it has to do with something I did or said before I fainted, but I can't remember what I did! What if me losing my job is all it takes for him to decide he's not interested?

I bury my head in my hands as I pace up and down the path. Burying it in the sand would've been a much more fitting option, but I doubt others would find it socially acceptable. What am I going to do?

Chapter Eighteen

THE STOWAWAY DECISION

I turn around, intending to head back to the campfire, but I stop in my tracks. Bruce is blocking my path. In the darkening night, his usually jovial features look menacing. The lines around his mouth are more pronounced and the hollows under his eyes make him look soulless.

"You startled me!" I try to sound friendly, hoping to mask the sound of blood pulsing in my veins.

"I was just trying to find my way to the bathroom, but I think I took a wrong turn," his voice sounds kind, but as he speaks, he shifts so that his face falls into the shadows, and I can't quite make out his expression. "It's also good to be up and about."

"I'm happy to hear that you're feeling better after earlier today," I say.

"I certainly hadn't intended for my kayaking trip to end the way it did," he says. "I'm feeling much better though."

"Weren't you feeling ill before kayaking?" the thought slips through my lips.

I had forgotten that Captain Lorenzo had claimed that Bruce had been sick to his stomach. Harry and I had become so caught up in his kayak rescue that the supposed fact that he had been sick earlier hadn't been reinvestigated. But now that I think of it, it is odd that Bruce would take on such a grand adventure across the seas in a state of ailment.

"Right, Cap' helped me out a bit. I think I was dehydrated," he mumbles quickly. "Anyway, must be on my way to the bathroom."

He glides by and hurries down the path. It's rather peculiar. A lot of things seem to have happened to Bruce today, but somehow, none of them have affected him for more than a few minutes. First, he hurt his ankle, which suddenly healed, then he got sick, but only for a short bit. Even his kayak rescue seemed to leave him unfazed. There is something off about Bruce, but I don't have time to ponder it. My phone buzzes in my hand. Maybe Mr. Hawking is calling me back, and I'm not fired. Maybe we just had a bad signal.

I look at the number. It's Charlie.

"Hey," I say. I try to keep the disappointment out of my voice, but I know I don't do a very good job.

"That's one of the most depressing *heys* I've ever heard. I take it there isn't good news on the murder mystery front?" Charlie's voice is chipper.

"On the mystery front, there's no news."

"Then why the sad greeting?"

I bite down on my lip. Should I tell Charlie that I might be out of a job? What would he think of me?

"Earth to Emma!" Charlie snaps. "Are you there?"

"I'm here." I take a deep breath. "I might've lost my job."

Charlie gasps. "What happened?"

"My editor forgot that I had gone on vacation, and I didn't send him an article when he wanted it. I don't know what to do. What will my parents think? What will Harry think?"

"I wouldn't be too worried about Harry."

"Why do you say that?" I ask.

"Emma, I'm not sure if you've noticed, but I don't think Harry is dating you because you write for a bird magazine. You might find this shocking, but Harry isn't even interested in birds. If you worked for a tree planting magazine, Harry would probably go and watch documentaries about tree farms. The boy is crazy about you, and it's not because you write about birds."

Even though Charlie isn't even on the same land mass as me, my cheeks still burn with embarrassment. He's right. Harry would never think less of me just because I lost my job. We've been through too much together.

"Really, Emma. If you worked for a publisher who specialized in whale watching, Harry would be listening to podcasts about whale songs. If you worked for a pepper magazine, that man would be in the garden—"

"Okay, okay, I get it," I stifle a laugh.

"Feel better?"

"I always feel better after a chat with my favorite food writer."

"Speaking of food, the pepper festival I flew all the way out here for is a total bust."

"Why? What happened?" It's hard to imagine a pepper festival going up in flames, but I don't know much about the culinary world.

"The most scandalous thing. There is a rumor going around that the main attraction, scheduled for tomorrow, opening day, might not happen," Charlie whispers as if someone might be eavesdropping.

"What was the main event?"

"Really, Emma, I'm surprised you don't know. This pepper festival is all that has been trending on my social media these past few months."

I don't tell Charlie that I have a strong suspicion that we follow different social media accounts. Mine tend to be ornithologists, bird bloggers, and writers. I don't even know who I would need to follow to learn about pepper festivals.

"I heard from my friend John, he's a chef from Turks and Caicos, his oxtail and fried conch is to die for, that the company bringing the Swirl Delicious pepper might not show!"

"Swirl Delicious?"

"It's one of the rarest peppers in the world. It can only be grown in a few places on Earth. It's the major attraction at the festival. I've never seen one before."

"Definitely an odd name," I say.

"Not really. It's no more strange than other fruit. Think of apples. Golden Delicious, Red Delicious, Granny Smith, Pink Lady."

"Pepper is a fruit?"

"Well, it's not a fish or dairy."

I had more been thinking it was a vegetable, but I trust Charlie's food knowledge enough not to question it. "I take it the Swirl Delicious has a swirl."

"Bingo! It's a red and yellow color that tapers out into a light gold. All in a lovely swirl pattern."

"What happens if the pepper never shows up?"

"The festival will be a complete failure. I'll have no choice but to tell all my readers about it. Several big publications are already vying for the article that I'm writing about the festival. I received several lucrative offers before I even arrived in Perfect Sands Islands."

"Yikes. Let's hope the rumors aren't true then. Maybe the company responsible for transporting the pepper is just hyping everyone up by starting whispers that they may not come."

"One can hope. Emma, I am so sorry to cut our phone call short, but your parents and I are about to be seated at our table."

"Are you all back on the ship?"

"Nope, we're all ashore. Bye for now." Charlie hangs up.

I put my phone away, and a flurry of emotions fall heavily in my stomach. I'm relieved after talking to Charlie about possibly being fired from the magazine. He really did put things into perspective. No one, especially Harry, would ditch me just because I don't work there anymore. Along with that, I've probably been misreading all those odd looks and awkward moments between Harry and myself as well. I've just had too much sun today.

But while one part of me feels relief, another part feels unsteady. Evening has come and gone, and it is officially night, but my parents don't seem very concerned about where Harry and I disappeared to. It's been easier to work on the case without them fretting, but Harry and I could have been kidnapped by pirates for all they know. I suppose Charlie could've told them about the murder on the tender, but if he did, then they definitely would have called. No, they must think that Harry and I are off on some romantic jaunt by ourselves. The thought makes me feel guilty, but thankful at the same time. I wouldn't want their anniversary trip to be ruined.

I head back to the beach, but as I do, I step too close to a killdeer nest because one comes running out at me. The little bird flops around in a dramatic circle, trying to distract me from a nearby treasure of eggs. Normally, the bird would make me smile, but a sour feeling just floats in my stomach. I should've just typed out a short article about killdeers on my phone and sent it to Mr. Hawking. I know that they're not exactly backyard birds, but hey, some people do live at the beach.

Back on the beach, the fire is still aglow. Bruce isn't back yet, but everyone else is present. If I didn't know about the murder on the tender, I might think that a group of friends had gathered around for a friendly bonfire. Of course, the mood is more obvious as I get closer. The smoke holds a somberness that stifles my breath. Samara and Opal both look uneasy while Harry and Dane look glum. Captain Lorenzo doesn't look much better. Lines furrow the spot between his dark eyes as he ponders over something.

"What'd I miss?" I ask Harry.

I expect him to shrug his shoulders and tell me nothing happened while I was gone, but that isn't the answer I get. "We discussed the stowaway theory, and we've all come to an agreement."

"You think that the person who attacked Lloyd had been hiding on the ship?" I keep my voice low. I don't want to disturb the others around the fire.

Apparently, my voice carries because Opal butts in. "Yes, Sherlock. While you and Bruce were gone, we all concluded that the only possible way for someone to have committed murder on the tender was if there was an extra person on board."

"Are they on the island then?" I tighten my hands on the armrests of my chair, and my knuckles whiten.

"No, they swam to Lapis Rock," Opal bites.

"That's the main concern," Captain Lorenzo ignores her. "If there is someone on the island who killed Lloyd, we may all be in big danger."

Opal scoffs. "We've always been in danger. I've been trying to point that out to everyone since we landed here. I was the only one with any sense." Opal flaps her hand around to indicate the rest of us gathered around the fire haven't been thinking properly.

Her assessment isn't exactly correct. While some people like Dane may have been more concerned with their marital affairs than Lloyd's murder, others have most certainly been preoccupied with their own safety. Captain Lorenzo has been on the phone with the police for half the day, Harry and I have been sleuthing, poor Bruce attempted to kayak across the water, and Samara spent almost all her time on Killdeer Cay hiding.

I stare into the raging fire in front of me. The idea of a stowaway on the island is much worse than one of the seven of us being a suspect. Before, Harry and I had a trail to follow, but now, we'll be lost. Who could've wanted Lloyd dead so bad that they hid away on the tender? The only way Harry and I can figure it out is if we try to figure out who Lloyd Alapha was.

CHAPTER NINETEEN

SNAKES IN HIGH GRASS

T he fire has died down to winking embers. Harry holds my hand in his, and the night air stills my skin with an icy chill. I hadn't expected the Caribbean to get very cold at night, and while I'm sure the temperature is still tropical compared to what it would be at home, the fact that I'm stuck in my bathing suit coverup probably isn't helping matters.

"We packed extra towels in the beach backpack. Let me go find one for you," Harry says, and he gets up.

"Don't you have the backpack with you?"

"I left it in the eating area," he says.

This surprises me. After someone stole the notebook from the backpack, I had expected Harry to have kept a closer eye on the bag. I suppose that there's not much of anything important in the bag now that it's been pillaged. Harry trudges across the compact sand until he disappears somewhere near the dining area.

Opal smacks her arm, and a light smear of pink blood appears across her sinewy bicep. "Disgusting. Now there's bugs."

Samara looks away from the streak of blood and digs her toes into the sand. Her freshly painted, blue nails disappear.

"What was the name of the beach club that was on this island before it closed?" Dane asks Captain Lorenzo.

"I'm not sure," Captain Lorenzo replies. "I didn't visit it. It was mostly for the tourists."

I don't pay attention to the rest of the conversation. Harry has come back with a fluffy towel for me to snuggle up in. He drapes it over my shoulders and gives me a light kiss on the head as he settles into his own chair.

"I might tucker in for the night." I turn around to see Bruce behind me. He's made his way back from the bathrooms.

"If you go now, I'll follow. There's no point in me staying up. My phone has died, and it's impossible for me to put a call through to Jill. She's going to grill me when we all get back to the boat." Dane stretches his long limbs towards the night sky and yawns. "Once again, nothing is working in my favor."

"At least you have a phone. Mine was stolen," Opal eyes Bruce.

Bruce holds his hands up in innocence. "I had nothing to do with your phone."

"Sure," Opal says.

"I doubt anyone is trying to contact you anyway," Bruce mumbles under his breath.

"Everyone should take some towels and cushions with them to the cabanas," Captain Lorenzo says. "There are plenty over in the dining area."

The group of us shuffles through the cool sand over to the bar where Captain Lorenzo has arranged a stack of towels and cushions. Opal snags hers without much enthusiasm and Dane follows.

"Are we keeping the arrangements from earlier?" Dane asks.

"I don't care what other people do, but I'll be staying in the cabana that I claimed when we first arrived on this treacherous island," Opal says.

"As long as the cabana I'm in is nowhere near her, I'll be happy," Bruce says.

"We will keep the arrangements then," Captain Lorenzo says. "Mrs. Halladay and Ms. Loweton will be with me on the beach here while everyone else goes to the other side of the island."

"Let's get the field trip started then!" Bruce looks at Harry, Dane, and me. "The path should take us right where we need to be."

The four of us set out into the night. If someone had told me that the day would be ending with me going on a night jaunt with Bruce and Dane, I probably would've laughed. I suppose stranger things have happened though. Before we get far, Harry suddenly stops.

"I forgot the backpack near the campfire. I'll be right back!" Harry runs off.

I gnaw at the inside of my cheek as he fades down the path. He hasn't been himself. It's twice now that he's forgotten the backpack somewhere. Harry is one of the most attentive and detail-oriented people I know. Something must be bothering him. I make a mental note to ask him about it once we're alone in the cabana. If it's something I did before I fainted, it would be best if he told me.

"How long have you two lovebirds been together?" Bruce looks at me and wiggles his eyebrows. I sea of nausea washes over me.

"Not too long," I say quickly. Something about the way Bruce calls Harry and I lovebirds rubs me wrong, and I want the conversation to end.

"Where'd you meet?"

"At my great aunt's house," I say.

I don't want Bruce to know too much about me. While Harry seems to be onboard with the whole concept of a stowaway being to blame for Lloyd's murder, I'm not sure that I'm as open to the idea.

"If Jill had been stuck on this island with me, like you and Harry are together, then I know she wouldn't be so mad at me," Dane says. "If only I hadn't missed the first tender. She hates me now. Why did I have to be on that tender?"

Dane's words strike me. Why did so many of us end up on that tender, and could the fact that we all missed our original boat point to something sinister? I know Harry and I missed our scheduled ride to the island because we couldn't find each other at the gangway, but what of the other guests? Why had they ended up on a boat with Lloyd Alapha? And had they ended up on that boat intentionally? I now have two pieces of homework for Harry and I. One is to learn more about who Lloyd was and why someone would hurt him, and two is to learn why everyone ended up on the tender in the first place.

Harry returns to us with the backpack slung over his shoulder. Bits of sand cling to his pale skin where the bag has brushed against his muscular chest.

"I'm ready. Sorry about that," he says.

Bruce leads the way to the southern beach. We pass by the same plants and underbrush that were present during the day, but in the night, they look eerie and otherworldly. The dried, yellow grass, so easy to see in the day, looks like spindly hands reaching up from the earth, hoping to grab whoever is unfortunate enough to walk by. Every once in a while, something soft flutters across my back. Most likely a spider web or a moth, but in the dark, alien ideas run through my mind. The sooner we get to the cabanas, the better.

"Shoot!" Dane calls out from behind me.

I turn to see him holding his ankle. In the strong moonlight, I see something slither away into the tall grass.

"Snake!" I scream.

"Yikes!" Bruce springs into the air like a cartoon figure.

Harry jumps into action. He hurries over to the spot where the grass is shifting. He pulls his phone out and activates the flashlight. "I can't see anything," he says. "The captain might know what we should do. We're not too far from the other beach, let's hurry."

I imagine we make a rag-tag team as we high-tail it back to the beach. Bruce, having recovered quickly from his injury earlier in the day, is doing some sort of high-kneed jig in an attempt to avoid any possible snakes. Dane, on the other hand, is limping. The long cut across Harry's face is reflecting in the moonlight, flashing silver here and there, and myself, I'm not sure what I look like, but I imagine it can't be anything too attractive considering I've spent the day trapped on an island. Not only that, but my headache has returned with rage.

Captain Lorenzo is standing by the dead fire when we come down from the path. His face shows concern at the sight of us.

"Is everything okay?" He asks, looking mostly at Bruce who hasn't stopped his ridiculous jumping.

"Dane was bitten by a snake. I tried to find it after the bite, but it was long gone," Harry says.

Dane holds out his swollen ankle. There are two tiny prick marks with drizzles of blood seeping from them.

Captain Lorenzo lets out a breath. "That is nothing. I was worried for a moment."

"It doesn't feel like nothing," Dane says.

"Yes, it must hurt," Captain Lorenzo says apologetically. "You will need some antiseptic and maybe a bandage to help with the blood."

"What if the snake was poisonous?" Harry asks. "We could be in real trouble."

At this, Dane's face pales.

"There are no dangerous snakes in Perfect Sands Islands. There are only three types, and they are all harmless."

Dane grumbles at the word harmless.

"You will feel better when it's all cleaned up. Snakes on this island are no worse than crickets." Captain Lorenzo walks off to find the first aid kit.

"What is all this ruckus?" Opal Halladay appears at the edge of the cabanas. "I was trying to get some shut-eye, and all I hear is obnoxious yelling."

Samara also appears, poking her head out from behind Opal.

"Dane was bitten by a snake when we were walking towards the cabanas. We came back to get some help from the captain," Harry says.

"Snakes!" Opal trills. "We were never told that there were snakes on this island! There could be one in my cabana."

"He said they were harmless," Harry replies.

Opal points at Dane's ankle. "That doesn't look harmless to me! It looks like some sort of bear has attacked him! There's enough blood there to satisfy a blood drive!"

The pain in my head flares at Opal's loud voice, and I bite down on my lip. I hope Opal has a background in acting because she's by far one of the most dramatic people I've ever met. Sure, Dane has some blood on his ankle, but his injury hardly resembles something from a bear.

"I'm back," Captain Lorenzo kneels on the ground with the kit. "You all need to stop getting hurt. I will run out of supplies soon," he says this with a smile, but it's probably one of the worst possible things to say in front of Opal.

"I knew something like this would happen. Ever since I got on the cruise, I've been waking up with crow's feet around my eyes. I haven't had a wrinkle in years," Opal says. "Had I known that asking for a semi-private tender to take me to Lapis Rock would've led to this mess, I would've just taken the crowded one with everyone else."

The rest of Opal's monologue is lost on me. Only one question reverberates in my mind. "You requested a semi-private tender?" I ask.

"Of course, didn't you all?" Opal looks around.

I shake my head. "Harry and I missed our scheduled tender, and one of the crew members told Harry that there had been an issue with over-scheduling and that a second tender happened to be available. Dane said the same happened to him."

"Ouch!" Dane grits his teeth together as Captain Lorenzo pats his injury with rubbing alcohol.

"Sorry. I always forget that alcohol stings," Captain Lorenzo apologizes.

"Can we not focus?" Opal places her hands on her hips. "How was it possible for me to have ordered a semi-private tender, yet you were all told that there had been a scheduling accident?"

"I'm as focused as I can be right now," Dane groans.

"Let it go, Opal. We're trying to help Dane. You'll just have to hold your horses for once in your life," Bruce says.

While I know Bruce is right, I was hoping the conversation would continue in the way Opal had been driving it as I also wanted to know how we had all ended up on a tender with Lloyd Alapha.

As Captain Lorenzo dabs ointment onto Dane's injury, I notice Samara shift uncomfortably, pressing her feet rhythmically into the smooth sand. Something is bothering her. Whether it's the conversation about how we all ended up on the tender, or Dane's wound, she seems distraught.

"Captain, who exactly was Lloyd Alapha?" Harry pipes up while Captain Lorenzo unfurls a long, white bandage.

Captain Lorenzo pulls his eyebrows together. "He was the passenger on the ship who was killed," he says as he wraps Dane's ankle. "But you all know this."

"Sorry, I wasn't clear. Did the cruise give you any information on Lloyd Alapha? Like why was he traveling? Or if he was traveling alone?"

Captain Lorenzo readjusts a section of the bandage as he thinks.

"I have a passenger list if that is what you mean, but you have all already seen that. Otherwise, I have no details about the man."

"Why so many questions?" Opal asks.

"I was thinking that maybe if we all knew a bit more about Lloyd, then we might be able to piece together who would want him dead," Harry replies.

"But I thought we all agreed it was a stowaway?" Samara's voice is squeaky as she glances around at everyone's moonlit face. "If it wasn't a stowaway, then who was it?"

"Please, stop the dramatics. It was a stowaway. Harry is just bored and wanting to play at detective. Don't mind him." Opal flutters her hand in the air as if Harry is some sort of housefly that needs to disappear.

"I think you are all done," Captain Lorenzo says to Dane.

"I appreciate it," Dane runs a hand over his patched-up ankle and winces.

"It will be sore, but there is no poison," Captain Lorenzo says.

"It'll be a bit of a hike for Dane to make it out to the other cabanas," Bruce says.

"It might be a bit uncomfortable, but like I said, he will be alright," Captain Lorenzo replies. "He has no need to have concern."

"Time for bed then!" Bruce announces. "Let's get a move on."

A panic flies through my mind. This might be one of my last chances to talk to everyone together before daybreak. Other than Opal and Captain Lorenzo, I have no idea how or why the others ended up on the tender with Lloyd Alapha, and I also have no idea who Lloyd Alapha was.

"Wait!" I take a gulp of air. "I think Opal was right."

"I usually am." Opal smirks.

"It's odd that Opal scheduled an extra tender to pick her up, but Harry, Dane, and I were all told that the extra tender was due to a scheduling mishap."

I look around at the faces of the group. While Opal and Samara appear to be interested in what I have to say, I'm not sure that the others are.

"Captain Lorenzo, do you have an idea about why we were all told different things?"

Captain Lorenzo shrugs his shoulders. "I wish I could be more help. I work with a company that contracts smaller vessels to help cruises shuttle guests from the ships to Lapis Island. When I arrived at work this morning, I was given a schedule and time to go to the ship to pick up passengers. They usually don't give me any details other than that. Even the passenger list I got from the cruise security before we left the gangway."

A small bug buzzes past me before disappearing into the night just like every clue I've found since arriving on Killdeer Cay. Every time I think I might've figured out something that will lead me to an answer, it turns out to be a false path, another useless thought flying away on the night wind.

Chapter Twenty

HIGH TIDE

A fter a long discussion that turns into several rounds of each person promising that they have never met Lloyd and had no reason to charter a tender with the purpose of killing him, Captain Lorenzo produces the passenger list for the second time. True to his word, the list Captain Lorenzo shows us only has seven passengers listed. Lloyd A Alapha is the first name written on the list in loopy, cursive writing. Next to his name, his cabin number is written, 567.

"He must've been staying on the fifth level of the ship," I point to the number. "Was anyone else on that floor? Maybe one of us passed by him when he was near his room?"

"I always book my rooms on the first deck," Bruce says.

"I'm in the VIP sun deck," Opal says.

"Not surprised," Bruce mumbles.

"My cabin is on that deck," Samara whispers. She grasps at the hem of her cover up. "What if the murderer mixed Lloyd and me up because of our room numbers?"

Opal lets out an exhausted sigh. "Even in the rare event that the murderer had difficulty reading numbers, he most likely didn't choose his victim based on their room assignments."

"I think we can all agree that the passenger list isn't very helpful," Dane speaks up. He's become ornery since his injury. "We've delayed long enough. Let's go to bed."

"Would you like me to walk the group of you to the far cabanas?" Captain Lorenzo offers.

I'm sure he'd rather stay here, but considering people keep getting hurt whenever they leave his sight, he's probably starting to wonder if we can all be left to ourselves safely.

"We'll be careful this time," Harry says.

"We know what things to look out for," I add.

"Maybe you should take the kit?" Captain Lorenzo holds out a red box with a large, white cross on it. "If something happens, you won't have to run back here again."

Bruce readily accepts the first aid kit. "Better safe than sorry," he says.

The four of us set out again to the remote cabanas. Normally, I would expect my headache to worsen due to the physical exertion, but being away from the noisy group is helping. When we reach the part on the path where Dane had been bitten by the snake, we take precaution to walk slowly and look where we step. Bruce walks on his tiptoes as if he's auditioning for some sort of ballet.

We pass the rocky cove. In the moonlight, the limestone rocks that jut out in the shallow water look spectral. It's funny to think about how different everything looks in the light of day. I doubt Bruce would attempt to venture across the water now.

As my skin begins to prickle from the cool sea breeze, the path dips down into the soft sand. We've finally arrived at the far beach. The day has been hectic, and I haven't noticed how worn out I feel. My muscles ache from hiking around the island all day, my arms and legs sting from the slight sunburn grazing my skin, my shoulder and wrist throb from my fall, and my eyelids are heavy and my vision blurred. Suddenly, the idea of cuddling up on a lounge chair with a towel seems wonderful. I'm curious if the others feel the same. It's not as if anyone else has had an easy day on Killdeer Cay.

Bruce yawns loudly as he crosses the sand to the cabanas. Dane follows him, but he does so slowly, limping from his snakebite. The moonlight makes the small beach shacks look silver.

Dane is the first to notice that something is wrong. As he nears the front of the nearest cabana, he lets out a yelp.

"Shoot!" His voice travels across the vacant beach.

"Well, isn't this a doozy!" Bruce chimes.

"What's wrong?" Harry asks.

I follow behind Harry, but it only takes one wave to realize the problem. A crash of salty water sprays my ankles and seeps into the cabana's opening, soaking the bottoms of the lounge chairs.

"I think we found out why they abandoned these cabanas," I say.

The water recedes slowly back to its watery home, but it's not long before another powerful push of water invades the tiny beach cabana. There's no way any of us will be sleeping in here tonight unless we are hoping to float away.

"It must be the high tide," Harry says. "I read something once about the moon impacting it, and tonight is a full moon."

"We'll have to go back to the other beach," I say in disappointment. Will we ever catch a break on this island? This night seems like it will never end. I can't imagine the others will be too pleased when we show up again after they've gone to bed.

"Can we at least rest for a bit before we head back?" Dane asks. "I know Captain Lorenzo said my wound wasn't a big deal, but it's hurting."

"Of course, let's find someplace for you to sit," I scan the barren beach.

At first glance, there aren't many options for Dane unless he wants to sit on the sand, but then I spot an old, driftwood log that's washed ashore where the beach meets the path. I point it out, and the four of us settle into the spots of the dead tree's hooked roots and smooth hollows.

"This is the worst vacation I've ever been on, and it's my honeymoon," Dane looks at the large moon that glows above us. His face is sullen in the silver lighting. "First off, I think my wife doesn't like me very much. Second, I ended up on the wrong tender where someone got murdered which led to being stranded on an island, and now, I have some sort of tropical snakebite."

Bruce scratches at his bald spot. "Don't be too much of a downer. Most of what you're talking about is just life. My missus is going to lay into me once I get back to the cruise, but she'll forget about everything soon enough." Bruce chuckles. "I'm sure she'll give me a good telling off when she finds out I took the up elevator instead of the down elevator when I was on my way to the gangway. That's why I missed the earlier tender."

"You're married?" I hold my hand over my mouth as soon as the words escape. I had imagined Bruce to be a forever-bachelor with his nonchalant attitude.

"Disappointed?" Bruce chuckles.

"Isn't your wife wondering where you went?" I ask.

Bruce shakes his head. "I was able to borrow Opal's phone earlier and send a text to her. I don't exactly have one of those fancy international plans on my phone. Millie, that's my wife, is a tough broad. Served twenty years in the Navy. She'll be fine by herself on Lapis Rock and the ship."

I would have thought Bruce would've mentioned his wife a bit more considering that we had all spent the whole day together.

"Is that why Opal thinks you stole her phone? Because she let you borrow it?" Dane asks.

At the mention of Opal, Bruce's jolly face transforms. "That woman thinks I took her phone because she's unbalanced. I have no interest in her phone."

Dane makes a passive gesture with his hands. "I was just asking."

"Is your bite feeling any better?" I ask. It's best to change the route of conversation considering Bruce's sour attitude.

Dane reaches down and taps his bandage, poking what must be a tender spot.

"It's a little better," he says. "Give me another minute, and I'll be good to get up."

The four of us sit on the washed-up tree trunk. As the water erases the marks in the sand, I think about all the things that happened today that cannot be erased from my mind. I'm pretty sure Mr. Hawking fired me from the magazine, but that seems small compared to the death of the mysterious Lloyd Alapha. Who was he? And how did he end up on the tender? Who had placed that bloody knife in the house across the island? Was it really possible a stowaway was behind everything? And if so, where were they now?

The palms behind me rustle as if someone is pulling back a curtain. I peek behind me, but only darkness stretches through the island.

Chapter Twenty-One

Night Owl

We spend a little longer than intended sitting on the battered log. The rhythmic swish and shush of the waves hypnotize the four of us so that we all travel far from Killdeer Cay in our thoughts. Harry sits far from me on the other end of the log. He looks discontent. As my eyes trace the outline of his nose and jaw, I note the rigid sinews of his neck. He glances in my direction, catching me staring.

"Do you think you'll be ready to go in a few minutes?" Harry asks Dane.

Dane pokes at his ankle. "I think that would work. Sorry about putting everyone behind schedule."

"I don't mind having a little sit and chat," Bruce leans back on the driftwood, taking up more room than is necessary. "Anything to keep me far away from *that woman.*"

Harry gets up and stretches, a small section of his stomach appears as his shirt inches up, revealing his taut stomach. Turning towards me, he catches me staring. Immediately, he lowers his eyes. Something is definitely wrong. The Harry I know would've cracked a joke and teased me, not avoided my gaze.

"Want to go for a short walk?" he asks me.

"I'd be delighted to," I say.

Inside, I am anything but delighted. My stomach tightens so much that I wonder if it hasn't permanently shrunk. Why do I feel this way? It's just Harry. We're probably going to discuss Lloyd Alapha.

We walk up the path until we're far enough away from the beach that the others won't be able to hear us. Other than the buzzing of a few cicadas and the croaking of a tree frog, the island is quiet. If anything is loud, it's the sound of my heart beating against my chest, trying to escape.

"What's up?" I ask.

Harry doesn't look at me. He stares at the ground, fidgeting with a pebble, lightly pushing it back and forth between his sandaled feet. The whole scene reminds me of when I was back in high school, and my prom date told me he had a crush on another girl right in the school parking lot. Harry and I are too old for petty breakups like that, aren't we?

"Sorry, Emma, I don't mean to stall. I'm just trying to figure out what I want to say." Harry's eyes stay glued to the ground as an uncomfortable silence hovers before us.

From somewhere up in the trees, an eerie screeching wails through the leaves and branches. It almost sounds like an old door on unoiled hinges or two iron hulled ships scraping against one another.

"Is that someone screaming?" Harry looks up at the trees.

"It's a barn owl!"

As soon as I say the words, a large, ghostly bird swoops from the highest branches. Its face is a pale orb with large, black eyes. The creature's claws are out and bent. Quickly, it pulls its wings back as it snatches something off the ground and disappears into the darkness.

"It's hunting. It caught dinner." I look up to where some of the dark canopy's leaves tremble, but there's nothing to see. The bird is gone.

"I thought owls hooted," Harry says. "Do we have those things back home?"

I don't answer Harry's question because I hear him speaking different words to me. Words he spoke to me earlier before I fainted. Almost as if I'm dreaming, I envision Harry's face and boyish grin as he tells me that *Everyone loves owls. They're hunters. They hide in trees and wait until its dark and quiet and then they snatch their prey.* It had only been a few hours since that conversation, but it unfolds in my mind as if it's happening now. I had told Harry that *I loved him!* The conversation had occurred shortly before I fainted, which would explain why I had forgotten about it. No wonder why he's been acting strange tonight. Avoiding eye contact and repeatedly forgetting his backpack among other things. Worse, was that why he had pulled me aside to have a talk in private?

The top of my forehead feels hot and moist while my heart knocks against my chest. When I had said that to Harry, it had been a slip of the tongue. I haven't thought much about my feelings for him beyond that I like him. But what if Harry feels differently? What if he is about to profess his love for me! Am I supposed to say it back, even if I'm not ready?

Another thought flies through my mind, like the barn owl, aggressive and unapologetic, it appears out of nowhere and ceases my whole attention. Maybe Harry asked me over here because he thinks I'm too invested in the relationship too early. Harry is busy, and very handsome, he probably has lots of girls he could go out with who aren't clingy, and now, I look clingy.

"Emma? Are you okay?" Harry steps closer to me. His face is next to mine, and his eyes shine with concern. "You look like you're about to throw up."

I try to smile, but it feels like a frog is about to spill forth from my stomach. Had it really only been an hour or so ago that Charlie had reassured me that Harry was incredibly into me? That memory feels years away, adrift in the long-lost sea of the time before Harry and I got stranded on this island.

"Emma?" Harry places a steady hand on my hip. His grip is strong and warm. "Do you need water? I have some in my bag."

Harry sets his backpack on the ground and reaches down to unzip one of the pockets. I study the raised veins running through his forearms and the slight rise of his bicep. This might be the last time I see him like this, caring for me so tenderly.

I take a big gulp of the Caribbean air. "Did you pull me aside because you wanted to talk about how I said I love you earlier? You've been off ever since that happened," the words tumble out like granules of sand fighting to be the first through the small center of an hourglass.

Harry pauses. The silver moonlight rests on his back. He stops what he's doing in his backpack and looks up at me. A look of some emotion crosses his face, but I can't tell if it's good or bad.

"Emma, I'm so sorry," Harry stands and ruffles his hair.

He lets a long silence fall between us, which isn't making me feel much better. What is he sorry about? Sorry he's about to dump me? Sorry he didn't say I love you back? I take another deep breath, but the island air has grown more humid. I suck in as much oxygen as I can, but only a thick air enters my lungs, making it hard to breathe.

"I hope you haven't been worrying about that all day," Harry says to me. "I really, really like you, and nothing you say could ever change that. What you said gave me a lot to think about, and I know I've never felt this way about anyone before." Harry pulls me into a tight hug. Against his chest, I feel his heart throbbing. He smells like smoky firewood. "I'm sorry if that wasn't the answer you wanted," he whispers in my ear.

I pull my head away from where it rests on his chest so that I can see his eyes. "It's exactly the answer I wanted. I was worried that you were going to dump me or say the words right back. I wasn't ready for either one."

Harry rests his forehead against mine. "Emma, nothing you ever say will stop me from wanting to be with you. I'm happy you told me what was on your mind. Do you feel a bit better?"

I don't answer. Instead, I tip forward and let our lips meet. Harry's soft mouth is familiar against mine. All around us, the cicadas buzz and the wind flutters through the leafy trees, but all I notice is the trust that blooms inside my chest.

Chapter Twenty-Two

A Possible Connection

We don't have time to discuss the original reason Harry wanted to talk to me alone. Time has passed us at speed, and we need to get back to Dane and Bruce. When we get back to the beach, the two men are sitting on the log where we last left them. They're in deep conversation. By the sounds of it, Bruce is giving Dane advice on marriage. As we get closer, I hear bits and pieces.

"And if she says she doesn't want Italian food, that doesn't mean she doesn't want pasta. In her mind, those things are very different. For example, macaroni and cheese, is that Italian? I have no clue. Is it pasta? I would say yes. But to her, it might be a completely different food group."

Dane nods his head, taking in the advice. "But what if she says she's not hungry?"

Bruce never gets to answer the question. He's too distracted by Harry and I as we come down the path.

"About ready to go, lovebirds?" Bruce yawns loudly. He opens his mouth wide enough that I can see his tonsils. "Or are you two looking for relationship advice too?"

"I think we're alright," Harry looks at me with a small grin. He's probably thinking about our embrace in the woods just moments ago. I don't think we need any relationship advice.

Back on the path, it's easy to see where we step. The moon has risen so that it's high in the sky, and it spreads its white glow across the corners of Killdeer Cay. I notice that Dane stays close behind Harry and me. He's probably worried that we'll run into a snake again. Bruce takes up the rear of our troupe. He hums to himself some sort of song that is out of his vocal range based on the number of high notes he misses.

As we reach the bend in the path to the beach, I cringe at the thought of disturbing everyone for a second time tonight. Opal isn't exactly welcoming when she's fully awake. She might be a true bear if we disturb her in deep sleep.

It turns out there's no need for us to wake anyone. When we arrive at the beach, Captain Lorenzo, Samara, and Opal are all wide awake and standing in the dining area. Opal's hair has grown into a massive lion's mane. It poofs around her face like some sort of dark cloud. When she sees us, her eyes turn into little slits, making her look even more feline.

"I'm surprised you're all up!" Bruce booms to the group. "Having a second wind?"

Samara looks exhausted. She has puffs under her dark eyes, and her lips are dry and cracked. Captain Lorenzo is the only one that looks mildly okay, but even his eyes and mouth have an uncharacteristic droop to them that suggests a lack of sleep.

"We had an incident," Captain Lorenzo's voice is so hoarse that there's almost no trace of an accent in it.

"It was more than an incident," Opal roars. "Someone tried to get into my cabana. I could've been killed had I not been a fast thinker."

Bruce chuckles.

"Is me being attacked funny to you?" Opal glares at him.

"It just seems like you think someone is always out to get you," Bruce says.

"No, no, she's telling the truth," Samara says in her soft voice. "I heard everything. There was someone trying to get into her cabana."

"Did they hurt you?" Harry asks Opal.

"No. I saw the curtains near the entrance of the cabana move as if someone had pulled them back, so I screamed and scared him off."

"How do you know it wasn't just the wind if you never saw anyone?" Bruce asks.

"I saw him too," Captain Lorenzo says. "Someone disappeared into the trees. A shadow of a man."

I stare off into the wilderness beyond the beach. It appears closer than it did in the light. If the thick palm trees and heavy grasses can keep a barn owl secret, I'm sure a man could hide amongst them too.

"We can't sleep here," I say. "What if that person comes back?"

"We'll have to sleep in the other cabanas then. The older ones that the four of you were going to use," Captain Lorenzo says.

"Not possible," Harry says. "We found out why those cabanas had been abandoned by the beach club. It turns out when there's high tide, they flood."

Opal digs her fingers through her hair. "Flooding! What more can this wonderful island surprise us with?"

"Opal, can you think of any reason someone would want to attack you?" I ask, trying to redirect the conversation to the cabana attack. "No one has been targeted since Lloyd's death. Why do you think someone would be after you?"

Opal eyes Bruce suspiciously.

Her look doesn't escape Bruce. He puffs up defensively. "I was with Dane the whole time. Don't point fingers at me."

Opal opens her mouth, but Bruce stretches himself just a bit taller and continues, "I also didn't steal your phone! I have my own life, and I have no interest in ruining it because I want to attack you."

"The shadow I saw didn't look like Mr. Misemueller," Captain Lorenzo says.

"What did the man look like?" Harry asks.

Captain Lorenzo thinks for a moment. "I couldn't see much because of the darkness, but he was tall. He moved like a young man."

"I bet he was after me," Samara's voice is high and light, but the words she says are heavy. "That sounds exactly like the type of person my great aunt would hire to get rid of me."

Normally, Opal is the first person to remind Samara that the idea of her being the original target of murder is preposterous, but this time, she stays quiet. Is it possible that Samara has been right this whole time? Maybe her great aunt did send someone to get rid of her, and Lloyd Alapha somehow got in the way, and now, the killer is trying to get rid of Opal because they've mistaken which young woman they are being asked to kill.

"Samara, I know you said your great aunt was unhappy about your grandfather's will, and you mentioned that some odd things had happened to people that your great aunt didn't get along with, but could you maybe tell us more? You never know, any little detail might help us understand something we previously didn't see."

Samara is quiet for a moment as she plays with her pendant necklace. I hadn't noticed before, but it's a light blue color, similar to the ocean waters that surround us. I wonder if there's any significance attached to it, or if she just clutches it out of nervous habit. She gives her pendant one final squeeze and then begins to talk.

"Ever since I was young, my great aunt was incredibly jealous of my grandfather. When my grandfather was growing up, his parents had a lot more money than when my great aunt was around. After their parents died, they left my grandfather and her equal amounts, but she squandered hers somehow. From then on, she was always relying on my grandfather to help her pay for things."

"His death would've been difficult for her, knowing that she couldn't rely on him financially anymore," Harry says.

Samara nods her head. "It was. Any bit of his property or money that she didn't get after his death, she wants now."

"Earlier you said sometimes bad things happen to people who are close to her, could you tell us more?" I ask Samara. While I know the topic might be tough for her to discuss, if Samara thinks she might be in danger, we have to understand more of her story.

"Several of my great aunt's close friends have died not long after they had falling outs with my great aunt. Her one friend who she was close to for years suddenly got ill right after my great aunt stopped speaking to her. They had a disagreement over a bracelet. Another time, my great aunt opened a business. I think it was some sort of grocer or restaurant. The business didn't thrive like she had hoped, and her business partner went missing not long after the business went bankrupt. They never did find the woman."

Samara's stories don't make me feel better. It sounds like her great aunt really could be nefarious. Maybe she had sent someone to try and kill Samara on the tender. This idea gives me another thought.

"Samara, did you end up on the tender today by accident or on purpose?"

"What do you mean?" she asks.

"Harry, myself, and Dane all missed our scheduled tender to Lapis Rock, so we ended up on the tender operated by Captain Lorenzo, but that isn't what happened to Opal. She reserved semi-private transportation to take her to the island."

"So, if Samara had been scheduled to be on the semi-private tender, the chance of this murder being related to her is higher," Harry finishes my thought for me.

Samara twists her lips. "I'm not sure."

"How can you not be sure if you were on the right boat or not?" Opal puts her hands on her narrow hips.

Samara shrugs. "I remember seeing in my itinerary that I was scheduled for an early tender, so I went to the gangway and boarded one."

Opal scowls. "Well, being in la-la land didn't pay off very well, did it?"

"There's no need for that," Bruce says to Opal. "No one knew what was going to happen on that tender."

"Even if Samara doesn't know if she was supposed to be on that boat, I think we should still consider the idea that the murderer is after her as our top theory," Harry says. "We don't have much else to go off of at the moment."

Opal's face transforms into one that has bitten into a sour lemon. "What about me? I was in the cabana that the murderer went into, and I'm the one who had my phone stolen."

"That's fair," I say. "Can you think of a reason someone might want to kill you?" The words come out a bit harsher than I mean. Opal doesn't respond and instead glares at me. I shouldn't have said anything. It's about to be a long night.

CHAPTER TWENTY-THREE

LIGHTS IN THE TENDER

A debate ensues about where we should sleep for the night. Bruce suggests that we all try and share the three cabanas on the nearby beach. He argues that the murderer won't come back now that he's been seen. Dane supports this, pointing out that if there are multiple people in each cabana, we're all safer, but I secretly think he just doesn't want to take another trek around the island. He keeps poking at the ankle that's been nipped by the snake.

Samara and Opal won't agree to sleeping in the cabanas though. Samara is convinced that the cabanas make us all easy targets. The murderer already knows where we all are, and they already have an easy escape route through the trees and grass. Opal agrees, stating that she won't be able to sleep because every time the light breeze touches the cabana's curtains, she's apt to call out in fear.

Harry suggests we all sleep in the eating area, and while Dane is open to this idea, no one else is. Opal is worried about bugs, reminding us all of the bees that congregated around our snack food, and Samara says sleeping under the open-air setup will only make it easier for someone to attack her.

Bruce adds that the dining area isn't ideal in the rare event of a rain shower because we might get wet if the wind blows the right way.

"There is one more option," Captain Lorenzo says. "*The House of Safety.*"

"*The House of Safety*?" Bruce repeats.

"It's a small, stone house on the island. It is on the north end. It would provide us with shelter for the night, and it is big enough for us all to sleep in. We could gather the cushions from the lounge chairs and the beach towels and bring them there."

"There's been a house on this island the whole time, and you are just now telling us?" Opal screeches.

"I wouldn't call it a real house. It is more a structure. It is very old," Captain Lorenzo responds.

As the others think the proposition through, my mind goes straight to the dagger hiding under the floorboards in *The House of Safety*. I hadn't intended to find it when I was exploring the island earlier. When I had mentioned discovering the weapon to Harry, he had suggested to stay as far away from the house as possible. How was I to do that if we all decided to sleep there tonight?

Not only that, but when I had first learned about the hidden dagger, Harry and I hadn't been entertaining the idea that a stowaway might've killed Lloyd. Now that a stowaway seems like a real possibility, *The House of Safety* might be the least safe place on the island. It could be where the stowaway has been hiding.

"Why is it called *The House of Safety*?" Samara asks.

"I am not sure," Captain Lorenzo says. "It is just what everyone calls it."

"There's a plaque outside the house," I speak up. "I explored the place earlier. I guess long ago, when bad storms hit these islands, ships would have to wait out the weather on Killdeer Cay, and usually people would camp out in the house."

"Why were you at the house?" Opal eyes me.

"I was exploring the northern part of the island today when I found it."

I hope there aren't any more follow up questions. If someone asks me why I didn't go and tell the others about the house, it'll be hard to explain my reasoning without looking a bit suspicious.

"We all agree to spend the night at *The House of Safety*?" Captain Lorenzo asks the group.

"I'm find with it," Bruce says, but the others are more reserved. They need more convincing.

"Wouldn't the north end of the island be a far walk?" Dane asks. "I won't make it with my ankle."

"While I agree it's safer that no one sleeps alone, I don't think it's necessary for all of us to sleep in the same room," Opal purposely lets her eyes settle on Bruce.

"The only other option is the dining area," Captain Lorenzo says. "I am fine with either one, but we must decide soon. I know I cannot be the only one getting tired."

There's a bit of chatter, but finally, everyone agrees that the best place to sleep is *The House of Safety*. Since it'll take Dane the longest to get to the north side of the island, he, with the help of Bruce, start out on the path towards the direction of the house before anyone else. Opal and Samara go to the kitchen to see if they can gather extra beach towels. Captain Lorenzo says the north will be windier than where we are now, so it might be a bit colder.

Harry, Captain Lorenzo, and I all go down to the cabanas to collect the seat cushions from the lounge chairs. There should be just enough for everyone to sleep somewhat comfortably on the stone floor. When we get to the cabanas, Captain Lorenzo goes to the one he was sleeping in while Harry heads for Samara's. That leaves me to gather cushions from Opal's.

Inside the cabana, it's apparent that Opal has reconfigured the tiny room. The two chairs are pushed together to create a double cot, and there are about five beach towels on the makeshift bed. Somehow, I'm not too surprised.

I go to gather up the things when something in the corner catches my eye. Right under the cabana's striped curtains, there is a small, red journal. The exact same one Harry and I had found earlier with the coded sentences. How had it ended up in Opal's cabana? Had she taken it out of Harry's backpack for some reason? Or worse, had the mysterious stowaway stolen it from Harry's bag and dropped it when he had been sneaking up on Opal, and if so, what did the journal contain that was so important? I grab the journal and wrap a beach towel around it so that it's hidden from sight. I don't need anyone knowing what I've found.

Just as I'm finishing up with the journal, Captain Lorenzo pokes his head through the entrance. "I was wondering what was taking you so long. I see that Mrs. Halladay had some extra towels."

"She did," I say. "It's probably a little more than I can carry."

"Let me help," Captain Lorenzo picks up some of the towels and folds them neatly before moving onto the lounge cushions and tucking them under his arms.

"Looks good, are we all set?"

"I think so," I say back.

The two of us exit the cabana. Harry is waiting for us, but his hands are nowhere near as full. He has a few cushions and one towel. Opal really had been hoarding a good portion of the supplies. No wonder she had been so possessive over her cabana.

We head back up to the eating area. While Captain Lorenzo and Harry make small talk, all I can think about is the red journal that I have hiding under the towel that I hold in my hands. Was it possible that it contained the key to why Lloyd had been murdered and why someone had gone into Opal's cabana? And if so, how long would it take Harry and I to crack the code?

Back at the eating area, Opal and Samara have gathered some extra towels, and they're ready to head out to *The House of Safety*. Captain Lorenzo guides us to the path, and he shows us which way to go so that we'll get to the house quickly. The route isn't the same one I took during the day, but it's in a similar direction.

It's not long before I notice that the trail widens. The last time the path had been this wide was when we had all gotten off of the tender. Is it possible that we will pass by the boat? My thoughts are answered fast. In the distance, the large, white tender bobs gracefully up and down in the ocean water. In the night, the tender looks like some sort of sleeping beast.

As we pass by the boat, something makes me stop in my tracks. On the lower deck of the ship, I think I see a light dance across the windows. It's almost as if someone has boarded the boat with a flashlight. I try to get Harry's attention, but he's up at the front of the group with Captain Lorenzo, and when I look back at the boat, the light is gone. I blink my eyes a few times, but all that remains is the outline of the boat against the dark sea. High above, the bright moon shines down on us. Maybe it was just the moon's reflection.

CHAPTER TWENTY-FOUR
NIGHT WALK

Maybe Dane had been onto something when he pointed out the walk to the northern end of the island would be a long one. I'm not sure why, but without adequate light, it feels like our small group has been trekking through Killdeer Cay forever. The humidity along with the bugs isn't helping. Twice I've walked face first through something that has felt uncannily like a spider web, and the amount of sweat that has gathered on my lower back is akin to what I might produce during a workout class.

At least I'm not having the worst time in the group. Opal has been complaining non-stop since we went by the tender. First, she was upset because she felt certain that she had a bug in her hair. Then, she became convinced that some sort of frog had leaped out of the tall grasses and grazed her foot. Finally, she concocted the idea that a large rat had run across her shoes and was clinging to her leg. Harry actually had to take his cellphone light out and show her that there was no frog or rat, or any type of animal, on her leg despite her insistence.

Captain Lorenzo was remarkably patient throughout the ordeal. He never once huffed or rolled his eyes at Opal. He really is a gentleman. I wonder how he had ended up in the Caribbean, so far away from his home of Italy. I can't imagine dealing with people like Opal was what he had been hoping for when he signed up to captain a tender.

My phone buzzes in my pocket, and I take it out. I have a text from Mom.

MOM: DAD AND I HAD LATE NIGHT. GOING TO BED NOW. SEE YOU IN MORNING

Following her text, an image comes through of her and my dad smiling at dinner with Charlie and a whole slew of people I've never seen before. At least I know they won't be losing any sleep tonight.

Before I put my phone away, I see that it's just a little past midnight. Funny, it feels so much later. I do the math in my head. Harry and I boarded the tender shortly after eight in the morning, which means we've probably been on Killdeer Cay for over 16 hours. No wonder why I feel like I need to sleep in a crypt.

As we pass a tree with large, fuchsia blooms dangling off of it, Harry sidles up next to me. He holds out the metal water bottle and prods me with it. I take it from his hands and gulp down most of the remaining contents.

"Thanks," I say. "I didn't realize how thirsty I was."

"We can't have you passing out on us again," Harry screws the bottle's lid back on. "You don't feel faint at all, do you?"

Harry's concern makes my insides bubble. Sometimes I forget how sweet he can be when he thinks I might need some extra tending to.

"Other than really wanting to sleep, I feel pretty much like my regular self. I haven't had a headache since around the time Dane was bitten by the snake."

"That's good to hear, but if anything starts to feel off, tell me right away."

Harry's words remind me of the red journal wrapped in the beach towel that I'm cradling against me. Glancing behind me, I see that Opal and Samara are a good distance away. Opal is grunting and swinging her hands erratically in the air as if a cloud of mosquitos is surrounding her while Samara is staring up at the starry sky. Captain Lorenzo is a good few feet in front of us. I think it's safe for me to tell Harry about the journal.

I lean towards him so that our shoulders touch. From far away, someone might think we are just two young people in love. They would never know I'm trying to tell Harry a secret that might just help us solve a murder.

"When we were gathering the cushions from the cabanas, I found the red journal that had disappeared from your backpack."

Harry straightens his back and stands up a bit taller. "Where did you find it? Was it under one of the lounge chairs? Do you think Opal took it?"

"No, it was by the doorway. I'm assuming that the intruder dropped it on accident when Opal let out her scream."

"This isn't good," Harry whispers. "I'll be honest. I thought Opal might've been exaggerating about someone trying to enter her cabana, but if you found the journal that was stolen right in the doorway, it's looking more and more like there is someone on this island who is very dangerous, and very determined to hurt one of the seven of us."

I tilt my head back just a centimeter so that I can view Samara. She's now looking at the moon, the large celestial satellite makes her face shine.

"I'm confident the person they want to hurt is Samara. Right from the start, she thought her great aunt might try to go after her, and now it looks like someone on this island is causing a lot of mischief."

"We'll keep her close then," Harry's voice is soft in my ear. "When we get to *The House of Safety*, we'll try to get a spot next to her."

"What about the journal?" I whisper. "Do you think we should find a moment to look it over? If the person who tried to attack Opal stole it from your bag, it must be important."

"That'll be tricky. We'll have to come up for an excuse to leave the house once everyone is settled."

An idea strikes me. "I could say I need to use the bathroom, and I want you to come with me. No one would question that."

"What about Samara though? We can't leave her alone."

I hadn't thought of that. Harry and I will have to come up with some way to keep Samara safe and snatch a moment away from everyone so that we can look at the journal.

Before we can think of a new plan, my phone buzzes again in my pocket. This time it's Charlie. I answer right away.

"Emma!" A voice sings through the phone. "I thought I'd check in with you, but more importantly, I wanted to update you on the Swirl Delicious debacle."

"Swirl Delicious?"

"Really, Emma. It hasn't even been a day, and you can't remember the name of one of the most important peppers in the world? The Swirl Delicious is the pepper that is the main attraction of the pepper festival on Lapis Rock."

"Right, sorry, a lot is going on today. I'm having trouble keeping things straight. Go ahead, what happened to the famous pepper?"

Harry gives me a funny look, so I smile back at him and wave my hand casually in the air, trying to convey to him that Charlie is having one of his food moments.

"The pepper is lost!" Charlie yells.

"Lost?"

"That's right. They don't know where it went. Can you imagine that?" Charlie talks faster in excitement. "Whoever could've predicted that one of the most famous peppers in the world would go missing? There are rumors swirling—no pun intended—that someone accidently ate it!"

"Oh, I'm sorry, Charlie. It must be a big bummer for you to travel all this way and not get to see that pepper," I say.

"I'm not too upset. I figure I'll still be able to write a great article about the pepper festival. Lots of people will be interested in a food mystery." I know I can't see Charlie while I talk to him on the phone, but I have a gut feeling that he's shrugging his shoulders nonchalantly.

"You're not wrong about that."

"Speaking of writing, did you tell Harry about how you might've lost your job yet?"

At the mention of his name, Harry perks his head in my direction. I'm hoping he didn't overhear what Charlie said about me losing my job. Our relationship doesn't need much more drama at the moment.

"Charlie, I actually need to get going. Is it okay if I talk to you in the morning?"

"Wait!" Charlie yelps down the line. "You never told me when the police would arrive on the island."

"We don't know much yet. Bye, Charlie!" I end the call before Charlie can say anything else.

It's too late though. The corners of Harry's mouth are pulling downward and his forehead is etched with lines.

"Why didn't you tell me you lost your job?"

"Technically, I don't know if I lost my job."

"What does that mean?" Harry asks.

"The last time I talked to Mr. Hawking, he had forgotten that I was on vacation, so he thinks I blew off "The Backyard Bird Blurb."

"But you would never blow off the magazine," Harry says.

"I know that, and you know that, but I don't know if Mr. Hawking knows that. Half the time, I don't even think he knows who I am. I just hope that I still have a job at the magazine when I get back."

Harry wraps his arm around my shoulder and gives me a tight squeeze. I shudder. My shoulder is still sore. He drops his arm. "I forgot about the shoulder," he gives me a tender kiss on my temple instead. "Whatever happens with your job, it'll be okay. You're the best birding journalist I know. Anyone would kill to have you work on their magazine."

I'm pretty sure I'm the only birding journalist that Harry has every met in his life, but his words still mean a lot. He believes in me, and if he believes in me, I should believe in myself. I'll give Mr. Hawking a call in the morning and have a chat with him. He's a bit scatterbrained, but he's a reasonable man. Maybe I can convince him everything was all a big misunderstanding.

From up ahead, Captain Lorenzo calls out a greeting into the night. It looks like we've caught up to Bruce and Dane. Hopefully their walk to *The House of Safety* has been as uneventful as ours.

CHAPTER TWENTY-FIVE

PLAYING WITH KNIVES

"Some sort of giant rat came at us from the grass," Dane says as soon as everyone in our group is close enough to hear.

Dane points to an area thick with dried vegetation. "I think it was around this area. At first, I thought a snake was coming out to bite me again, but then I saw the size of the thing. It was round and fat. It was covered in feathers too."

"The rat was covered in feathers?" Opal scoffs. "Rats don't have feathers."

"What do you think hopped out at us then?" Dane asks.

"Obviously one of those little birds the island is named after," Opal shrugs in an uninterested manner.

I have to cover my mouth to keep from giggles escaping. She hadn't been this suave when she first came across a killdeer defending its nest, nor had she been so calm when she thought she had seen a rat. She sure is something.

"That's right!" Bruce jumps in. He's as jolly as ever. "Harry and I ran into one of those little things. Little imps. They just kind of run at you for no reason."

I want to pipe up and point out that killdeers have a very valid reason for charging at people. It can't be easy having to look after ground nests all day long, and if a group of strange creatures kept coming near my house, I imagine I wouldn't be too happy either. I keep my mouth shut though. I want to get to shelter as soon as possible, and I don't want to delay the group by talking about birds.

"The house is only a little way from here," Captain Lorenzo cuts into the conversation. Like me, he must be ready to end our midnight hike sooner rather than later.

My feet began to hurt with each step we take towards the house. I don't think I've ever done so much walking before. I wonder if anyone else's feet hurt. Finally, a large shape appears outlined in silver ahead. It's *The House of Safety.* When I had first come upon it, it had looked ancient and rundown, but now the building is a welcome sight, glowing with comfort. The stones that make up its outer facade look quaint and cozy, and the lopsided steps leading up to the doorway give the house a sort of charm.

"Home sweet home!" Bruce sings out into the air. "I thought we would never make it here. Let's hope there aren't any surprises inside."

"You're not the only one hoping that," Opal grumbles behind him. This might be one of the first things that they've agreed about all night.

"Let's go inside," Captain Lorenzo herds us up the steps.

The house is large and airy. A cool breeze shivers through the doorway and out the far window as it had done in the hotter part of the day. In the night, the room doesn't appear anywhere as dusty as it did earlier. It's amazing what a little lighting can do.

People start arranging themselves around the room. Opal, unsurprisingly, is the first person to claim her spot in the center of the room. I assume it has the best access to the cool Caribbean breeze. She isn't one to short herself, after all. Bruce is far from her. He places a few cushions under the window. I look around for Samara. Harry and I need to try and get a spot near her. She is settling on the edge of the room, against one of the walls. I go ahead and drop the towel I'm carrying onto the floor next to her. As the towel hits the old, wooden planks, it makes a thud. Samara jumps slightly and gives me a curious look. I forgot I had wrapped the journal up in the towel. Thankfully, it hasn't spilled onto the floor.

I give Samara an awkward grimace. "Heavy beach towels," I say.

Harry makes his own bed up next to me with his collection of cushions. Against the hard floor, the lounge pads don't look nearly as thick as they did out on the beach. I have a feeling we're in for a lumpy night.

Across the room, the floorboards squeak under Bruce's weight. He shifts and turns and grumbles. His acrobatics don't seem to help. With every movement he makes, he sounds more and more in pain, and the floorboards squeal more and more in protest.

"Could you do that a bit quieter?" Opal snaps at him.

"I have a bad back! I'm being as quiet as I can. It's the floors that are making all the commotion."

Bruce stands up, and his back lets out a symphony of cracks. He bends over and starts throwing the cushions around.

"What are you doing? Trying to make it so that none of us will sleep?" Opal scoffs at him.

"I'm going to figure out why these floors are so loud!"

Bruce gets on his knees and starts poking around. It's then that I realize he's chosen to sleep right above where I had found the dagger. Sweat breaks out across my forehead. What will happen if he finds it? Will my finger prints still be in the same area somehow?

"Ah ha!" Bruce cries out. "It's this one right here."

He's found the loose floorboard. Wiggling his fingers in the cracks like little garden snakes, he pulls up the thin plank of wood. Part of me hopes there won't be anything there, but I know better. Bruce leaps into the air like some sort of dancer. He lands right next to Opal on her pile of cushions, causing Opal to scream. Samara whimpers next to Harry and me, and Dane loses his balance and falls against one of the walls.

"What is wrong with you?" Opal scolds Bruce. "You're acting like a maniac!"

"I'm not a maniac! Take a look at what's under the floor!"

Opal uses Bruce to balance herself as she stands up from her large collection of pillows and slightly pushes him over in the process. I'm not sure how she managed to get so many cushions to sleep on. I don't even remember her carrying any on the walk over here.

Opal peeks over the opening of the floor as if she's looking down at the sewer. Her nose is raised high, and her eyes are squinted. Unlike Bruce, she doesn't seem surprised by what she finds.

"What is it?" Captain Lorenzo takes a few steps towards Opal and shines the flashlight of his phone over the opening.

"An old, rusty knife. Not sure we needed all those theatrics," Opal says.

"A rusty knife?" I get to my feet.

Is it possible for knives to rust so fast? Or, had I misunderstood what I saw earlier in the day? I join Opal and Captain Lorenzo near the window.

Peering down, I see that Opal is right. The knife I saw earlier isn't gleaming with fresh blood. Now that the sun has set and most of the light is gone, I'm able to tell that the knife under the floorboards has a blade rusted to a deep red. A flash of heat hits my neck and the back of my ears. It makes sense. I hadn't exactly looked at the knife in great detail. Plus, knowing that Lloyd had just been murdered, it would make sense for my mind to assume the dagger had something to do with him.

"Why is your face so red?" Opal asks me.

I bring a hand to my cheek and feel the warmth of my dewy skin. "I think it's hot in here."

Opal stomps back to her bed in the middle of the house, and settles into her nest of cushions and towels.

"That was interesting. Maybe next Samara will find a broken fishing pole or Dane will see a sand dollar." She wiggles down into her pillows. "If we're all done being dramatic for the night, I am going to attempt to sleep. Please don't disturb me unless there is an actual emergency." She pulls one of the beach towels over her head. It's unnecessary considering that while the moonlight brightens the room, it's not exactly florescent lighting.

Bruce puts the plank back where it was, and remakes his cushion bed so that it won't make sounds when he moves. Across the room, Dane has laid down. His eyes are already drifting shut into sleep. I imagine we all feel drained after today.

I lay down on my own cushions. I can't believe how relieved I am to learn that the dagger has nothing to do with Lloyd's death. All along, it was just an old knife. Maybe used for scaling fish or cutting rope. Harry nudges me with his foot. He glances at the beach towel hiding the red journal before glancing back at me. I had forgotten that we needed to come up with an excuse to check out the journal alone.

Harry suddenly grabs his stomach and winces in pain.

"What's wrong?" I grab his shoulder.

"If he thinks he needs to throw up, he needs to leave the room!" Opal springs up.

"My stomach," Harry moans.

"I had a bit of that earlier," Bruce says. "It's best to just let it out."

"I need to go outside," Harry stumbles to his feet.

"I'll come with you!" I jump up.

Harry grabs the towel lying next to our cushions and rushes out the doorway.

CHAPTER TWENTY-SIX

CIPHERS AND CLUES

H arry doesn't stop groaning until we're far enough away from *The House of Safety* that we can't see it through the trees.

"Harry, stop running. If you need to be sick, just do it here." I gently caress his back.

Harry stands up straight and grins at me. His mischievous smiles always send a little thrill down my spine. He holds up the beach towel and pulls the red journal out from underneath.

"I thought pretending to be sick would be a big deterrent for anyone to follow us."

I shake my head and playfully roll my eyes at Harry. I should've realized it was all an act. Harry is always thinking two steps ahead.

"Wait, what about Samara? Will she be safe without us in the house?" I ask.

"There are enough people there that I don't think anything will happen to her," Harry says. "I wanted to ask you a question myself about the dagger Bruce found. Is that the same one you told me about earlier?"

"It is. I guess when I originally saw it, the sunrays were streaming through the window, and with the way they were glinting against the knife, I thought the rust was blood. Couple that with Lloyd's murder, and my mind ran away with the idea that I had found the murder weapon."

"It's a bit of a relief," Harry says. "Here we thought we had someone dangerous on the island, but maybe we don't."

"What do you mean?"

"Now that the dagger is ruled out, it's possible that Lloyd was never attacked. Maybe he just had an accident."

I shake my head. "What about the person that tried to attack Opal? Samara said she heard someone sneaking around, and Captain Lorenzo saw someone on the beach. Not only that, but when we were walking by the tender tonight, I thought I saw some movement on the lower deck. It looked almost like someone had a flashlight."

Harry leans against one of the nearby trees. "I suppose you're right."

"I think we should look at the journal. If we can break whatever code is written inside, maybe we'll have all the answers that we need."

Harry pulls out my large crossword book from the backpack. Between the thin, newspaper-like pages, I had stuck a writing pencil.

"Good thing you like puzzles. Otherwise, we wouldn't have anything to write with," he winks at me.

Harry and I get to work on the journal with its mysterious list of numbers. I don't imagine that we have much time to decipher the secret message hidden in the pages. Given that we left the group under the guise that Harry was ill, someone is bound to come looking for us if we don't come back soon, but we might not actually have to do much code cracking. Harry still has the small strip of paper that he found in the kitchen. If it has the key to the code, then all we have to do is translate the journal.

But after multiple attempts, it turns out the code doesn't work, so Harry and I start with a simple cipher. We cross out the letters on the scrap paper and start anew. For each number written on the slip of paper, we write a letter of the alphabet above it. We start with the alphabet in order, but this doesn't pan out. There are less than 26 numbers on the one scrap paper.

"I remember reading somewhere that it's easiest to crack the small words first," Harry says.

"What do you mean?"

Harry points to a section of the journal where five numbers are listed before being followed by a space and then one number. He points to the lone number. "Any place in the journal where there's a stand-alone number, we can assume that the number must represent either *A* or *I* since those are the only words in English that are spelt with only one letter."

What Harry says makes sense, so we get started again. I've never been particularly good at math, but I must have a gift for patterns. As I study the paper, I quickly see where letters can easily replace numbers to form words. In a way, it's like solving a crossword puzzle. If I can figure out a certain number represents a certain letter, then I can figure out the rest of the word.

I scratch down letters below numbers as I study the journal with Harry. He adds a couple himself. Harry and I become lost in our decoding. It's not until I pick up the pencil to write the letter *U* under the number 11 when I hear footsteps on the path.

"Hurry!" Harry whispers as he grabs the notebook and shoves it back under the beach towel.

I pick up the pencil and the crossword book that Harry had left on the ground and plunge them into the backpack. The footsteps come closer until Captain Lorenzo steps out of the darkness.

"Are you two alright? We were getting worried," he studies Harry.

Thankfully, Harry had worked up a sweat while we had been code breaking, so his face looks clammy.

"I think I feel a little better, but not a hundred percent. The fresh air helps."

"This is good to hear," Captain Lorenzo gives him a friendly smile. "Do you think you are well enough to go back?"

It would look suspicious if Harry and I insisted on staying outside by ourselves, especially when the others thought there was a stowaway on the loose.

"I think Harry should give it a try," I look up at him. "It couldn't hurt to see if you feel a bit better once we lay down again."

"I think I'll give it a go," Harry grabs my hand.

As the three of us set out on the path, a lone cloud covers the shiny moon, plunging us in darkness. I can't see anything in front of me. Other than Harry's hand, it's as if I'm stuck in a cave.

"That was sudden," Captain Lorenzo says. "I would say it's a bit spooky."

"I think I have my phone with me," Harry lets go of my hand.

"Wait, don't," Captain Lorenzo says. "You might attract the bugs. If it is just a cloud, it will pass soon."

Captain Lorenzo has a point. Turning on the phone flashlight in the middle of the trees and grass will draw the bugs to us like ants to sweet wine. We wait for a few minutes, but we're still enveloped in the night's black cape.

"Should I turn the flashlight on now?" Harry asks.

"I think maybe a moment?" Captain Lorenzo says. "It is a bit like being a child when your parents send you to bed with no nightlight. At first, it is upsetting, but then it is fine."

I get what Captain Lorenzo is saying, but standing in the middle of a pitch-black island when something perilous could happen at any moment feels a tad bit different from being tucked into bed as a child.

"When I was young, my mother would sing a lullaby. It was about the darkness coming to help me sleep."

"I think my mom stuck with the one about the sheep," Harry says. "It never made me feel much better. I've never really liked sheep. Their eyes remind me of vending machine coin slots."

I'm not sure if I should giggle or tease Harry. Being in the dark has made him vulnerable because I doubt he would ever reveal information like that in the light. Slowly, the path in front of us is illuminated. The cloud must've finally passed through.

"Shall we continue?" Captain Lorenzo looks back at us.

"I think that would be a good idea," I say.

We start walking, but Harry doesn't let the silence settle around us.

"Captain, how did you end up all the way in the Caribbean, working in Perfect Sands Islands, when you're from Italy? I imagine you are far from your family."

"My family?" Captain Lorenzo's voice breaks off. He suddenly stumbles and hops around the path.

I expect to see a snake because his movements are so similar to that of Dane's when he was bitten, but instead, a round, white ball scuttles into the middle of the path. I blink and see that the ball has two eyes and dark rings around its neck. It's another killdeer. They're everywhere on the island!

This bird isn't alone. Two little babies run after the parent, and together, they cross the road and disappear. It's like watching a small group of snowballs run on stick legs.

"My apologies. These little birds come out of everywhere. I can never get used to them."

"Are there a lot of them on Lapis Rock too? Or just out here on Killdeer Cay?" I ask. For some reason, imagining my parents and the killdeers sharing the beach together makes me want to laugh.

"There are lots of different bird species here," Captain Lorenzo says. "The islands are a beautiful place. Sometimes, I can hardly believe all the different wildlife."

"Are there any dangerous animals in Perfect Sands Islands?" I ask. Being on the lookout for a murderer is exhausting. I'm not sure if I can deal with adding a puma or bear to the list of things to watch out for.

"I believe no," Captain Lorenzo says.

Up ahead, *The House of Safety* comes into view. I suppose Harry and I were not as far from the house as we had thought.

Captain Lorenzo leads the way up the steps and we go inside, but the room is empty. Only cushions and a few scattered beach towels remain.

CHAPTER TWENTY-SEVEN

AN EMPTY ROOM

The House of Safety feels like a cathedral. Without Bruce's jolly laugh or Opal's sighs of discontent, it is as if our shallow breaths are echoing through the vacant room. Where had everyone gone? Harry and I hadn't left that long ago.

"Did something happen before you left?" Harry asks Captain Lorenzo.

Captain Lorenzo shakes his head. He blinks slowly, his charming face looking almost angry. "I don't understand."

"Maybe some sort of animal got in the room, and they all ran?" I say, thinking back to the snake that bit Dane.

"It is a possibility, but it is still not normal," Captain Lorenzo picks his way through some of the cushions.

"Everyone took their personal things," Harry says. He's standing in the middle of the room where Opal had been moments ago.

"I think some of the towels are missing too." There are a couple towels scattered here and there, but there had definitely been more in the room when Harry and I left.

"Do you think they all went somewhere together?" Harry asks.

"I don't know," Captain Lorenzo replies.

I let my eyes carefully roam the room, looking for any tiny clues, but there's nothing.

"Maybe they had a fight? We know Opal and Bruce don't get along. I could see them going off and Dane following Bruce while Samara followed Opal," Harry suggests.

I pick up some of the cushions off the floor and flip them over, checking to see if anyone left anything, but I find nothing. Where could they have all gone? And why would they all leave?

"I think we should look for them," I say.

"Do you think they are in trouble?" Captain Lorenzo asks.

I shake my head. "If someone tried to attack them, the four of them would've overpowered the attacker. Not only that, but people don't usually gather up their things in a moment of panic. I'm confident that the four of them left because they wanted to, not because they were forced to."

"That rules out the possibility of some sort of animal getting into the room," Harry says.

"Should we split up and search the island?" Captain Lorenzo asks.

"We would cover more ground that way," Harry agrees.

"I am comfortable being by myself," Captain Lorenzo says. "It may be best for you two to stay together if you prefer."

"What will we do if we find someone?" I ask.

"We all meet back here in an hour. If we haven't found anyone, so be it. We at least need to try and locate the others. This is too bizarre to ignore," Harry says.

Captain Lorenzo agrees to take the northern part of the island. The terrain is tougher to navigate, and he feels more confident than Harry and I do about searching the dense vegetation. Harry and I head south on the path. We decide to stop at the bathrooms first. It wouldn't be too outlandish to think everyone took a bathroom break together. Maybe a couple people had to go, and everyone joined in on the excursion.

When we get to the bathrooms though, no one is in sight. Harry goes through the men's room and I the women's, but they're deserted.

"This doesn't make any sense," Harry says to me. "Why would everyone leave the house? It was by far the safest place on the island."

"I think when we left, they must've started discussing something, and one thing led to another, and somehow, they decided the house wasn't safe anymore," I say.

"Or, they decided one of them wasn't safe anymore," he poses.

"What do you mean?" I ask.

"Remember how we discussed our doubts around the idea of a stowaway? Maybe they did too. If they felt like one of the seven of us was dangerous, I could see them choosing to spend the night alone."

"That's a possibility," I say.

"I don't think we'll know for sure until we find someone," Harry replies. "Let's keep looking."

I take the lead and guide us to the beach with the dining area. I figure that if Bruce, Opal, Samara, and Dane split up, at least one of them would've chosen to return to the main beach. It was the area that was most familiar after all, and it had lots of resources like lounge chairs and food and water.

When we get to the beach though, it's completely unoccupied. The dining area and unfilled chairs look otherworldly while the cabanas appear as if they haven't been used in years. Harry and I take a walk through the seats and table, but there's no sign of anyone recently visiting.

"Should we try the other beach?" Harry asks. His eyes glitter as they stare out onto the vast ocean.

"Which one? The one with the old cabanas? Or the one where Bruce tried to leave on that kayak?" As soon as I ask the question, my body fills with dread. What if everyone decided to leave the island like Bruce did earlier? The ocean was hazardous enough when Bruce took his outing, but in the night, it will be much worse. "Let's go to the one where we found Bruce, the cove," I say. "I know it sounds irrational, but it's possible that they tried to leave the island. If Bruce suggested the kayaks, they could've gone down to the beach and given it a try if desperate enough."

"Let's head that way now. I really hope you're wrong. I was able to help Bruce when he capsized, but I don't think I could help four people at once, especially at night."

We pick our way through the island path. My feet are beginning to hurt again, and while I'm hoping that no one has taken a kayak out into the water, I wouldn't mind if we found a few people at the cove. The path curves downward, and we stumble onto the thick sand. Like the other beach, there's not a person in sight. Where is everyone? While Harry calls out various names, I check the stack of kayaks on the beach, but none of them are missing.

"Should we try the other beach?" I look back towards the path. If we keep it up, I'll know every twist and turn on the island before sunrise.

Some of the large palm leaves near the opening of the path shiver in the wind. My ears perk up for a moment. If I hold my breath, I can hear the slightest sound of human voices somewhere close. I check on Harry and see that his face is also in deep concentration. He must've heard what I did.

The voices sound like they are approaching us. At the end of the path, Bruce's bald head pops up above the leaves. He's not alone. He's with Dane who is limping. When the two men see us, they almost break out into a sprint (which must be quite the feat for Dane). I don't think my simple presence has ever made someone so happy before.

"Are you okay?" Harry approaches the men.

"Where did you all disappear to?" I follow Harry up to the path.

Bruce looks exhausted. Purple blots his face, and his eyes are hooded with sleepiness. Dane doesn't look too much better. His hair is sticking up in odd directions, and his ankle looks swollen under its bandage.

"After Captain Lorenzo left the house, a few people revealed their true colors to the group," Bruce says.

"Did someone get hurt?" I ask.

"No, but Opal can't be trusted," Dane says. "I think she might've had something to do with Lloyd's death."

Dane's declaration surprises me. While Opal isn't exactly easy to get along with, I don't think she's capable of killing.

"Is that why you all left? You think Opal killed Lloyd?" Harry asks.

"Not exactly," Dane says. "But I think she set me up somehow. While we were all trying to sleep in that room, someone's phone started ringing. Apparently, Opal recognized the ringtone as belonging to her phone. Everyone started searching, checking under towels, moving around cushions. Somehow, her phone was right next to me."

"She pounced on him!" Bruce raises his voice and cuts in again. "I thought Dane was done for. Her nails are sharp. I thought for sure she would go for his eyes!"

"Are you hurt?" Harry asks Dane.

Dane's nostrils flair, and he stutters. "Technically, she didn't pounce on me. She jumped across the room when I announced I had found a phone."

"That's when the birds flew south so to say," Bruce says.

"What does that mean?" Harry raises his eyebrows.

I imagine Dane and Opal in a tussle, flailing on the floor of *The House of Safety* while Samara screams and Bruce tries to separate them. Was it possible that all of that occurred while Harry and I were gone for less than maybe twenty minutes? I suppose it's possible. Fights aren't exactly organized events. It also explains why everyone left so suddenly.

"It was like Bruce said. I thought she was going for me. We've all seen her lose it a few times." Dane continues, "She had this wild look in her eye like she was no longer human."

"Did you attack Opal?" I cringe as the words leave my mouth.

"I would never hit a woman!" Dane looks offended.

"Then what happened?" Harry prods. "You said she looked like a wild animal."

"She did! So, I threw her phone across the room," Dane says.

"When it hit the wall, you would've thought the building had been struck by lightning. There was a huge bang, and Opal went berserk!" Bruce says with animation. "She was howling like a cat in the night! She ran to the wall where her phone landed and got on her knees before bawling her eyes out. I've never seen anything like it."

"That was when I grabbed my stuff and made a run for it," Dane says. "I knew if I didn't get out then, I might never make it off the island."

Bruce leans in towards Harry and whispers, "She had the eyes of a killer."

"But what happened where you think she killed Lloyd?" Harry asks. "Did she mention that something similar happened while the two of them were on the tender?"

"Did you not hear the story?" Bruce's eyes widen. "We saw the killer instinct in her eyes!"

I frown. Opal's eyes flaring with heat isn't exactly evidence that would stand up in court. It sounds like Dane and Bruce don't have much to go on when it comes to linking Opal to Lloyd. At least we know why everyone left the house. There's also a decent chance we'll get everyone to return if we can talk some sense into them.

"I think we should check the far beach with the abandoned cabanas to see if Opal and Samara are down there, and then head back to the house," I say.

"Emma is right," Harry says. "We all know about Opal's dramatics, but she's not a killer. The safest place for everyone tonight is *The House of Safety*. Hanging out in the open won't do us any good."

Bruce crosses his sunburnt arms. They've already begun to peel. "The three of you are welcome to do whatever your hearts' desire, but I'm spending the night here near the cove. That woman is bound to kill one of us in our sleep."

Dane cracks his neck and stays quiet. He seems to be weighing his choices. Stay with Bruce on the beach or go back to the house with Harry and me.

"I'll stay with Bruce for now, but when you guys come back from checking the flooded cabanas, I'll head back with you to the house," Dane declares.

"You're okay with sleeping in the same room as that woman? Don't you remember her eyes? Her pupils had teeth!" Bruce spits a bit as he talks.

Dane looks around as a breeze strolls through the green palms and heavy coconuts. "I'm not sure we have much of a choice."

Bruce shakes his head. He stalks off towards a more covered area of the beach where the trees lean low.

"Are you sure you don't want to come with us now?" I ask Dane.

"I want to stay here for awhile. Opal needs to calm down before she sees me again." Dane scratches his long nose. "My ankle needs rest too."

Harry runs a hand through his dark hair, giving himself natural waves. "This might be awkward to ask, but how did Opal's phone end up next to you?"

Dane blanches. "Are you asking if I stole Opal's phone?"

Harry shrugs. "Kind of."

Dane shakes his head. "I didn't steal Opal's phone. There's no reason I would want her phone. I have my own phone. I can't believe you would think I stole Opal's phone."

Harry makes a placating gesture. "I had to ask."

"Right," Dane shakes his head in disappointment. "The two of you should get going if you're going to the other beach to look for Samara and Opal. They might be anywhere on the island."

"We'll be back soon." I give Dane a friendly smile, but he doesn't return one.

Chapter Twenty-Eight

Nursery Rhymes

"You don't think Dane actually was the one that stole Opal's phone, do you?" Harry and I are on our way to the beach at the southern end of the island. I'm not sure if we'll find Opal or Samara there, but it's worth a shot.

"I don't know what I think anymore," Harry says. "The stowaway theory made a lot of sense when paired with the bloody dagger, but now we know that there was never a bloody dagger to begin with. What if Dane or one of the other passengers attacked Lloyd?"

"Someone would've seen it. The tender is large, but it's not that big."

"What if it was more than just one person though? Maybe a few people were in on the murder, and now everyone is covering each other's tracks."

"Someone would've noticed if a group of three or more people got up and went to the bottom deck," I say.

"True, but what if only one person went down to deal with Lloyd while the other two stayed on the top deck? Those two on the top would be able to cover for the third person."

"Okay, let's go with that theory. What people on the island would we group into three? Not us, we know we had nothing to do with it."

"Captain Lorenzo was driving the boat, so he's no help for alibis," Harry says.

"That leaves Samara, Opal, Bruce, and Dane," I list everyone off on my fingers.

"Maybe they were all in on it together?"

"What?" I say louder than intended. Some animal rustles in the grass next to us and squeaks in surprise.

"Is my idea that out there?" Harry asks.

"Opal doesn't like one person here, and she's made it clear that being on Killdeer Cay is worse than being imprisoned. Dane is also on his honeymoon. Why would he plan a murder while on his honeymoon? And Samara is here because her grandfather died."

"What if they're all lying though?" Harry's voice is low in the dark night.

I bite my lip. That's the one thing I can't counter. What if everyone is lying? We're all trapped on the island. We can't exactly jog over to the local coffee shop and ask around to see if Dane really is a newlywed or if Bruce really is retired. There's no way of knowing if anyone is telling the truth.

The path dips down, and we're now standing on the sandy beach of the south shore of the island. The tide has ebbed a fair bit, and the cabanas look like they won't be impacted by the salty sea water for much longer.

"It doesn't look like anyone is around here," Harry says as we walk by the cabana where I had fallen off the step during the day and found the red journal.

I glance down at the cut on my foot I had received here earlier, but the shallow scratch has already started to heal. I had been so busy that I hadn't thought about the cut all day or night. Even the cut Harry got on his face feels of little importance after the day we've had.

"I wonder why that journal was hidden here in these cabanas," I watch the wet sand rise around the footsteps Harry and I have made. It almost looks like the beach is breathing. "If the idea of a stowaway ends up being correct, would it have been possible for a stowaway to hide this journal?" I look up at Harry who is looking out at the sea.

"We weren't on the island that long when we found this beach, so if the stowaway did hide the journal here, he would've had to have gone straight here."

"Right, but how would he even know that the tender would be stopping at Killdeer Cay? How would he even know about this beach?"

"He wouldn't," Harry says.

"Also, if the journal was important, why wouldn't he just keep it with him? I know if I was running around murdering people, I wouldn't be leaving my journal around for someone else to stumble upon."

Harry sighs. "I know we want the journal to be important, but maybe it really is some random notebook, and someone took it because they were bored," Harry says.

I try to let the idea that the notebook means nothing sink in, but for some reason, it doesn't feel right. If the notebook means nothing, then why steal it from Harry? If the notebook means nothing, then why did it appear again right after the attempted attack on Opal?

A new thought comes to me, and I grab Harry's arm. "What if the journal is a communication tool? Maybe the stowaway hid it on the beach because he wanted someone to find it, but he just wasn't expecting us to be the ones to find it? Think about it, the journal could be the stowaway communicating with someone else in our group of seven!"

Harry grabs my arm and gives it a squeeze. "That would also explain why someone took it from my bag. Maybe the stowaway put it here, and someone else saw I had it and took it."

"Weren't we alone when we found the journal?"

"No, Samara was with us, remember!"

The thought of Samara helping a stowaway murder someone seems absurd. She's spent her whole time on the island hiding. Why would she do that if she was friends with the killer or orchestrated the killing herself?

"She has a motive," Harry goes on. "Her family is going to try and interfere with her inheritance. If Lloyd is somehow connected to any of that, she could've teamed up with someone to take care of him."

"It can't be Samara. It just can't."

"But why not?"

"It's a gut feeling," I say. "It's just not possible for her to kill someone. It's not who she is."

"Alright, if it's not Samara, then who would it be? Opal? Bruce? They both have fiery personalities."

I shake my head. "No, that doesn't fit either. If they were part of Lloyd's murder, they would lay low.

"Okay, Captain Lorenzo?"

"Definitely not. He didn't even know who was going to be on the tender until this morning. Plus, all he's done since we've arrived here is try to solve problems. And he was the one who notified the police so quickly. Murderers don't call the police on themselves."

"Dane?"

"Absolutely not him. He might seem a bit off sometimes, but that's because he's lovesick. His new wife is temperamental, and he can't do anything to comfort her since he's stuck on the island."

"Okay, unless it's me or you, we've run out of people," Harry says.

"It has to be someone though."

"You just ruled everyone out," Harry replies.

I'm growing frustrated. I know I've ruled everyone out, but somehow, someway, someone on this island is responsible for Lloyd's death.

Harry gives my arm another tight squeeze. He must be able to read the frustration on my face. "Let's look at the journal again. We had almost cracked the code when the captain found us."

We go and sit on the washed-out log that we had rested on with Bruce and Dane not long ago. Harry pulls out the journal along with the scraps of paper we had been working with and a pencil. It's a good thing Captain Lorenzo didn't see what we were doing. We could've been deemed suspicious ourselves.

Harry opens up the journal to where we left off. He places the scrap papers near the top of the page. We're about halfway done. Maybe we'll finally translate all the numbers into letters this time.

"The numbers we have left to crack might be letters that are used rarely," Harry says.

"Like *Q*?"

"Yeah, like *Q*."

"We've managed to decipher a lot of the small words like *and* and *the*. Why don't we look for the words with double letters," I suggest.

"Double letters?"

"Words like *spill* where there are two *Ls* next to each other," I clarify.

Harry takes up the pencil and circles the few instances where numbers repeat. As he does so, I notice another pattern emerging towards the bottom of the page.

"Look!" I point to the last paragraph. "Almost all the words at the end of the first page start with the same letter. That's weird, isn't it?"

Harry taps the pencil's eraser to the paper. "Maybe it's some sort of alliterative poem?"

"It could be a tongue-twister," I try to think of some common ones my sisters and I used to try and say as kids.

"What letters do we have left?" Harry asks. "Other than *Q* of course."

I take the one scrap paper that we've been working on and look over the numbers that we've matched up with letters. "*W, Y, L, F, G, P, V, X,* and *B*. Oh, and *Z* and *C*," I say the missing ones.

"That's a lot of letters left," Harry says.

"If we know most of the words at the bottom of the page all start with the same letter, let's just systematically plug them in. It'll take some time, but we're guaranteed to figure out part of the code through trial and error," I say.

Harry and I start with the letter *G*, but we end up with a lot of silly words that make us sound like we're speaking some sort of made-up language. The letter *C* isn't much more of a success. We don't even bother to try out *X* and *Z*.

"Let's plug in *P* next," Harry erases some of the letters we've written on the bottom of the page and scratches in several *Ps*.

As he does so, some of the words start to emerge. It's almost like wiping dust off of an old mirror. It's a bit startling when an image begins to appear.

"Harry! It's working! Look!"

I point to the first few words. It spells out the name *Peter Piper*.

Harry's hand picks up speed. He's now filling in all the letter of the code. He references the scrap paper occasionally, but for the most part, it's almost like he's writing from memory.

"Emma, it's the nursery rhyme!" Harry's voice turns into a lofty tenor. "*Peter Piper picked a peck of pickled peppers.*"

I laugh at our discovery. "Of course! My sisters and I loved that one when we were little. I always got caught up on the last line."

"*Where's the peck of pickled peppers Peter Piper picked?*" Harry sings back. "What in the world is a peck though?" Harry looks at me.

"I think it's like a punnet of berries."

"What's a punnet then?"

"I don't know. It's just one of those old farmer measurements I guess." I lean back on my elbows. "Harry, I don't think this journal is anything more than just a couple of kids having some fun by turning nursery rhymes into secret codes."

Harry sighs. "You're probably right. I really thought there might be something important in here."

"I thought so too, especially since someone stole it and then it was found in Opal's cabana right after some mysterious person tried to attack her," I add on to Harry's point.

"Maybe Opal took it," Harry says.

"You think Opal would steal an old journal?"

Harry shrugs. "Maybe she was bored. Face it, Emma, we don't really know any of the people on this island, and from what we do know about Opal, she's not exactly the picture of a perfect citizen."

I look out onto the black sea. From where Harry and I sit, I can't tell where the ocean stops and the sky begins. The two things are so dark in the night. While I'm disappointed that the journal meant nothing, knowing that Harry and I have at least solved one small mystery brings me a semblance of calm. Maybe the answer to a bigger mystery is just around the corner.

CHAPTER TWENTY-NINE

FRESH FRUIT AND CHARCOAL

Back at the cove, the ocean is a different sight. The waves are thrashing against the rocks that jut out of the waters like broken bones. The sound is akin to summer thunder. Bruce and Dane are standing in a grove near a stack of kayaks, paddles, and life preservers. They're easy to spot since the kayaks are colored so brightly.

I give them a friendly wave when they see us, and they return one back.

"Find Mrs. Opal down in the flooded cabanas?" Bruce asks.

"The beach didn't have a soul around," Harry says. "The water was nowhere as choppy as here though."

"It has to do with the winds," Bruce says.

"Were you thinking of trying to paddle to Lapis Rock again?" Harry's eyes dart from Bruce and Dane to the kayaks behind them.

Bruce doesn't find any humor in the question. "At least I was trying to do something when I got in that kayak. We've all spent the day boiling on this island. If the police don't show up soon, I'm bound to try the kayaks again, I won't lie."

Dane eyes the kayak near his swollen ankle. "If we're still stuck here tomorrow morning, I might think about trying to cross myself. I did crew in high school."

Harry shakes his head, and I can tell a lecture is sitting on the tip of his tongue.

"Are you two ready to go back to the house? Harry and I told Captain Lorenzo we would only be gone an hour, and that time is approaching." I glance between the two men's faces. Bruce's is dry and puckered from too much sun and Dane's is tired and gaunt from stressing over his wife. I hope they're both able to take another vacation after this one.

"You are coming back with us, right?" Harry presses the two men, a little more forcefully than I would've.

"If Opal is back there, it might be best for us to just stay here," Dane says. "She tore into Bruce when she *thought* he might've taken her phone, but she *knows* I broke her phone. Who knows what she'll do?"

I try to suppress a grin. It's a bit odd looking at these two grown men who cower at the name of Opal Halladay.

"Let's at least walk back to the house together. Emma and I will go in first, and if Opal is anywhere around, we'll say her name really loud so that you two can run back here," Harry proposes.

Bruce shakes his head. "Every time I'm anywhere near *that woman*, something bad happens. I'm happy as a clam on this beach right here."

"Dane?" Harry turns towards the younger man.

Dane looks down at his ankle which has swelled up considerably since the snake bite.

"I'm going to stay with Bruce. If I walk much more on my ankle, I might not be able to stand come morning."

"Fair enough," Harry says. "I'm not sure what the plans are going forward, so you might not see us again until morning." Harry directs his gaze at Dane as if to say this is the last chance to change his mind.

"Thanks. I'll head back to the house if there's an emergency," Dane says.

The two men remain standing by the colorful kayaks as Harry and I disappear into the Caribbean night.

I wonder if Captain Lorenzo has managed to find Opal or Samara. It would be helpful to get their side of the story about the cellphone. I know both Bruce and Dane swear up and down that they didn't take it, but then how did it end up right next to Dane?

"Has it really been an hour since we last saw the captain?" Harry asks me.

"I think so, but I'll double check the time."

I pull out my phone and see two missed calls from Charlie. He's up late. I would call him back, but it's possible he had just been checking in with me before bed.

"Everything okay?" Harry asks.

"Charlie called me a few times, but he was probably just checking in. He's got that big festival tomorrow, so he's just excited."

Harry nods his head. I'm sure Charlie has sent him a slew of text messages as well. Harry is as good of friends with Charlie as I am. It's still funny to think we met him less than a year ago. It's hard to imagine life without him.

"I think the killdeers are nesting around here," Harry whispers as we enter a part of the path where the grass stands a little taller and the leaves grow on the trees in thick bouquets.

"We'll have to make sure to stay in the center of the path. As long as the birds don't think we're going for their nests, they shouldn't bother us."

"How come I never see killdeers when I go to the beach at home?" Harry asks. "Are they some Caribbean bird?"

"No, they're common in the US. They like rocky areas when they nest, and I'm going to guess that when you go to the beach, you don't usually spread your towel out on the rocks?"

Harry laughs. "I don't. This might surprise you, but I usually plant myself under a large umbrella."

I giggle. I lightly bump my good shoulder against Harry's. Talking about the beach like this reminds me that this is supposed to be our vacation. It's the most stressful trip I've ever taken.

Harry stops walking, and I run into his back.

"What's wrong?" I ask.

"Did we take a wrong turn?"

Harry is right. Wherever we are on the path is unfamiliar, but it's also night, and the full moon, while providing us with plenty of light, has been getting lower and lower in the sky.

"Look over there!" Harry points to something off to our left some distance away. From where I stand, I don't see much.

"I think there's a building," he says.

"Do you think we looped around to *The House of Safety* somehow?"

"I'm not sure," he says.

Harry detours off the path and into the grass because there's no direct walkway to the structure. As we get closer, the outline of a small fishing shack becomes apparent.

"That's odd," I say. "The island has so little infrastructure. I would think that something like this would be labeled on those maps that Bruce gave us earlier."

"My guess is that those maps were for guests, and this place is for the workers. Or maybe it was abandoned long before the beach club was founded."

As we get closer to the fishing shack, I notice that the wooden panels have paint peeling off of them like ripe bananas. The roof is also in bad need of a repair. We circle the building, looking for a way in, but the trees in this part of the island have grown tall and close together, so it's difficult to see.

"This place looks like it hasn't been occupied in years. Are you sure it's safe to go in?"

Harry pulls his phone out and turns the flashlight app on. A flutter of moths flocks to the beam. Harry turns to me and gives me one of his irresistible grins. "No, I'm not sure if it's safe, but I've found the door."

Harry pushes some long vines out of the way, and a handle appears along with a door that has been scratched and chewed on by various creatures. Harry tries the handle, but the door doesn't budge. He puts a bit more weight behind his second try, but still, nothing happens.

Harry tests the door in different places, but he doesn't find any weaknesses. "It doesn't make sense."

"What doesn't?" I ask.

"The beach club is abandoned. Why would they bother to lock up an old fishing shack before they left?"

Harry is right. Why would someone lock up an old building if nothing important was inside?

"Even if there is something important in there, we might as well leave it. It's not like it has any connection to what happened to Lloyd."

Harry nods his head, but I can tell something is gnawing away at him. Something deep inside is telling him that the fishing shack is more important than it looks. I turn back to the path, but I step on something hard that crunches against the rocky ground. I shift my foot, and a solo beam of moonlight lands on a metal object. It's a silver key.

"Harry! I found something."

I pick up the key. It's next to a larger rock that has recently been disturbed. Most likely the key was meant to rest underneath the rock and used in case of an emergency.

I hold the key up so that Harry can see it. "Should we use it?" I ask him.

"I think we should. Opal or Samara could be hiding in there."

"That's true. It looked like someone had disturbed a large rock nearby. Maybe one of them tripped over it when they found the shack."

I pass Harry the key, and he slots the key into the hole. The handle twists easily. As Harry pushes against the door, this time it opens with only slight resistance.

Harry shines the light from his phone into the small structure. At first, all I see are dust motes floating in the air, but then, a clearer picture emerges. The building holds an array of fishing gear. There are buckets, and poles, and colorful neon lures. Amongst the supplies, there's a bunk in the corner of the room with a messily made bed. Next to that, there's a desk covered in papers and books. Clearly, the fishing shack was once used as an emergency place for workers to sleep in times of need.

Something about the room isn't right though. Next to the door, there's some sort of makeshift kitchenette. A well-used basin sits next to a small bowl of fruit. The fruit is not just fresh, it's ripe enough to eat. If the shack had been abandoned for a long time, I doubt the fruit would've looked the way it does.

"Someone has been living here," I say.

"And they've been here recently," Harry adds.

He picks up something near the basin and rotates it in his hand. It looks like a black rock. There's a small pile of them next to the fruit.

"What is that?" I ask.

"Charcoal."

"Why would someone have so much of it?"

"It can be used to filter water." Harry looks around the small room. "Emma, I think we should leave. Someone has been living here, and they've been here a lot longer than we have. This can't be some stowaway who arrived on the island with us. No, this must be another person."

Harry sets the charcoal back where he found it. We're about to head out the door when there is a thump outside. Harry grabs me and pulls me against the wall. He turns his cellphone light off so that it's just us breathing against each other.

Outside, a twig snaps. Someone or something is moving rocks and leaves around, searching for something. In my hand, I still hold the silver key. Is that what they are hunting for out there? The key I have in my hand? The thought makes me grip it tighter against my palm, so tight that the little teeth bite into my hand.

"Did we lock the door when we came in?" I whisper to Harry.

"I'll check," he whispers back.

Harry leaves me and inches towards the door. Without him next to me, it feels like I'm floating. Every step he takes away from me, I feel less attached to the Earth. One of the floorboard creeks under Harry's weight, but whoever is outside doesn't hear it. They keep searching for whatever it is that they're convinced they'll find.

There's a sharp click, and I know Harry's locked the door. He creeps back to me in silence because I don't know he's next to me until I feel the warmth of his breath as he whispers in my ear, "I locked it. I don't think they can get in since we have the key."

"Who could it be?" I ask. "If someone is living on this island, why have they been hiding from all of us?"

"I'm not sure," Harry says.

Something sour rubs against my stomach. It doesn't make sense for someone to be hiding on the island other than a stowaway, but Harry said the amount of charcoal in the fishing hut didn't make sense for someone who had recently arrived. It is possible that the charcoal is old, and the fruit is new. Samara had been crafty with finding hiding spots around the island. I could see her discovering the fishing shack and the key but choosing to keep it secret. The stack of ripe fruit could be from earlier in the day. Or even Bruce. He had been exploring the island the whole day. If he found a comfy bed, he would keep it secret to prevent Opal from claiming the spot as her own.

The rustling outside the fishing shack finally pauses. I focus my best to listen to the sound of retreating footsteps, but it's silent.

"Did they leave?" I ask Harry.

"They must have," he says. "I don't think someone would stand that still for that long."

We try our best to be quiet as we cross the room to the door. Harry unlocks it by gently flipping the deadbolt. With extra care, he opens the door. We scream.

CHAPTER THIRTY

A COMFORTABLE BED

It takes me a second to catch my breath. Harry pulls his phone out and turns the flashlight on so that the night is once again alive with light. Opal is right in front of us. She looks horribly disheveled. Part of her swimsuit cover up is ripped, and there's smudges of dirt under her eyes.

"What are you two doing here?" she hisses.

"We were exploring," Harry says.

"Actually, we were trying to find you and Samara," I speak up. "What is going on?"

"I'll tell you what's going on! Everyone has lost their minds!" Opal raises her voice. "Shortly after you and Captain Lorenzo left us all in that awful house, I discovered that Dane had my phone."

I want to let Opal know that we've already heard the story, but I have a feeling interrupting her wouldn't do anyone any good.

"When I caught him with it, he threw it against the wall! I gathered my things and left. While I was tramping around the island, I found this little place. It's a bit dusty, but it's better to spend the night here than somewhere else. The door even locks so no random attacker can come get me."

"Is all the fruit on the counter yours too?" I ask.

"Fruit?" Opal looks at me like I've grown an extra head.

"There's a bunch of fresh fruit in here. Did you bring all that with you?"

"Oh, that," Opal says disinterestedly. "No, that was all here when I found the place." Opal pushes past Harry and I and enters the small shack. "Normally, I wouldn't share such a small room with others, but the two of you are welcome to the floor if you like." Opal settles herself onto the bunk and fluffs her hair.

"Opal, we can't stay here," I say.

Opal shrugs. "Up to you. I'm sure there's still lots of room for the two of you back at that little stone house."

"You're not understanding," I say. "Opal, if you didn't bring that fruit here, then someone else has been here recently, and we don't know who it is. It could be someone dangerous who isn't happy that we're all on the island. We need to leave right now."

Opal crosses her arms and a look of defiance darkens her features. "I know exactly what the two of you are doing."

"We're not doing anything other than trying to get out of here before we make the wrong person mad," I reply.

Opal scoffs. "You two want this place all to yourself. That's not happening. I have been through so much today. I deserve to have my bed. You can leave if you want, but I won't go with you. I'm staying right here."

"Opal, Emma and I aren't trying to pull one on you. We really think that someone might be living here. They won't be happy if they come home and find a bunch of people in their house."

Opal doesn't bother even looking at Harry. She pulls back the covers on the bed and wiggles under the sheets as if she's in a hotel room at a resort.

"You have to listen to us," I take a step towards her.

"I don't have to listen to you." She sniffs at me over her shoulder. "If you haven't noticed, this place has a lock. As soon as the two of you leave, I can lock myself in here and enjoy a quiet night away from rude and obnoxious people."

Harry tugs at my arm. "I think we should go. If she wants to risk it, she can stay here. She's an adult. Let her make her own choices."

I frown. I know Opal is an adult, but I don't think she's truly grasping the type of trouble she might be in if she stays in the fishing shack. She could get seriously hurt.

"Opal, you need to come with us. If the police show up, and they find out you spent the night in this fishing shack, they'll think you killed Lloyd," I say.

"Why would they think that?" Harry asks. His face is filled with confusion. He has no idea where I'm going with this train of thought.

"They'll figure that you were more than happy to sleep by yourself even though there is a murderer on the loose. It'll make you look suspicious. Not only that, but when they see all the supplies in here, the police might think that you were planning to hide out after you killed Lloyd. This place is well stocked," I point to the pile of fruit on the table.

Opal's bottom lip juts out into a pout. I think I've won her over. For once, she doesn't have a comment to bite us back with.

"Fine," she mumbles and stands up from the bed. "This is ridiculous though. I found this place, so I should be able to sleep in the bed." She looks longingly at the crumpled sheets and sagging mattress.

When we're all outside, I go ahead and return the key to where I found it. In the scenario that a lone fisherman does live on the island, I don't want to accidently lock them out of their house. Hopefully when they get home, they're not upset to see a few people have been exploring.

Chapter Thirty-One

LULLABY

On our way back to *The House of Safety*, my phone buzzes in my pocket. I pull it out and see that Charlie is trying to reach me again.

"Hey, Charlie. Everything alright?" I would have thought Charlie to be asleep right now, especially considering his big festival.

Unfortunately, our connection is no good near the fishing shack.

"Night...parents at the...pepper...called..." Charlie's voice hiccups through the phone. All I hear are blurbs and random words.

"Charlie, my phone isn't picking up what you're saying."

"Contacted earlier...someone...festival..." Charlie's voice is all broken up again.

"Charlie, I really can't understand. Maybe you could text?"

"It...safe...away...Emma?" Charlie and I might as well be playing a game of password at this point.

"Charlie, I'm going to hang up. Just send a text," I end the call. Hopefully Charlie doesn't get too mad at me, but there's no point in us talking when I can only hear snippets of the conversation.

"It's late for him to be calling," Harry says.

I shrug. "I think he must be really enjoying himself. He's bound to be exhausted tomorrow at the pepper festival."

Suddenly, Opal squeezes her purse to her chest and quickens her pace. She must've heard an animal or something rummaging in the grasses. We walk faster to catch up with her. A dull throb stretches itself across my head as we hurry down the path. It's amazing how I never notice when I don't have a headache, but as soon as one comes on, it's all I can think about. I haven't had any water in a while. Harry and I might have to let Opal outpace us so that I can stop.

I tug on Harry's shirt and mimic me drinking water. He stops right away and pulls his backpack off his broad shoulders. It takes him a moment, but he produces the metal water bottle I have been nursing since I first passed out. The water tastes sweet with every gulp I let rush down my throat. Soon, there won't be much left. When I'm done, Harry takes a turn before twisting the top and storing the bottle safely away.

"I think we lost Opal." I glance up and down the path, but it's just Harry and me once again.

"It felt like she was trying to run away from us," he says.

"I thought that too. My guess is she saw a snake or a killdeer. She's not much of an outdoorsy type. She's probably heading to the house by herself."

"The house isn't too far from here, and we still have a little bit of time before Captain Lorenzo is expecting us back. Do you want to look at the journal again?" Harry pulls the red notebook out of his backpack.

I frown. "Why? It's just filled with children's nursery rhymes. It doesn't have anything to do with what happened to Lloyd."

"But we found those scrap papers, and someone took it from my backpack. Emma, I think it might be more important than we realize."

I'm not exactly buying what Harry is saying, but I would feel horrible if I ignored him, and the journal turned out to be important. "Alright. Let's do one more page."

Harry opens the journal to the next coded section while we both take a seat on the path. A lot of the journal is empty. Based on how beat up it is, I had thought that it would be a bit fuller, but I guess not.

Harry and I rely on the code from the first page once again, but it doesn't do us any good.

"I think the writer changed the code," Harry says. "Let's look at the scrap paper I found that we didn't use, maybe that piece of paper better fits this section of the journal."

While Harry's plan sounds good, in actuality, it's not. This code is much more difficult. There are moments where I'm certain we've figured something out, only for the realization to set in that what we thought was right is incorrect.

"This code is shifting or something." I tie my curly hair into a messy bun on the top of my head so that the loose pieces are no longer falling into my eyes. My headache paired with our attempted code cracking is causing frustration to blare through my veins.

"Whatever is in this section of the journal must be important. Otherwise, the writer wouldn't have employed a difficult cipher." Harry continues to pencil away as his brain twists numbers into letters.

I lean back on my hands and stare up at the night sky. I can't think of the last time that I saw the stars so bright. If Harry and I had made our scheduled tender, we wouldn't be here on Killdeer Cay right now. No, we might be back on the ship sampling rum cake with my parents at dinner.

"I got it!" Harry leans forward on his knees and scribbles intensely in the journal. "It wasn't as bad as we thought. After every word, the code shifts one space."

I let Harry finish with the cipher. If I try now, my head might burst into flames.

"You're not going to like this," Harry says to me.

"Why? What does it say?"

A string of different things enters my mind. Is it some type of confession from the person who killed Lloyd? Is it instructions on how to identify Samara so that she doesn't get in the way of a large inheritance?

I sit up and peer over Harry's shoulder.

"It's another nursery rhyme!" I cry.

"It's "Hush Little Baby," a classic," Harry reads the title of the nursery rhyme to me.

"Harry, I really think this might be some random journal a group of kids played around with back when the beach club was open. "Peter Piper" and "Hush Little Baby" aren't exactly helpful when it comes to what happened to Lloyd.

"I know, but for some reason, these feel important." Harry slips the beaten notebook back into his bag.

I know I shouldn't think too much about Harry's behavior, but I can't help noticing that he's not himself. Normally when we get tangled up in mysteries, Harry is logical and clear cut about his decisions and choices. I'm the one who is usually distracted by her gut. Maybe being stuck on the island and having not found even one clue as to what happened to Lloyd is making Harry lose his detective touch. I wouldn't dare say things like that out loud to him. If anything, we both just need a night of sleep.

"Let's head back to meet the captain. If we stay much longer, he'll wonder where we are," Harry says.

I get up from the ground slowly, but my head is still woozy when I stand. Harry must notice because he grabs my arm and steadies me.

"You need more water."

"I'm fine," I say even though I know I am far from fine. I'm exhausted and I can barely think.

Harry gives me the water bottle, and I take a sip from it. It feels lighter in my hand than it has all day. We're running out of water. I hadn't thought about what would happen if the police weren't here before we ran out of potable water. Was there any on the island somewhere? Everyone else must've been keeping hydrated somehow.

"We should ask Captain Lorenzo if he has water bottles on the tender when we see him. I know we're not supposed to go back to the murder scene, but if we all start falling sick, that won't do anyone any good." I pass Harry the water bottle back. I barely drank anything out of it, but I don't want to waste what little we have left.

Harry presses the bottle back into my hands. "I'm sure there's water stored in the kitchens too. Don't try and save water when you need it now."

I undo the lid and drink the remaining sips. I hope Harry is right because if we don't have access to fresh water for the rest of the night, things might be rough.

CHAPTER THIRTY-TWO

REUNITED WITH THE CAPTAIN

I have "Hush Little Baby" repeating over and over in my head as we walk back to *The House of Safety*. I remember reading an article once on how to get rid of earworms, but being trapped on an island has erased any of those suggestions from my mind. In fact, the only things I can think of are from the nursery rhyme like mockingbirds and diamond rings.

Up ahead, the shadowy outline of the house comes into view. It looks like the last place I want to spend the night, but I know it's the best choice we have. I also know that the first thing we'll have to do when we see Captain Lorenzo is tell him about the fishing shack.

"Harry, wait," I grab Harry's hand and pull him away from the path.

We're hidden under a tree with large palm leaves and clusters of fruit. A couple of tree frogs climb up the trunk when they see Harry and I standing so close.

"What's wrong?" Harry pushes a loose curl behind my ear. "Is it your headache?"

"It's not that." My head has been feeling slightly better after my last guzzle of water. "I think before we go in and talk to Captain Lorenzo, we need to talk about the fishing shack."

"The fresh fruit?"

I nod my head. "Unless one of us who was on the tender has known about the fishing shack the whole time and chosen to keep it a secret, that means that the fruit is either from a stowaway or someone else who lives on the island. I have a theory, but it's a bit out there." I take a step towards Harry and lower my voice. "What if there was a stowaway and someone on the island. Both things could be true. The two people could even be working with each other."

"How would the stowaway know that we would be stopping here on Killdeer Cay?" Harry shakes his head. "No, it doesn't make sense. That fruit had to have been left by either the stowaway or one of the seven of us. The pile of charcoal must be old."

"Alright, let's go with that then. Who do you think left the fruit?"

"Not me and not you. Not Opal, she would've owned up to it." He lists off people.

"Bruce?"

"Possibly. But does the fruit really matter? I mean, Samara could've been hiding in there. Hiding doesn't mean someone is guilty. In fact, it implies they're innocent because they don't want someone to hurt them. I think the fishing shack is a fluke."

Harry is probably right. The fishing shack doesn't fit into a narrative. The only possible narrative that makes sense when it comes to Lloyd's death is a stowaway. And without knowing anything about Lloyd, Harry and I have no way of knowing who would want to kill him.

"Harry, I hate to say it, but I think maybe we should just give up."

Harry's brows rise. "Give up?"

"On the mystery. Harry, we've solved lots of mysteries before, but this is different. There's no way we can solve what happened to Lloyd. We just don't have enough information."

Harry looks heartbroken. Out of all the things that have happened on this trip, me admitting that I think we can't solve Lloyd's death seems to be the one thing that has truly hurt his feelings.

"Emma," Harry grasps my one hand as if he's about to plead with me. "We can figure this out. If we give up, someone could get hurt. We could get hurt."

I pull my hand away from Harry. "The main reason we started looking into Lloyd's death was because we thought I had accidently put my finger-prints on a murder weapon. It turned out that what I thought happened didn't happen."

"But what about everyone else?" Harry asks. "Samara or even Opal could really be in trouble. We have to help them."

"They've been doing fine by themselves so far. Plus, the police will be here by morning. I think we should just sit this one out."

Harry's face is filled with hurt. He doesn't agree to give up on the mystery, but he does nod his head to acknowledge he's heard me.

"There you two are!" Captain Lorenzo spots us hidden under the trees.

He strides towards us, coming out of the house and down the stone steps. The late night has caught up with him. His shirt is a bit disheveled, and his shiny shoes are scuffed from running around. I wonder if he had any luck finding Samara in the northern part of the island. Harry and I certainly didn't see any signs of her.

Captain Lorenzo's mind is in the same spot as mine. "Did you find anyone?"

"We did," Harry steps away from me and meets Captain Lorenzo on the path. Next to the ship captain, Harry looks smaller than usual.

"We found everyone but Samara," Harry says as I pick my way through the weeds.

"Where are they?" Captain Lorenzo peers around me like I'm hiding three people behind me.

"They wouldn't come with us," Harry says.

This confuses Captain Lorenzo. He tilts his head to the side, and the corners of his mouth tip down. "They wouldn't come back? Why not?"

"Bruce and Dane are together. They're down by the cove. Dane ruined Opal's phone, and that's what caused everyone to scatter."

"Opal's phone?" Captain Lorenzo scratches his head.

"Yeah, the one she claimed Bruce stole. Apparently, somehow, it ended up next to Dane. When Opal saw the phone, he panicked and thought she might attack him, so he threw it across the room, and it hit a wall," I say, joining the men on the path. "That's one reason why Dane won't come back. He doesn't know what Opal will do to him. Also, his injury isn't doing too well, and he doesn't want to keep walking around until the swelling in his ankle calms down."

"This is news," Captain Lorenzo looks surprised. I can't blame him. The story sounds like something that happened amongst middle schoolers and not a group of grown adults.

"Mrs. Halladay. Where is she?" he asks.

"We found her by an old fishing shack," Harry says.

Captain Lorenzo's eyes grow wide. "What?"

"There's another structure on the island that we didn't know about. It looks like an old bunkhouse that was once used to store fishing gear. Harry and I were thinking that maybe the workers at the beach club used it once in a while if they had to stay on the island overnight. There's a bed and everything," I explain.

Captain Lorenzo is silent, deep in thought.

"There was a good bit of supplies in there like Emma said. There was charcoal and fresh fruit."

"Was she with Ms. Loweton?" Captain Lorenzo asks.

"We were hoping you had found Samara," I say. "We never ran into her, and we checked the southern part of the island thoroughly."

"This is not good," Captain Lorenzo says.

Harry gives me a heavy look. I know what he's thinking. On the beach when we first cracked the "Peter Piper" code, he had put forth the theory that Samara may not be as innocent as she looks, and I had disagreed based solely on my gut. Harry probably thinks Samara's absence might point to her guilt, but I think it's the opposite. Samara's absence might mean trouble. I'm about to say just that when I clamp my mouth shut. The police will be here in a few hours. There's no point in causing panic over something that may be trivial.

"Why would Mrs. Halladay go to this fishing shack by herself?"

"Everyone left the house after Dane threw the phone," I remind Captain Lorenzo.

He shakes his head. "It's not that. Mrs. Halladay said someone tried to go into her cabana, so we all came here, to *The House of Safety*, to be together. If someone tried to attack her, why would she suddenly go off by herself?"

Harry and are both silent. Why would Opal go off by herself if she thought she was in dire danger? It didn't make sense.

"And she stayed in this shack after you two found her?"

"She wanted to," I say, "but we convinced her to come with us, but on the way back, she ended up getting ahead of us, and we lost her. We were hoping she'd be here when we showed up."

"This is not good," Captain Lorenzo says. "Not good at all."

"What should we do?" I ask, but it's as if no one hears me. Only the island breeze answers with a soft hush.

CHAPTER THIRTY-THREE

A CAPTAIN'S TALE

The rough wind coming off of the ocean makes the leaves in the trees waltz and spin and the grass sway. We're back at the cove with Dane and Bruce. After a lot of discussion, it was decided that Captain Lorenzo, Harry, and I would go join the men at the cove and convince them to come with us to look for Opal and Samara.

"I can't understand what you want Dane and I to do," Bruce leans against a coconut tree while the moon shines off of the bald spot on his head.

"Because it doesn't make sense," Harry answers. He's been trying to convince Bruce and Dane to help us for several minutes now. "Opal said that she had been attacked, so it wouldn't make sense for her to want to be alone on the island."

Bruce makes a dismissive gesture. "I got that part."

"But no one saw Mrs. Halladay get attacked with their own eyes. Samara said she *heard* something, but she never saw anything," Captain Lorenzo emphasizes the word heard.

"You think Opal wasn't attacked, and she made it up?" Bruce asks.

"I do," Captain Lorenzo says.

"But you yourself said you saw some shadowy guy retreating into the woods or forest or whatever it's called," Bruce holds his finger in the air, and I wonder if he had been a lawyer before he retired. He quizzes Captain Lorenzo with the ease of a cross-examiner.

"I did see someone retreating towards the trees, but that doesn't mean Mrs. Halladay was attacked. At the time, I thought it meant that because that's what she said happened, but now I think differently," Captain Lorenzo says.

"Then who was the shadow if it wasn't the attacker? It wasn't any of us," Bruce points his thumb at himself, Dane, Harry, and me. "We were all at the other beach."

"It could've been the stowaway," Captain Lorenzo says, his voice lowered.

Bruce looks bewildered. He starts laughing. "But you just said you thought that woman had never been attacked! Was she attacked or not?"

"She wasn't attacked, but the stowaway was there!" Captain Lorenzo raises his voice. "Do you not see?"

"I don't," Bruce cuts in before Captain Lorenzo can better explain.

"Mrs. Halladay has been insisting that Ms. Loweton was not the target of murder on the boat. She has been most confident. Now, she goes off into the night after she says she is attacked. This does not make sense unless Mrs. Halladay is lying." Captain Lorenzo is now yelling. "I say Mrs. Halladay never was attacked. I say she knows the stowaway, and she and the stowaway intend to hurt Ms. Loweton!"

For once, Bruce doesn't have an argument to contest what Captain Lorenzo has said.

"What should we do?" Dane whispers.

"We must find Mrs. Halladay," Captain Lorenzo says. "It is the only way to prevent something from happening."

"Should we split up and look for her?" Dane asks. "My ankle is swollen, but if it's for the good of the group, I can get past the pain."

"We will cover more ground that way," Captain Lorenzo says. "I am okay going by myself. I feel confident that if I catch her, I will be okay."

"But she could be with the stowaway," Bruce says.

"I think I will take the risk. If we stay together, we will lose time."

"I can't go by myself," Dane says. "But whoever I go with will be significantly slowed down."

"I'll go with you," Harry says.

"You will?" I'm taken aback.

I had assumed that if we were splitting into smaller groups, Harry and I would naturally stick together. Why would he ever pair up with Dane over me? Was he still hurt that I wanted to put a pause on looking into the mystery? Surely, he must understand that that was before Captain Lorenzo shared his beliefs about Opal.

"But you should come with us, Emma," Harry adds. "That way, Bruce can go with Captain Lorenzo. No one will be left alone, and we will still cover plenty of ground."

Now I'm confused. What exactly is Harry up to?

"No, I don't like this. We will waste time. If we have only two groups, it will be easy for Mrs. Halladay to avoid us," Captain Lorenzo shakes his head.

"We're wasting time by twiddling our thumbs trying to figure out who is going to go with who," Bruce says.

Captain Lorenzo seems to take Bruce's comment rather literally. He nods his head sharply. "I agree. I will head northeast on the paths. You all can figure out your groups yourself." He disappears into the humid night.

Bruce, Dane, Harry, and I are left at the sandy cove by ourselves. I'm too stunned by Captain Lorenzo's idea that Opal is behind everything to even think about how much time we might be wasting by standing around. How had Opal pulled it off? She had done almost everything possible to attract attention to herself. It seemed almost impossible for her to be responsible for Lloyd's death let alone determined to hurt Samara. What even was the connection between Samara and Lloyd?

"I'm not sure Captain Lorenzo is right," I blurt.

All the men stare at me, but I keep going.

"In order for Captain Lorenzo's theory to be right, that would mean Opal had something to do with Lloyd's death, but there's no connection between Opal, Lloyd, or Samara."

"Maybe the stowaway got confused and accidently killed Lloyd?" Bruce suggests.

I shake my head. "We all heard Opal say it a thousand times. No one is going to confuse Samara with a random man. That can't be it."

Before we have time to discuss it, my phone is buzzing in my pocket. Who could possibly be calling me at this moment? It's almost two in the morning, and I know for certain that my parents are tucked away in their cruise cabin. I also doubt that Mr. Hawking is dropping a line to have a friendly post-midnight chat.

"I have to get this," I say and move towards an abandoned fire pit that has makeshift chairs of jetsam and driftwood circled around it. I take a seat and answer the call.

"Emma!" It's Charlie. He sounds almost out of breath.

"Hey, Charlie. Is everything alright? We're kind of in the middle of something here," I try to say without being too rude.

"Were you able to hear anything from my last call?"

"No, your voice was broken up," I say. "I must've been on a part of the island without good service."

"Alright, I'll try to say everything as fast as I can. It's about the pepper festival."

I internally grown. I really don't have time to listen to Charlie update me on the pepper festival. As if to confirm my point, Harry waves me back over to Dane and Bruce, encouraging me to get off the phone.

"I'm so sorry, Charlie. I hope they work everything out, but I really can't talk right now. I'll call you as soon as I can. Bye!"

I hang up my phone and put it on silent. I can't have any more distractions. I won't be letting anything derail me, especially news about the pepper festival.

Chapter Thirty-Four

A Late Reunion

I pick my way across a scattering of sand dollars and seashells until I'm back with the group. They've migrated a bit away from the shore and closer to a small grove of fern-like plants that grow in close clusters.

"Sorry about that," I say. "My friend Charlie called. He wanted to talk to me about some pepper festival."

"Pepper festival?" Bruce asks. "What's a pepper festival?"

"It's a long story," I make a dismissive gesture with my hand. "I don't want to waste any time on that. We need to find Captain Lorenzo before he finds Opal."

I'm not sure what I expect, but it's not the reaction I get. Dane plops himself down on the sand and leans his back against a tree while Bruce lets out a laugh and shakes his head.

"I don't get it," I say. "We know Opal couldn't have been the one who killed Lloyd, we need to find Captain Lorenzo so that we can tell him that she's innocent."

"I can't hobble around the island anymore. My wife will already have my head when she realizes that I have a bum ankle. I'm not going to make it worse. I'm staying here. Opal is an adult. She can take care of herself," Dane says.

I can't argue with him. He looks awful. The circles are so dark under his eyes it looks like he got in a fistfight, and the hollows of his cheeks are so deep that he's starting to resemble a skeleton. Even his nose looks longer than it did earlier in the day.

"I won't have anything to do with *that woman*," Bruce says. "She's been nothing but a nuisance. Everything that happens to her, she's brought on herself." Bruce takes a seat next to Dane. His skin is flaking on his arms and his face is red and puffy with excess sun. "I'm staying right here."

"What about Samara?" I try to take a different approach. "She hasn't done anything to either of you. She's spent her whole time on the island staying out of the way of everyone. She's out on the island all alone."

"And that's her choice," Bruce shrugs his shoulders.

"Dane?" I look at the younger man.

"Bruce is right. Samara knows where the cove is. If she wants to be around other people, all she has to do is look around. We'll be right here when she decides she wants to socialize."

An acidic lemon of disappointment twists in my stomach. I suppose I had thought that Bruce and Dane might've been a bit more empathetic, but apparently, they aren't.

I turn to Harry. "I guess you and I should get going."

"I think we can stay here," Harry says.

My mouth falls open. What is going on? Since when has Harry ever wanted to just sit put and let things play out without trying to be helpful?

He must read my thoughts because he points behind me. "Captain Lorenzo is back. There's no need to go looking."

I turn and see the captain appear at the edge of the path. He doesn't look too happy. His dark eyes cut across the beach and fall on the group of us.

"Hey there Cap'," Bruce waves his hand in the air. "Any luck?"

Captain Lorenzo stalks over to us. "No," he puts his hands on his hips. His muscular arms are illuminated by the silver of the moonlight.

"What happened?" Bruce asks.

Captain Lorenzo hesitates for a moment, almost as if he doesn't want to tell us what happened. "I thought I saw a strange man on the path, so I came back here."

"A strange man!" Harry raises his brows. "Do you think it could be the stowaway? All of us stayed here in the cove."

"Yes, I think it must've been."

"It's good you came back," I say. "Shortly after you left, we realized that Opal couldn't possibly be in cahoots with whoever killed Lloyd." I go on to explain how there's just no connection between Lloyd, Opal, and Samara.

"You think Mrs. Halladay is innocent?"

I nod. "Confident of it. No, I think that whoever hurt Lloyd must've been a stowaway. We didn't have much evidence that there had been a stowaway, but you've seen him twice now. I also thought I saw some lights in the tender when we were on the way to *The House of Safety*. At the time, I wrote it off as the moon's reflection, but now, I'm not so sure."

Captain Lorenzo stands up a bit straighter. "Lights on the tender? It must be the stowaway."

"Now we're back to where we were earlier tonight," Bruce says from his seat on the sand. "We wait until the police show."

"But Opal and Samara are still out there, and they're all alone." I remind everyone.

"I will go back and find them," Captain Lorenzo declares.

"Let me go with you," Harry says. "The stowaway won't be able to attack both of us at the same time."

Captain Lorenzo shakes his head. Defiance darkens his face, and he tilts his head up. "I will go alone. The stowaway has now been near me twice, and he has not made to strike. He is intimidated by me. I will not let a guest put themselves in danger. Everyone will stay here except me."

"Captain, I can help," Harry protests.

Captain Lorenzo won't hear it though. He looks Harry in the eye. "It is best if you stay here. If the stowaway comes to the cove, you all could be in danger. Mr. Cassigan is injured, and Mr. Misemueller may not be an equal match for the stranger. Also, your girlfriend will be here. Someone must protect her."

Harry doesn't say anything, but I know he'll stay with us when he takes a small step towards me. As much as he wants to help Opal and Samara, he would never risk anything happening to me.

"How will we know if you need help?" I ask.

"I have my phone with me. I can call for help if I must. I will be back soon," Captain Lorenzo's figure morphs into the darkness as he takes to the path.

Harry sits on the sand with Bruce and Dane. I don't want to sit. I want to keep standing, but my feet hurt, and my head is still a bit delicate. I plop myself down next to Harry and cross my legs, but something sharp jabs me in the bum.

I get on my knees and turn myself around. I've sat on the pointed edge of a paper that's sticking out of the sand. The paper has been folded over several times.

"What is that?" Harry asks.

"I sat on this paper." I hold the folded note out to him.

He takes it from my hand and unfolds it. While we have the moonlight, it's not enough for him to read the details, so he pulls his phone out to get more light.

"Looks like trash to me." Bruce lets out a big yawn.

"It's not. It's the passenger list from the tender trip. Captain Lorenzo must've dropped it," Harry shows the list to Bruce.

"Is it the same one he showed us earlier?" I ask.

"Yup. Everyone is on here. There's me and Emma, Bruce Misemueller, Dane Cassigan, Opal Halladay, Samara Loweton, and Lloyd A. Alapha," Harry reads the list. "You can look at if you like." He gives the list to Bruce.

As Bruce skims it, the rolling sound of a small pebble that's been kicked makes me jolt my head in the direction of the path. Harry and Dane hear it too. They both look in the same direction. Bruce starts to ask us what's happening, but Harry holds a finger up to his lips, and Bruce goes quiet.

The crisp crunch of a leaf is the next thing to be heard in the night. These aren't the sounds of snakes or birds scurrying. No, these sounds are from a much larger being.

"I'm not going down without a fight," Bruce grumbles and gets to his feet.

Harry tries to grab his arm to stop him from storming towards the path, but Bruce is surprising fast, especially for a man who claimed to have an ankle injury only a couple of hours ago.

"Who's there?" Bruce yells into the night, his voice booming and echoing around us. "There's a whole group of us, so if you've come here to start trouble, get ready to have some fun, buddy!"

The noises on the path abruptly stop, and two dark eyes blink out from behind the trunk of a coconut tree.

"It's, it's me," Samara reveals herself. "I didn't mean to surprise anyone."

I stand up and brush the sand from my legs before running over to Samara. I couldn't be happier to see her.

"Where were you?" I ask. "Harry and I looked all over the island for you."

"After Dane broke Opal's phone, I left the house at the same time as everyone else. I'm not sure what I was thinking, but I ended up taking the path towards a part of the island I hadn't been to before and wound up getting myself lost. The area was mostly just a rocky beachline."

"I wonder if you were on the northern tip of the island," Harry says. He's joined us on the edge of the path.

"It's possible. There was one point where I thought I saw Captain Lorenzo, but I called out, and no one was there. I'm just so thankful I found the rest of the group." Samara takes a deep breath.

"Did you see anyone else while you were out there?" Harry asks.

Samara runs a thumb down the rope of her necklace. "No, no, it was just me. I ran into a couple of those birds that are a bit loud, but other than the one time when I mistakenly thought I saw Captain Lorenzo, I was all alone."

"That's good to hear," Harry says.

"Why?" Samara asks. Her hand has moved to the pendant on her necklace, and she's now gripping it.

"Captain Lorenzo thinks he saw what must be the stowaway on the island. He just left a few minutes ago to find you and Opal," Harry replies.

Samara's eyes widen. "It's true then? Lloyd was killed by someone hiding on the boat."

"We won't let them hurt you though," Bruce puts a comforting arm around Samara in a fatherly show. "The five of us are going to stay right here, and there's no way some person can overtake all of us."

Bruce guides Samara over to Dane, and Harry and I follow them. I hope Bruce's words are true and that we do have safety in numbers. The five of us sit and make a circle in the sand. It's odd sitting out on the beach when so many other things are happening around us. While the waves crash against the shore and retreat with their soothing melody, the five of us have thoughts racing in our minds.

If Captain Lorenzo doesn't show up with Opal soon, we might have to come up with a new plan. We can't let this mysterious stowaway hurt Opal or Captain Lorenzo. I know Opal hasn't been the easiest person to be around today, but I won't let her share the same fate as Lloyd, and I know Harry won't let her either.

Across from me, Samara pulls on her necklace while she stares up at the stars. She has a few twigs in her hair and a leaf hanging off of her netted cover up. Bruce closes his eyes and rests his head against a tree trunk until light snores leave his lips, and Dane massages his ankle. We've all been thrown into a mess, but I know we can get out of it.

CHAPTER THIRTY-FIVE

GAMES IN THE SAND

B ruce's snores come and go in a beat that matches the crashing of the nearby waves. Part of me is annoyed, but another part of me is amazed at the musicality of it.

I let out a groan and hold a hand against my forehead.

"What's wrong?" Harry places a hand on my knee. "Is your headache back?"

"No, I think I need sleep. I was just thinking about how Bruce's snores are matching up with the sound of the waves."

"You do need sleep," Harry says with a grin.

"I thought I was imagining that," Dane says. He pokes Bruce in the arm, and the older man stirs, awakening in a fit of coughs.

"Everything dandy?" Bruce looks around and blinks.

"You were snoring," Dane says.

"It's the sinuses." Bruce pinches the bridge of his nose. "My wife has slept in the guestroom for the past twenty years."

"That rough?" Dane's face falls. He's probably thinking about his own unhappy wife.

"What are you talking about? We have two king beds. It's great! We wouldn't have it any other way."

"It's good to know some people have it figured out," Dane mopes.

Bruce thwacks him on the back. "Don't get down on yourself again. You'll get the hang of it."

"Being stranded on this island isn't helping. Every moment that passes, I think about how my phone has died, and I have no way of contacting Jill." Dane buries his head in his hands.

Bruce lets out a long whistle. "We could play a game?"

"A game?" Harry's brows pull together.

"Yeah, a game. Does anyone have a game?"

No one replies. Part of me imagines Opal sarcastically telling Bruce that she managed to fit a few boardgames in her purse just for this moment.

Bruce seems to catch on that no one planned accordingly to get stuck on an island, so he charges ahead. "That's okay. I've got a game! Let's guess what's in each other's bags."

Harry shrugs his shoulders and drags his backpack into the circle. Samara straightens her back and plops her purse down in front of her while Dane removes the drawstring bag on his back and holds it in his lap. Bruce and I don't have any bags.

"How do we play?" Harry asks.

"We go around in a circle, and we each guess an item in the bag, and when we're all done, the person reveals what's in their bag," Bruce says. "Who wants to go first?"

Dane raises his hand. "I'll go." He glances at Samara's purse and then at Harry's bag. "I think Samara has some lipstick. My wife always has some in her purse."

"I can go next," Harry volunteers. "I think Samara has some sort of document related to her family. We know she's here to check on an inheritance."

"Good guess," Bruce says. "I'm going to say she has something sentimental with her, a small trinket. She brought it to give her some gumption!" Bruce looks at me. "Emma?"

I try to keep my face as neutral as possible. I'm spectacularly exhausted, desperate for news about Opal and Captain Lorenzo, and I feel a headache coming on. The last thing I want to do is play some sort of guessing game.

"I think you've got your room key," I cringe at my answer.

"That doesn't count!" Bruce exclaims, his voice much too loud. "We all have our room keys. You have to guess something exciting."

"Er, I think Samara has a book with her," I say.

"What kind of book?" Bruce prompts.

Internally, I groan. Why is Bruce picking on me? Can't he see we're all lacking sleep?

"It's a book about peppers," I say.

"Peppers?" Bruce says. "Where'd you come up with that?"

"I don't know. It's just what came to mind."

Samara ducks her head shyly now that it's her turn to have the spotlight. "Well, I don't have a book about peppers." She digs her hand around inside her purse. "I do have lipstick," she holds up a deep red that matches what she was wearing earlier. "I also have documents like Harry guessed, but I don't have anything sentimental in my bag." Samara grasps at her necklace when she's done speaking.

"Let's do Harry next," Bruce says. "I think he has something exciting in his bag."

"Exciting?" Harry chuckles.

"A pocketknife," Bruce says.

Dane nods his head. "I can see that. I think he probably has something in there for emergencies too. I'm going to say he has some of those military grade ready-to-go meals."

Harry's laughs. "You all make me sound like I was preparing for a survivalist mission and not a day at the beach."

Samara's next. She presses a thin finger against her lip as she thinks. "Maybe a compass?"

Harry's shaking his head now, but he's thoroughly entertained. "Good to know everyone thinks I'm an adult boy scout."

"Emma's turn," Dane says.

"She might already know what's in Harry's bag," Bruce points out.

"Technically, the backpack is for carrying both of our things," Harry says. "So yes, she knows what's in here."

"If we had known that, we might've guessed a bit differently."

"Too late." Harry tips the backpack over. Our water bottle, crossword book, and disposable camera all come tumbling out along with some towels. The last item to escape is the red journal."

"I haven't seen a disposable camera in years," Dane picks up the plastic contraption.

"What's this?" Bruce pokes the red journal. "A diary?"

Heat crawls up the back of my neck and scratches at my cheeks. Harry shouldn't have dumped everything out of the backpack. He should've done as Samara had and pulled items out one by one. I know the journal isn't important, but now we'll have to explain where we found it, and the others might find it odd that we have kept it a secret this whole time. And we have to tell the truth if anyone asks about it. Samara was with us when we discovered it, so she'll know if we lie.

"It's some sort of notebook we found by the cabanas that flooded. It's written in code," Harry holds the journal up with little interest.

"In code?" Bruce snatches the journal. "This could be important stuff! Why'd you two hide it?"

"It's not important," Harry says. "It's something that was probably left behind and forgotten by a bunch of kids. Emma and I decoded it, and all it contains is nursery rhymes."

Bruce flips through the book while Dane looks over his shoulder.

"It would be kind of fun to see if we could crack a few more of these," Dane says. "It's not like we have anything else to do."

For some reason, Dane's suggestion makes me uncomfortable. I know there's nothing of importance in the journal, but I feel protective over it as if it personally belongs to Harry and me. Not only that, but Dane or Bruce, or even Samara, could've been the person who stole it earlier, and I feel a need to protect it.

Harry isn't on the same wavelength as me though. "It could be fun if some of the other pages were cracked," he says.

Harry explains how we managed to decode the first two nursery rhymes before we get started on a new page. Bruce and Dane seem intrigued by the process, and lean forward to get a better look of the book and all the numbers. Samara is more reserved, but even she can't resist the idea of deciphering some nursery rhymes. We all might be drained, but we need to find something to keep us awake until Captain Lorenzo and Opal come back. Plus, more importantly, we need to stay awake in case the stowaway pays us a visit. We may have an advantage in our numbers, but if we're all asleep, numbers won't matter much.

We get to work, but this code is the most difficult of all. It's similar to the "Hush Little Baby" cipher, but different enough that no one seems to be able to catch a pattern. Bruce loses interest first. He reclines against the tree he slept against earlier, and I watch as his eyes grow heavy.

Dane is the next to give up. He doesn't quit like Bruce though. He burns out like a bright star. He cracks his knuckles, mutters under his breath, and chews on his nails. Finally, he scoots away from the code in defeat.

Samara is different. She leans over the book and stares at it with soft concentration. One of her coiled curls falls in front of her eyes, but she doesn't even notice. She occasionally picks up the pencil Harry set out and etches a word onto the paper, but otherwise, she sits still.

I shift how I sit on the sand, and my phone digs into my thigh. I pull it out to check the time. I want to know how long Captain Lorenzo and Opal have been gone. But when the screen lights up, I bite down on my bottom lip. I have 15 missed calls.

I stand up, and sand runs down my legs.

"What's wrong?" Harry hops up next to me. "Did something happen?"

"I'm not sure," I show him my phone.

His face registers all of the calls from Charlie, and lines of concern dig into his forehead.

Harry and I aren't invisible. The others all notice how we're behaving, and they know right away that something is very wrong.

"Looks like you're having a bit of a doozy," Bruce says. Despite that fact that he had been drifting off, Harry and I standing up caught his attention. "Anything we can do to help?"

"It's nothing," I say. "I just need to return a phone call."

Before I leave the group, I grab Harry's hand. I don't want to call Charlie alone. Whatever he wants to tell me must be incredibly important for him to have called so many times.

Harry and I stand near the wet, compact sand and let the sea nibble at our toes while I call Charlie back. I put him on speaker phone so that Harry can hear easily.

The first call goes to voicemail, so I try again. This time, Charlie picks up.

"Emma?" My name is rushed over the line. "Is that you?"

"It's me," I say. "Harry is also here. I put you on speaker phone. Are you okay, Charlie? It says you called me 15 times."

"I did," Charlie says. "I was trying to get ahold of you."

"That part appears obvious," Harry says. I think he forgets that Charlie can hear him.

"I don't need the extra attitude, Harry. You two both know me well. I don't call and harass people unless I have a very good reason, and in this case, I do."

"What's wrong?" I ask.

"It's the pepper festival," Charlie replies.

For a split second, I feel like throwing my phone into the water and watching it float away. I can't believe Charlie called me 15 times to give me an update on the pepper festival! Can't he understand that Harry and I are stuck on an island with a murderer?

"Charlie, Emma and I are in the middle of some scary stuff. Maybe we could talk to you later about the pepper festival?" Harry offers.

I can feel Charlie boiling across the phoneline. "No! We cannot talk about the pepper festival later. We need to talk about it now!"

Harry's about to open his mouth to protest, but Charlie keeps talking.

"The pepper festival is life or death! Will you listen to me now?"

"Life or death?" Harry repeats skeptically.

"Yes, Harry. Are you ready to listen? I think you'll want to hear what I have to say."

CHAPTER THIRTY-SIX

BEHIND THE SCENES

Charlie clears his throat, preparing for some sort of monologue. "I'm up late tonight because one of the festival organizers ran into me while I was with your parents at the restaurant and asked me if I was interested in having a behind-the-scenes tour before tomorrow's opening day. Naturally, I said yes. Who wouldn't?

"I met them several hours ago, and they took me around the venue, explained the setup, all that logistical stuff. It was a snooze-fest until we got to the area that was being prepared for the Swirl Delicious."

"What's the Swirl Delicious?" Harry cuts in.

"Emma, you didn't tell him about the Swirl Delicious?"

"I forgot?" It's the truth. I wasn't exactly spending my time informing Harry about various pepper species while we were stuck on Killdeer Cay trying to solve a mystery.

"It's one of the world's rarest peppers," Charlie answers.

"I see," Harry says. "Am I to believe it's the main event at the pepper festival then?"

"Bingo! The pepper is not only rare, it's also beautiful. It looks like a piece of gold from far away. Absolutely breathtaking, or so I've heard. I've never seen one in real life."

"I can see why it would be a big deal," Harry says.

"It's a huge deal." Charlie continues. "Back to the story, the organizer takes me to the area where the Swirl Delicious will be displayed. Most of the pepper festival will be outside in tents, but for the Swirl Delicious, they've rented a portable room so that they have full control over the climate, which is kind of ironic because the Swirl Delicious is hardy. When we enter the room, I see that they went for a minimalistic look in terms of the design for displaying the pepper. All white walls with a large glass case in the center of the room. It reminded me a bit of going to see the Crown Jewels. Security isn't limited though. They've hired outside contractors to guard the pepper while it's there, and there are at least three cameras with three-sixty views."

"How much is this pepper worth?" Harry asks.

"It's priceless. They're near impossible to grow, and I've heard some chefs have even resorted to the black market to get their hands on one."

Harry raises his eyebrows at me, and I shrug. Leave it to Charlie to find a pepper worth more money than I'll see in my lifetime.

"So, the organizer is showing me the fancy setup they have, and I'm barely paying attention. All that's on my mind is the rumor I heard about the Swirl Delicious being a no-show. I'm going over all these different ways that I could bring the subject up when the organizer turns to me and lowers her voice. She says *I'm guessing you heard what people are saying?* Immediately, I feign innocence. She totally buys it and spills everything. What I heard is true! The Swirl Delicious hasn't shown up yet on the island! Can you believe it?"

"Charlie, I don't mean to interrupt, but I thought you said your story was a matter of life or death?" Harry says. I can hear the twinge of annoyance in his voice. He thinks Charlie is overplaying his pepper story. It wouldn't be the first time Charlie has over-elevated the importance of food.

"Harry, do you know me to exaggerate? Would I say it was life or death if it wasn't life or death?"

I can tell Harry is about to say that yes, he believes Charlie exaggerates, so I pull the phone away and speak myself. "Keep going with the story, Charlie," I say.

"Here is what the organizer tells me. She says a private company was contracted to bring the pepper to the island. It's top security where the pepper never leaves the sight of the human carrier. Everything was going well until today when they suddenly lost all contact with the carrier. No one knows where they went. It's like they fell of the face of the Earth. It's complete panic. The security company thinks the carrier might've stolen the pepper themselves! To make matters worse, the company can't even disclose the name of the person carrying the pepper because they have so many safeguards in place that no one is a hundred percent certain who the carrier is!

"The organizers have spent almost the whole day trying to figure out what to do. They're in constant contact with the security company, and a few hours before midnight, they decided to pull in the local police."

"That sounds serious," I say.

"But what's the life or death part?" Harry rushes to speak before I can shoo him away from the phone again.

I give him a nudge in the ribs with my elbow. Charlie's story might be important, but he won't tell us if Harry keeps interrupting. I hate to say it, but he's picked up some bad habits from Opal.

"I'm getting to that part, Harry. Just listen," Charlie chides him.

"Go on, Charlie. Harry will be quiet for the rest. Right, Harry?" I raise my brows at him and tilt my chin down.

"Yes, I will stop interrupting," Harry says.

"The organizer tells me that when the police get there, they interrogate everyone, but no one has any idea what could've possibly happened to the pepper. Everyone is stumped, but then, according to the organizer, this forgotten intern suddenly speaks up. He's some sort of food researcher from one of those fancy-smancy schools that allow students to create their own major."

Harry opens his mouth to say something, but I hold my finger to my lips, reminding him of our deal.

"This intern gets a meeting with the head of the police, and not long after, the police call everyone together to make an announcement. This intern's research specialty turns out to be black market food. His whole PhD thesis is based on it. Apparently, in the last few months, an international crime ring has been abnormally active when it comes to the Swirl Delicious. There have been multiple thefts of the pepper reported around the world within the past few weeks, the most recent being out of Sicily. With this new information, the police go ahead and declare an island-wide emergency!"

"What? That's terrible!" I exclaim.

"It is! I asked the organizer what this meant, and she told me that essentially, unless there's a dire emergency, all the island's police are going to treat the disappearance of the Swirl Delicious as their top priority."

Harry groans next to me. "Charlie, are you saying what I think you're saying?"

"No interrupting," I whisper at Harry.

"I'm not interrupting. I'm adding to the conversation," Harry says. "What Charlie is saying is huge. This might mean that police won't be here in the morning like Captain Lorenzo thought they would be. All of them are treating this stolen pepper as their number one priority. They might make us wait here longer."

Harry's words register in my mind. Is it possible that we'll all be stuck here even longer? Could a missing pepper really supersede the death of a man?

"We're all on the same page," Charlie says. "My first thought was of you two, stuck on that island with a murderer. As soon as the organizer told me that the police would be occupied unless there was a dreadful emergency, I asked the organizer if the police would consider murder a serious enough situation to reallocate a few officers."

"You asked her that?" Harry says.

"Yes, it was a poor choice on my part. A look of sheer horror transformed her face. I think she was worried that I was about to kill her. I should've thought about context a bit." Charlie sighs. "I calmed her down though. I explained that I had a curiosity with the macabre, and she accepted that. She ended the tour shortly after, but when I was leaving the venue, I noticed a few young officers mingling around.

"They looked friendly, and also bored. They'd been there for a while at this point. I went up to the group, and I turned on my Charlie charm. I started a conversation. I told them that I was a food writer, and all that good stuff. Then, I brought up the missing pepper.

"They were more than happy to give me the details, which wasn't much. No one has any idea what happened to that pepper. All they know is that the carrier confirmed it had arrived in Perfect Sands Islands, and then after that, no one heard anything. We talked a bit more, and eventually, I wiggled in my question about murder."

"You flat out asked them if they would show up to a murder?" Harry asks. "Charlie, they probably think you killed someone!"

"They don't think I killed anyone. Stop interrupting, Harry. You're becoming rather rude."

"Charlie! You went up to a bunch of police and asked them if you had free rein to commit a crime," Harry says.

"I did not! Will you listen?" Charlie says. "As I was saying, I was chatting with them, and they were telling me about their day. They started talking about how rare crime is in Perfect Sands. They said the last major crime to occur on the island was over a year ago, and it involved a slew of thefts on Lapis Rock. After they said this, I pointed out that today must've been a particularly bad day then. No crime for over a year, and now, two in one day: a murder and a high-profile theft."

Charlie is right. That is odd. What are the chances that two major events would happen on one day, especially with a place with almost no crime like Perfect Sands Islands?

"This is the part where things get a bit complicated. The officers grew quiet, and a couple of them had looks on their faces like I had just insulted their mothers. I thought to myself *Shoot! I shouldn't have said anything. They'll be wondering how I knew about the murder.*"

"I can see why that would be a problem," Harry says. "What did you do?"

"I started explaining how I knew about the murder because I had friends who had been on the boat when it happened, but they stopped me." Charlie takes a deep breath. "They looked me straight in the eyes, and they said, *Sir, what are you talking about? There has not been a murder on Perfect Sands for twelve years.*"

"They said that?" Harry's voice comes out hoarse. "Why would they say that?"

"My thoughts too," Charlie replies. "I figured that these were lower-level officers, so maybe they didn't know about the murder. I tried to dismiss it, but they wouldn't let it go. I think at one point they thought I was confessing a murder."

"How did you convince them that you hadn't murdered anyone?" I ask. I'm not sure what I'll do if Harry and I are stuck on Killdeer Cay and unable to help Charlie.

"They ended up taking me to the local jail," Charlie says.

"Jail! Charlie, are you in jail right now? Is that why you called Emma so many times?"

"I am in the jail, but I'm not *in jail*. They took me here so that I could talk to a higher-ranking officer."

I let out a breath that I hadn't noticed I was holding. Charlie is okay. That's at least one positive thing to focus on.

"When I got here, I met with the officer, and I told him the same things I had told the younger guys. I expected him to know what was going on. The man I talked to was second-in-command. If anyone knew what was going on in Perfect Sands Islands, he would. But he reiterated what the other men had told me. *Perfect Sands hasn't seen a murder in over a decade.* He said to me.

"I argued. I told him that wasn't true. At this exact moment, two of my closest friends were stranded on a nearby cay because someone had been murdered on their tender while being taken from one of the cruise ships to the shore, and the captain had instructed them to wait until the police showed up.

"The officer shook his head, and he got up, and he brought me all the call logs from today. The islands don't see much crime, so there weren't that many calls, other than the missing pepper."

Charlie's story isn't making sense. Why would the police in Lapis Rock deny that there had been a murder? Harry and I knew there had been a murder. We had been on the tender when it happened! Lloyd's name had been on the passenger list, and he had never made it to shore!

"Charlie, none of that can be right. Harry and I were on the tender when the murder happened," I say.

"Technically, we never saw a murder though," Harry says. "We've been going off the theory that a stowaway killed Lloyd, but if a stowaway was able to keep himself hidden somewhere on the tender, maybe Lloyd never died either and he also hid on the tender. Maybe the stowaway everyone thinks they keep getting glimpses of is Lloyd!" Harry talks faster with excitement. "Emma, maybe there never was a murder!"

Could Harry be right? Could Lloyd be the shadowy figure we've been glimpsing this whole time around the island?

"Will you stop interrupting!" Charlie's voice is shrill. "It doesn't matter if Lloyd was a secret contortionist hiding on the boat or a magician who has pulled off the trick of the century! Don't you see what the problem is?"

"Charlie, I think we've solved the mystery!" I grab Harry's arm in excitement. Could it really be that simple?

"We have to go!" Harry reaches towards my phone to hang up.

"No!" Charlie screams down the phone. "Whether or not Lloyd is dead doesn't matter!"

Harry and I both exchanges looks. It wasn't like Charlie to be cruel and crass.

"Don't you see? That boat captain told you he had called the police, but he never called the police! He's been lying to you!" Charlie yells. "You can't keep trying to figure out what happened to Lloyd. You don't have time to solve a mystery right now. You have to get yourselves and everyone else away from that captain now!"

CHAPTER THIRTY-SEVEN

WORD GAMES

Harry's pupils are as dark and wide as the ocean in front of us. My own heart is fighting a war in my chest as it pounds and pounds against me. Captain Lorenzo never called the cops. But we had seen him and heard him talking on the phone with the police. Who had he actually been on the phone with?

"Hello? Hello?" Charlie says. "Are you two okay?"

"We're right here," Harry says. "Charlie, when you told the cops what happened, did they say they were on their way?"

"That's one of the reasons I'm calling you. I have no idea where the two of you are!"

"We're on Killdeer Cay," I say. "Charlie, go tell the police ASAP. Harry and I will go speak with the others. It sounds like Captain Lorenzo may have had a hand in the death of Lloyd."

Harry and I hang up the phone and hurry back to the group. Samara, Dane, and Bruce are still seated in the sand and gathered around the red journal. They seem to be debating something, and the discussion has become heated.

"It could be important," Samara pulls at her necklace. "It could be linked to Lloyd."

"I think it's a load of horse junk," Bruce declares.

"No, it means something," Dane says. "It definitely means something."

Samara is the first one to see us arrive. The men notice when they follow her large eyes that stare up at us.

"You two look like you've seen some sort of ghost! Bad phone call?" Bruce chuckles.

Harry ruffles his hair. "I wouldn't call it a good call."

"We've got some news ourselves. We cracked the code in the journal," Dane holds the journal up. "Let me read it to you."

I don't think we really have time to hear some more nursery rhymes, but the look on Samara's face tells me that what they found might be more than a child's song.

Dane cracks his neck to the left and then the right. "*Measurements: Five CM Across, Shape: Sphere, Stem: Brown, Flesh: Gold, Cab: Five-Six-Seven.*"

"Is that all it says?" Harry reaches his hand out for the journal, and Dane passes it to him.

Harry flips through the pages, but the rest is empty.

"Do you think it means anything?" Dane asks.

"I don't know how it could," Harry says. "It's just some nursery rhymes and a list of random specs."

Dane looks disappointed.

"Emma and I have other news," Harry redirects the conversation. "Our friend Charlie is on the main island in Lapis Rock, and he's met with the police."

"Will they be here soon?" Dane asks.

"Or are they delayed again?" Samara peers up at us.

Harry and I exchange a look.

"That doesn't look like good news," Bruce says. "You two need to spill the beans."

"Charlie told us that the police hadn't been contacted yet about the murder on the tender," Harry announces.

Everyone's reactions happen slowly. Samara blinks her eyes as they slowly fill with salty tears. Bruce's sunburnt face turns a carmine, and Dane looks like he's been frozen in time.

"That's not possible," Bruce says. "Simply not possible. Cap' told us that he had called the police."

"I saw him make one of the calls," Dane says. "He definitely called."

"It's true," I back Harry up. "Our friend went to the police, and they had no idea what he was talking about. No one had ever placed a call to them."

"How could this have happened?" Samara looks at the ground.

"The Cap' lied, that's how." Bruce shakes his head.

"They should be on their way to us now," Harry says. "We told our friend the name of the island, so hopefully the police will arrive soon."

"He probably killed Lloyd himself," Dane says. "Lucky us, not only were we on the boat where the murder happened, we were all tricked by the murderer into doing nothing about it."

Samara's knuckles tighten around her pendant. "Oh no," she says, her voice barely above a whisper.

"I can think of a few words that are stronger than oh no," Bruce says.

"No, it's Opal. She's out on the island all alone, and Captain Lorenzo is looking for her! What if he's going to hurt her?" Samara cries.

Things click into place, and the cogs of the mystery groan to life. Captain Lorenzo had been bent on finding Opal earlier. When Harry and I had told Captain Lorenzo about the fishing shack and the fact that Opal had been there, he had gone looking for it at once. Opal's phone had gone missing early in the day, but no one else had lost theirs. Opal had seen someone trying to come into her cabana while she slept, and Samara had heard the commotion, and while Captain Lorenzo claimed he saw a shadowy figure escaping into the trees, who is to say that he didn't make that up? Maybe it had been Captain Lorenzo the whole time.

"What's wrong?" Harry turns to me. "You look like you might be sick," he says.

"Something isn't right," I say. "Captain Lorenzo is definitely lying, and he's definitely out to get Opal, but how did he kill Lloyd? He was driving the tender the whole time."

"He did go to the lower deck right before we landed on Killdeer Cay," Dane says. "Maybe he went and killed Lloyd then."

"He was gone for about thirty seconds, and we were all aware enough at the time that we would've noticed or heard something going on," Harry says.

"Then why not call the police if he had nothing to do with the murder?" Bruce says.

"Bruce, do you still have the passenger list that Captain Lorenzo dropped when he was here?" I ask.

"Sure do," Bruce reaches into his back pocket and produces the folded paper.

I take it from his hands and open it. I skim the names on the list until I get to Lloyd's.

"I knew it!" I give Harry the list and point at Lloyd's entry. "Lloyd was in cabin 567. The journal page you decoded listed all those random things, and one of them was *Cab: five-six-seven.*"

"It's a clue!" Harry passes the list back to Bruce. "This journal must've been used by Captain Lorenzo in some way."

"It would explain why it was left in Opal's cabana after she was almost attacked. Captain Lorenzo must've dropped it," I say.

"If the five-six-seven represents Lloyd somehow, then what do all the other things in the note mean?" Dane asks.

"That's not the only problem," Bruce stands. "Even if that cabin number is connected to Lloyd, how in the world did Captain Lorenzo kill the man? We all saw him driving the tender."

"Someone had to kill him," Harry says. "It's not like he vanished into thin air."

"We can't forget about the stowaway theory," Dane says. "People can be anywhere at any time."

"What does that mean?" Bruce asks.

"It means if you aren't certain as to where someone is, then technically, they could be almost anywhere," Dane replies.

Bruce shakes his head. "Sounds like some mumbo-jumbo philosophy stuff to me."

"I know what he means," Harry says. "Our friend Charlie is in Perfect Sands Islands for a pepper festival at the exact same time that Emma's parents and we are here. The chances of that happening were low, but not impossible. The same concept can be applied to the stowaway. The chances of one are low, but not impossible."

There are so many ideas being tossed around, it's hard to keep track. What I'm certain of is that Captain Lorenzo never called the police because for some reason he is after Opal. There's a slight chance that he somehow killed Lloyd, but I'm not sure how unless he had the help of someone who was kept secretly hidden on the boat because, as Dane stated, *people can be anywhere at any time.*

This last thought wiggles in my mind, and I'm not sure why. It's just proof that a stowaway is possible, nothing more, but why does it bother me so much?

"What I'm hearing is that we need to be on the lookout for two people: Captain Lorenzo and a stowaway," Dane says.

"Three people," Harry corrects. "Technically, we need to find Opal too. We can't have her wandering around when the captain is intending to harm her."

Bruce says something else, but I can't focus. Dane's voice is an earworm. *People can be anywhere at any time.* It's an unoriginal idea, and yet my mind won't let it go. It clings to me like a salty barnacle. I can't detach it from my thoughts. But then, it hits me.

"We've all been fooled!" The words clamber out of my mouth. "Not only can people be anywhere at any time—people can also be nowhere at any time."

Bruce scrunches his face up, and Harry tilts his head.

"Don't you get it?" I ask. "It was impossible for anyone to have committed murder on that tender and gone unnoticed. There was no murder! Whoever Lloyd is, he was never on our boat! It was all a setup. Lloyd never existed. Lloyd doesn't exist."

Harry's eyes clear a bit. "You think Captain Lorenzo made it look like there had been a murder so that we would be forced to dock on Killdeer Cay?"

"That's exactly what happened," I nod. "How else was Captain Lorenzo going to be able to go after Opal without anyone else noticing?"

Samara hops up from the ground, flapping the passenger list in the air. It's the most vibrant that I've seen her. "We can prove it! Lloyd A Alapha is the only person on the passenger list with a middle initial. Why not include my middle initial or Opal's or Emma's? Lloyd Alapha can't be such a common name that a middle initial is needed for identification."

"You think the middle initial is a clue?" Harry asks.

Samara takes a shaky breath. "It's the answer. L-L-O-Y-D-A-A-L-A-P-H-A. Rearrange the letters. O-P-A-L-H-A-L-L-A-D-A-Y. Opal Halladay!"

"It's all linking up!" I say as my mind flashes. "The red journal was a code to look for the passenger in cabin 567, which was Lloyd A Alapha. When that name is rearranged, you end up with Opal Halladay. Whoever left that journal and the person who gave Captain Lorenzo that passenger list were covertly putting a target on Opal's back."

"But how did Captain Lorenzo know that Lloyd A Alapha was the pretend murder victim before he got his hands on the red journal?" Harry asks.

"When Captain Lorenzo originally read us the passenger list, he had no idea what name was supposed to represent the murder victim. He had read the list in a roll-call fashion so that we could identify ourselves. While Opal and Samara were absent, Opal had already identified herself to the group, and it wouldn't be too difficult to guess that Samara wasn't named Lloyd.

"Why would he be after Opal?" Harry asks. "She doesn't appear dangerous or important."

"She hasn't revealed much about herself to us. She hasn't told us anything about herself now that I think about it," I reply.

It's true. I know that Bruce is retired and married to a military veteran, I know that Samara is set to collect a large inheritance that her great aunt is jealous of, and I know that Dane is a newlywed, but what do I know about Opal? Nothing other than she likes to cling to her purse and dislikes Killdeer Cay.

"I don't have an answer, but I think we need to try and find her before Captain Lorenzo does," I say.

"Should we all go in one group?" Harry suggests.

"I can't," Dane points to his ankle. "I want to help, but I'm in too much pain. I would also slow everyone down."

"Maybe we shouldn't go," Samara says quietly.

Bruce pulls his head back in shock at her comment while Harry's brows come together in confusion. Dane's mouth hovers open in surprise too. Out of everyone here, Samara would be the last person I could imagine suggesting that Opal should have to go at it alone. Bruce I could imagine arguing against saving Opal. He's not exactly her biggest fan. Even Dane has just cause to not help her after she acted so aggressively when he found her phone, but Samara has no reason to have animosity towards Opal.

Bruce holds his hands up. "Look here, I don't like the woman either, but she might be in big trouble. We need to get past our differences and help her."

Samara looks down at the sand. "That's not what I meant. While I understand that Captain Lorenzo lied about the police, and lying isn't usually a good sign, we don't know what he wants with Opal."

"He wants to hurt her, obviously," Bruce answers,

Samara's eyes don't leave the sandy ground. "We don't know that. What if Captain Lorenzo set this whole thing up because Opal is dangerous, and he's trying to stop her or catch her? She could be a wanted criminal, and he could be working undercover." Samara takes a big breath. "She chose to go off by herself on the island. Perhaps there was a reason for that."

Normally, Samara's idea would sound far-fetched, but considering all that's happened since we docked at Killdeer Cay, every idea should be seriously entertained. Opal hadn't been the easiest person to get along with while Captain Lorenzo had been easy going and accommodating. I can see why someone might argue Opal is the threat.

"Maybe the journal has more information in it?" I suggest. "It was a way to communicate to Captain Lorenzo that Lloyd A Alapha was code for Opal Halladay. If we could figure out why Captain Lorenzo wants to find Opal, then we would have a better idea of what to do," I say.

"That's reasonable," Harry supports me.

"I can't see how it would hurt," Dane says.

"It's the safest thing to do," Bruce declares. "Samara has some good points. Captain Lorenzo seems a lot more reliable than *that woman* who has caused trouble for everyone. I'll help save her if she's in trouble, but if Captain Lorenzo is doing the right thing by trying to find her, then we shouldn't interfere."

We gather around the journal once again, studying the pages in depth. Bruce points out that the word diamond is underlined in "Hush, Little Baby," but Samara thinks it could be a subtle reference to Opal, both being precious stones. Dane says maybe the name Peter from "Peter Piper" is also a clue, but no one can come up with a connection to the name.

"Let's call the police again," Dane says. "We can't crack this journal, and if the police get here, no one has to worry about going anywhere. They'll bring enough officers to find both Opal and Captain Lorenzo without us."

"That's not a bad idea." Harry looks at me. "Emma, do you think Charlie would pick up if we called again?"

"Most likely," I reply.

I pull out my phone and see that I already have three missed calls from Charlie. They were only several minutes ago. Hopefully everything is okay.

I put my phone on the speaker so that everyone can hear it.

Charlie picks up on the first ring. "Emma? How's it going?"

"We've made a lot of progress," I say. "It's a bit much to explain right now."

"That's okay. I have some bad news on my end," Charlie announces.

I can't be the only one in our group who feels their heart collide with their stomach. How could there possibly be even more bad news?

"When I told the officers about Killdeer Cay, they were really confused. I guess some of the smaller cays around Lapis Rock get renamed frequently.

They're calling around to see if anyone can remember what Killdeer Cay would've been renamed."

Charlie's news isn't taken too well around the small circle. Bruce looks displeased as he aggressively rubs at the sunburn on his forehead while Samara's eyes are growing teary again.

"There has to be something we can do to help," I say to Charlie. "Let me think. It's an old beach club? Is that helpful?"

"I told them that, but they said there are a lot of cays with a lot of abandoned beach clubs. Is there a historic feature on the island? That would help."

"Yes!" I practically sing over the phone. "There's an old house called *The House of Safety*. It's a stone structure that people used as an emergency shelter during bad storms long ago."

"Perfect," Charlie says. "I'll let the police know."

Charlie hangs up the phone.

"That wasn't good news," Bruce says. "They aren't even on their way here because they don't know where we are!"

"They'll know where we are soon enough," Harry counters. He's trying to keep everyone calm.

"Who knows how many of those safety houses there are in Perfect Sands Islands. We could be here forever," Bruce laments.

Samara squeezes her knees to her chest and rocks lightly.

"We don't know that," I say. Harry and I have to keep the situation positive. We can't risk anyone losing it. "Let's get back to the journal." I push the red book into the center of the circle.

We all peer over the journal pages again, but this time, the buzz in the air is gone. We don't know how long it might take the police to find the island, and we don't know what will happen during the time when we are stranded here.

"The measurements on the one page seem the most important. Let's focus there," I suggest.

We read over the various specs written on the page. Dane suggests they might describe Opal in some way, but Harry doesn't see how that would make any sense. Bruce concentrates on the specifications of measurement and shape, and ends up listing things he knows that are spherical and five centimeters. Samara stays quiet, deep in her thoughts.

As Bruce adds kiwi to his list, I stare at the rest of the specifications on the page. *Stem: Brown, Flesh: Gold.* What could it mean?

"Maybe it has to do with a diamond?" Bruce says. "A diamond could be round and five centimeters."

"A diamond could also be gold," Dane says. "That would explain why diamond is underlined in that one nursery rhyme."

"The nursery rhyme!" I spring to standing. "That's it! We need to call Charlie back!"

A group of concerned faces peer up at me.

"The first nursery rhyme is "Peter Piper," and it's about peppers! That must be it."

Harry knows what I'm trying to say. He jumps up and slings his backpack over his shoulder.

"What is going on?" Bruce says. "Peppers?"

"There's a big pepper festival happening on Lapis Rock tomorrow. Actually, technically, it's happening today. This rare pepper called the Swirl Delicious is the focal point of the festival, and it has gone missing. No one knows where it went, and the police on Lapis Rock are heavily involved. The last anyone heard about it, the pepper was somewhere in Perfect Sands Islands. What if Opal has the pepper? What if that was why she had requested a semi-private tender to take her to Lapis Rock? Maybe she was hired to safely transport the pepper to the festival, and because we all got stranded here, now no one knows where it is!"

"And Captain Lorenzo wants it because it's worth a lot of money on the black market!" Harry chimes in.

"The description in the journal fits too. A pepper would have a stem, and the coloring is right, as is the shape!" My voice is rushed.

"But why would Captain Lorenzo steal a pepper for the black market?" Bruce asks. "He already has a job."

Dane speaks up. "Captain Lorenzo told us he was from Italy, but he's working all the way on Lapis Rock. Not only that, but no ones' stories added up as to why we all ended up on that tender. Remember? We all missed our scheduled tender, and there just happened to be an extra boat available because of a scheduling miscommunication, but according to Opal, she had been scheduled to be on that tender. How could the tender have accidently showed up and been scheduled to show up at the same time?"

"Our friend Charlie did mention that an international crime ring was involved with recent disappearances of these peppers," Harry adds.

"And, he said that some of the most recent robberies involving the peppers had occurred in Sicily," I supplement. "If Captain Lorenzo is Italian, Sicily makes sense."

"These connections are too strong to ignore," Harry says.

"Opal fits too," I say. "She has clung to her purse the whole time we've been stuck here because it probably contains the pepper."

"She lost her phone early on too, which would make it difficult for her to let anyone know that she was stuck on the island," Harry says.

"That must be how Opal's phone ended up near me when we were in *The House of Safety,*" Dane says. "Captain Lorenzo set up his bed near mine. It must've fallen out of his pocket."

"We've solved it," I say. "Captain Lorenzo, who isn't really a boat captain, but a member of an international crime ring, staged a murder of a fake man named Lloyd A Alapha on a tender so that he could get Opal Halladay alone on an abandoned island and steal the Swirl Delicious from her."

"What he didn't expect was for the five us to figure it out," Harry says.

I shake my head. How had we all been so easily tricked? "So, there was never a murder," I say.

As soon as the words leave my mouth, a dreadful scream scatters through the still night air.

"There hasn't been one yet, but there might be one soon if we don't help Opal." Harry's face is stony and serious. We have to hurry. Opal is about to run out of time.

"I'll stay here," Dane says. "My phone is dead, but if Emma or someone else gives me theirs, I can call the police and keep them updated on what's happening."

"The rest of us can stay in a group," Harry says. "It'll take us longer to find Opal, but if the captain, or Lorenzo rather, is part of a criminal organization as we suspect, he could be incredibly dangerous."

"In that case, Dane shouldn't be left alone either," Bruce says. "What if the Cap' comes around here, and we've left Dane all alone?"

"We don't have time for this," I cut in. "If you want to stay here in the cove, then stay here in the cove. Those of us who want to search for Opal need to go now! We just heard her scream. It could be too late already!"

I pull on Harry's arm. "We know Opal found the fishing shack, so she could still be there. Let's head that way."

Harry runs with me up the sandy beach. When we reach the path, I turn around to see that Samara has joined us.

"I'll follow you two. I can't let Opal get hurt. We're all stuck on this island together," she says.

"We're heading to the northern part of the island," I say. "Harry and I found an old fishing shack there that we know Opal knows about. She likes her creature comforts, and it's the closest thing to a hotel room on the island."

We take a step in the right direction when the bushes on our right swish and shake like their shedding themselves of their leafy extremities. Right before us, something large plunks itself into the center of the pathway.

Chapter Thirty-Eight

A Criminal Runs

In the middle of the path, a shadowy lump stirs and groans. Harry pulls his phone out and activates the flashlight app. Collapsed in a heap in front of us is Opal. She's clinging to her precious purse, and her fluffy hair is cascading down her back, smoothing the edges of her spine, making her look almost rock-like.

"Are you okay?" I take a knee and grab Opal's hand.

She groans before unfurling herself. "I got lost," she mumbles.

"You fell out of the bushes," Harry says. "Were you being chased?"

"Chased?" Opal shakes her head, and clarity snaps into her eyes. "Chased? No, I wasn't being chased. One of those repulsive birds tried to bite me, and I ran away. I ended up losing the path, and that's why I was in the bushes. I just now found my way out."

She limps to her feet. Harry tries to help balance her, but she swats him away like he's a mosquito. Her one knee is scraped and shiny with blood while the other one is bruised blue. She didn't take a gentle tumble.

"Stop gawking," she snaps at Harry, "Never seen a beautiful woman before get a bit scrapped up?"

Harry averts his eyes and his cheeks turn red. "Wasn't really what I was thinking," he mumbles low enough that only I can hear him.

"Did you see Captain Lorenzo while you were out there?" I ask her.

"Why would I have seen Captain Lorenzo?" She shifts her purse so that it is nestled closer to her chest. The behavior makes sense now that we all know what's in her bag.

"It doesn't matter," I say. "Let's get back to the cove. Everyone else is there. It's safer if we have big numbers."

It's a relief that Opal has quite literally fallen into our path. Having to search the island for her would've been a monumental task, and one made harder by the sheer exhaustion overpowering us.

When we get back to the cove, Bruce and Dane are surprised.

"That was lickety-split," Bruce says. "Where was she?"

"It's rather rude to talk as if I'm not here," Opal says to him.

"Should've left her out there," Bruce mutters as he retreats to a shadowy spot below a coconut tree.

"Did you see Captain Lorenzo?" Dane asks. He's lying on the ground with his ankle propped up on some driftwood.

"No, we barely got on the path when we found Opal," Harry says.

"What do we do if Captain Lorenzo shows up?" Samara's large eyes dart nervously to the path and its bordering tree line.

"Why is everyone being so cagy around Captain Lorenzo? Did something happen?" Opal pushes herself between Samara and Harry so that she can get everyone's full attention.

"Captain Lorenzo—" I start, but Harry cuts me off.

"Is right here!" Harry waves his hand in the air. "Hey, Captain."

Captain Lorenzo appears on the path. He looks as he has this whole day, but knowing that he's really a criminal after a priceless pepper has me noticing features that I had skimmed over before. He has a small scar above his lip, and there's something unforgiving about his eyes. They're sharp and intense, quick and calculating.

"You found Mrs. Halladay!" he says upon noticing Opal. "Where was she?"

"We found her right here," Harry says. He steps in front of her.

I try and read the situation, but I can't tell what Harry is hoping to do. Is he going to confront Captain Lorenzo? And if he does, what's the plan after that? We can't run. With Opal's knees beat up and Dane's ankle hurt, not to mention my throbbing feet, Captain Lorenzo would catch us. We can't fight for the same reasons, nor would I want to.

"The police are coming," my voice cracks as I say it. I had meant it to sound powerful, but instead, I sound weak and helpless.

"Yes, they will be here soon," Captain Lorenzo says. "I believe the morning time is when they will come."

"We got an update that they would be here sooner," Harry says.

"Oh?" Captain Lorenzo's eyes narrow. A thousand thoughts must be going through his head. There's no way he could possibly know that we've cracked the case, but he'll be scrambling for time nonetheless.

"There is an abandoned fire pit over there," he motions to the spot I took the phone call earlier. "I will gather some wood, and we can sit around the fire. That sounds nice, yes?"

I catch Harry's eye. His face is as confused as I am. Captain Lorenzo isn't dumb, and that's what makes him treacherous. He's planning something, but what is it?

"I'll help you," Harry says.

"The rest of you should gather round the fire," Captain Lorenzo says. He sidles up to Opal. "I can take your bag, Mrs. Halladay. I see you are exhausted."

"No!" I say rather loudly.

Captain Lorenzo takes a step back.

"I can help Opal," I say. "That way you can focus on the firewood."

"Of course," Captain Lorenzo says.

He and Harry stalk off towards the path. Bruce follows. I turn to Opal. Her hands hold her purse like two raptor claws. Somehow, I need to get the pepper out of her purse.

"Opal," I say, "set your bag down, and I can look at your knees for you. They look rather rough."

This makes Opal hold her purse tighter.

"I'm fine, thank you," she says coolly.

It's going to be near impossible to get Opal to let her bag out of her sight, but we need to remove the pepper from her possession. Captain Lorenzo could take her purse by force if he wanted, and if he does that, the pepper can't be inside of it.

"Can I help you?" Opal glares at me. "You're staring."

Heat creeps up the back of my neck like tendrils. "I'm just tired."

Opal raises her eyebrows and walks off to the fire pit.

"We're back," Harry says loudly as he, Captain Lorenzo, and Bruce come down from the path. "Lots of wood around."

Captain Lorenzo dumps the logs and sticks he's gathered into the pit and removes a lighter from his pocket. He's ready to get the fire going. He's got a plan in motion, and I need to stop it.

"Ladies, please, take a seat." Captain Lorenzo motions to two spots that face the ocean.

Samara takes a seat in the spot indicated. Opal waits a moment, but then she sits next to Samara after Bruce adds his kindling to the fire. I try to sit next to Opal, but Captain Lorenzo slides into the seat right as I come near.

"My apologies," he says to me in his charismatic way. "I didn't see you there."

"No worries," I say as Bruce plops down next to Samara.

Opal pulls her purse off her shoulder and puts it in her lap. It would be so easy for Captain Lorenzo to grab it and run. We would never find him on the island, and unless the police arrive within minutes, he'll be able to disappear with the pepper, possibly forever.

Harry puts the firewood he's found next to the fire and settles next to Bruce. He and I share a look. I hope he has a plan because I sure don't.

Captain Lorenzo stands up to stretch, but as he does, a huge gust of wind lifts itself off of the ocean and sends the smoke and flames of the fire directly into the faces of Samara and Opal. Samara gasps and tips back on her seat, falling to the sand while Opal screeches and her bag flies to the ground.

It's only a second, if that long, but Captain Lorenzo dashes to the ground and picks up the purse before springing back up and sprinting to the path.

"Stop him!" Opal cries. "That's my purse!"

Harry takes off, but there's no chance of him catching Captain Lorenzo who has already disappeared. Not only is Captain Lorenzo faster, he knows the island better. He and the other criminals he works with might have been preparing this island for months.

Harry stops in his tracks and kicks the sand. "He'll be gone."

"Maybe not," Bruce says. "We are on an island. He can only go so far."

Harry puts his hands on top of his heads while his jaw tightens. "He has the tender. He'll be gone as soon as he gets to the dock."

"Let's head there then," Dane tries to stand, but he grimaces.

"We'll never catch him," Harry says. "Also, he's dangerous. He might kill us, and no one should die over a pepper."

Opal steals a sharp breath from the air. "You knew! You knew about the Swirl Delicious?"

"We figured it out right before you showed up here," Harry says.

"It doesn't matter much now," Bruce says. "The Cap' has it. We'll never see it again. No one will."

Opal crumbles to the ground. I can't imagine what she must be feeling. She has gone through so much to try and keep that precious pepper safe, and in the end, it was still stolen.

Samara stands up and brushes the sand from her thighs and gives us a big smile. "I wouldn't be so sure about that," she says.

In her hands, she's holding something small. It's a silver case. She props it open and inside is the most beautiful pepper I've ever seen. Yellow and red swirls together until they birth a dark gold that glitters in the moonlight like an ancient jewel.

Samara smiles. "I haven't picked a pocket since I was in middle school, but it was nice to use the skills for something good for once."

Opal breaks into tears and hugs her so tightly that Samara almost falls to the ground.

"I've never been so thankful to be stuck on this island with all of you," Opal beams at us all as the waves ebb into the ocean behind her.

Chapter Thirty-Nine

THE ENDING

Captain Lorenzo ended up making it back to the tender with Opal's purse, but not with the pepper. Fortunately, it was around the same time that the police were arriving at Killdeer Cay, or Diamond Paradise Isle, as the police knew it as. We didn't know this at the time because the docks can't be seen in the cove, but Charlie let Harry and I know everything when we later saw him on Lapis Rock.

Shortly after the Perfect Sands Islands' police boarded the tender and arrested Captain Lorenzo, they took the rest of us to Lapis Rock. The island was as beautiful as I had imagined. The beaches were white and the waters full of gradient blues with light azures by the shores and dark navy farther out where the cruise ships hovered.

When we all got to the police station, everyone was given medical attention. It turned out Dane needed a strong round of antibiotics for his bite while Harry and Opal needed some minor patching up. I got an IV drip for my dehydration and ice packs for my sore wrist and shoulder. While Bruce insisted that he needed a full medical checkup, they didn't find anything wrong with him. Samara, despite being the hero of the day, didn't need any medical attention. She had faired the best out of all of us.

The police took statements from us about what happened. Because the crime ring that Captain Lorenzo belonged to was so high profile, they couldn't give us many details about what would happen to him. We did learn some interesting information about him though. He had been somewhat honest about his identity. His name really was Lorenzo, and he really was a boat captain from Italy, but that's where the similarities ended. It turned out he had only been in Perfect Sands Islands for a few days, and the police were working hard with INTERPOL to link Captain Lorenzo to the other thefts in Sicily. It was rumored that both of those crimes had also involved boats, one a yacht and one a fishing trolley. They also shared similarities in which the main evidence was a trail of dark red paint. Th e officers thought that might've been Captain Lorenzo's calling card as a professional thief. So, it turns out that what we thought had been blood on the tender, had been paint all along.

The police were also confident that Captain Lorenzo had had a lot of outside help. Someone had planted the red journal on Killdeer Cay, and someone else had helped pass Captain Lorenzo the coded passenger list with the fake Lloyd A Alapha listed on it. There had never been a stowaway, just lots of organized preparation.

It was a wild thinking that Harry and I had been caught up with such a dangerous group of people, but I guess there is a first for everything!

After everyone got their needed medical attention, and the police got their statements, they let us go. Dane's wife, Jill, met him right at the police station. The two hugged and kissed, and Jill doted on him and his injured ankle. I have a feeling that they will work everything out, and many years of happiness together are ahead of them. Maybe Dane being put in peril had put their relationship into perspective a bit.

Bruce's wife also met him at the station. She was taller than Bruce with muscular arms and a toothy smile. She greeted Bruce by thwacking him on the back and calling him a hero. They made a cute couple.

Samara was the most nervous to leave the station. She wasn't sure how meeting her extended family would go after so many years, but in the end, Opal was the one who gave her the courage she needed. She pointed out that nothing Samara's great aunt could say or do could be anywhere near as daunting as having to pickpocket a priceless pepper right in front of an international criminal. I hope Samara keeps in touch. I want everything to work out well for her. She deserves it, especially after her heroic actions on the island.

Most important of all, Opal was able to deliver the Swirl Delicious to the pepper festival. It was a huge success. Charlie said he had never seen so many people trying to look at one pepper in his life. It was cool to know that Harry and I had seen it up close.

As for myself, I had gotten so caught up in the events going on while we were stranded on Killdeer Cay that I had momentarily forgot about my job, or lack of job, at the birding magazine.

I try not to think about it as I splay out on a lounge chair on the sundeck of the cruise ship. Harry is next to me, reading a spy novel. He turns a page before looking over at me.

"What's on your mind? You look upset," he says.

"I guess when I get back, I'll have to start job hunting."

A shadow blocks the sun, and I lift my sunglasses to see my mother peering over me. "I got you an orange juice." She holds out a bottle to me.

While Harry and I had been trapped on Killdeer Cay, my parents had thoroughly enjoyed their time on Lapis Rock. They had visited most of the landmarks and spent a lot of time at the beach and restaurants along with Charlie. My mother was horrified when she realized why she hadn't seen Harry and I for the whole day, but she got over it quickly.

"Have you seen your father?" She sits on the edge of my chair. "He said some man has been texting him trying to get a hold of you."

"Me?" I sit up.

Harry puts his book down. "Did the person say who they were?"

"It was a Mr. Hawking. He said he's your boss and that he was wondering if you were interested in working on some sort of article for the magazine. He said it would require some travel. I'll have to ask your father when we find him."

Excitement bubbles in my chest. What I took to be Mr. Hawking hanging up the phone and firing me must've been a bad connection. It turned out I wouldn't be job hunting after all.

I lay back on the chair and stare up at the blue, cloudless sky above me. Hopefully whatever travel Mr. Hawking has in mind will be a little more restful than this trip has been. I could use a break from mysteries.

Chapter Forty

TO MY READERS

Thank you so much for reading Catastrophe at Killdeer Cay! Every single time someone chooses to read one of my novels, my whole day is made. So, truly, **thank you**, dear reader!

When I first embarked on this novel, I had some ideas about where I wanted it to go, but I wasn't completely sure how to get there. I had the inspiration for the main concept (a murder on a tender) while I was on a tender myself in the middle of the Caribbean. I think mystery writers try to challenge themselves by putting characters in seemingly impossible situations, and I couldn't resist doing exactly that to Emma and Harry.

I hope you enjoyed the book as much as I loved writing it. I'm so thankful to everyone who supported me during this endeavor (shoutout to my editor, M), and if you haven't read my other books, check out the rest of the birdwatching journalist series on Amazon, and don't be afraid to give this book a rating! Every little thing helps!

Until next time,

Nicolette

P.S. If you are hoping to keep up with me when I'm between writing projects, take a gander at my bird blog on **nicoletteharpford.com**

www.ingramcontent.com/pod-product-compliance
Lightning Source LLC
Chambersburg PA
CBHW061955170626
46813CB00006B/2651